Rainie Missed

Melody Muckenfuss

Copyright © 2011 by Melody Muckenfuss

Cover by Melody Muckenfuss & Ronald Hornbeck

All rights reserved

This book, or parts thereof, may not be reproduced in any form without permission of the author

Keep up with Rainie at www.rainieseries.com

Acknowledgements:

Once again, many thanks to Ron for all of your hard work. Your patience is amazing, and none of these books would have been published without your help. Thanks to Gerry for your editing skills and encouragement, and of course... thanks to everyone else for asking for more.

Chapter One

Rain mixed with snow: a phrase that can bring a chill to the heart of even the most intrepid Midwesterner.

When there was already a layer of snow on the ground it meant that some of it would melt and the streets would be hydroplaning nightmares of thick, dirty slush. If there wasn't any snow to start with you could be sure it would get cold enough to freeze everything before it was all over, and then everyone slid rather than drove wherever they needed to go. The morning commute would require ten cold, vigorous minutes of scraping ice from car windows before a person even pulled out of the driveway, and frozen slush would build up in wheel wells until they rubbed the tread off the snow tires.

Ah, Michiana in January.

My name is Rainie Lovingston, and I live in Buchanan, Michigan, a small town just a few miles up from the Indiana state line. The area is known as Michiana, I suppose since so many people live in one state but work or shop in the other and they needed some way to describe the relationship. The weather in our area is strongly affected by Lake Michigan, and all winter we hear our meteorologists warning of "lake effect snow." Lake effect is an interesting phenomena that can dump twelve inches of the white stuff in one spot but leave only a dusting a mile or so away. It can be beautiful and treacherous and soothing and a general pain in the butt, sometimes all at the same time.

Today there was plenty of snow on the ground, but it wasn't the pristine white covering of the picture postcard. We had just gone through a week of unseasonably warm temperatures after a month of way too much snow, and as a result we had a crusty covering of off-white to gray. Old snow mixed with dirt and grime was piled at every curb and in miniature hills in every parking lot. Some of the bigger ones probably wouldn't melt off until late April.

It was completely overcast, the clouds seeming to hang as low as a theatre ceiling. It was gloomy and monochromatic, as if someone had skimmed a gray crayon over the whole world. Rain was falling in a fine mist, almost a fog, leaving a thin rime of ice on every surface it touched.

I sipped my morning coffee and stared dispiritedly out the kitchen window. I had no desire to go anywhere or do anything. I could have stood right here in my jammies until bedtime and then rolled back into the covers without missing a beat.

Yep, it was definitely January in Michiana.

Like it or not, I had to get dressed and get moving. It was Monday and I had to be at Bob's by eight o'clock.

Bob is one of my clients. I provide homecare for the elderly. It's a great alternative to assisted living or even nursing homes for those who can afford it. I happen to love being a caregiver. I often think I get more from my clients than they do from me.

Bob just turned 93. He's a retired college professor and still pretty sharp mentally, although his short-term memory and his ability to focus for any length of time has gotten a little rocky. My job is to fix him meals and be sure he eats them, do the housework and laundry he can no longer do, and drive him wherever he needs or wants to go. I do my best to keep him active and mentally stimulated, and in general help him maintain the highest quality of life he can manage.

Lately he hasn't been feeling well, and I'm worried about him. He refuses to go to the doctor. As far as he's concerned he's lived a full life, and although he isn't depressed, he also isn't afraid to die. What he really fears, he told me, was some doctor prolonging his life well past the time that it was worth living.

People still in the bloom of youth or even the slightly faded glory of middle age might not understand that. What kind of person would choose to leave this life? In our culture suicide is against the law. Only a person of unsound mind would *choose* to die.

But the reality is that while drawing breath and registering a pulse might technically indicate life but they don't necessarily mean a person is l*iving*. Our medical technology has far outpaced our common sense, and too often our elders are provided the means to continue breathing without thought of whether they really should be.

I've seen it happen many times, and the truth is Bob is in a bit of a downhill slide. He gave up last year because of a torn rotator cuff, and in November he had a bad fall and was now required to use a walker. His eyesight is failing, making it difficult for him to read or do crossword puzzles, and he absolutely hates anything on TV except for the news, occasional programs on the Discovery channel, and now and then an episode of Jeopardy. He isn't a complainer, but he has confessed to me that his life has gotten almost excruciatingly dull, and in his words he is "about over it."

"I've lived a great life, Rainie, better than a lot of people. I have no regrets, nothing that I feel I've left undone. My kids are healthy and happy and better off than I was; my grandkids are in college or starting good careers. I'd rather die quick than linger for months in bed. Can you imagine what that would be like?" He shuddered. "My mother had a stroke, paralyzed her right side and took her speech. We couldn't even be sure how much she could comprehend, or if she was in any pain. She just lay there, day after day, staring at the ceiling, waiting to die for six long months. And do you know the whole time they were still giving her meds to keep her heart healthy? Now does that make sense to you?"

"I know, Bob. But what if you just have some little thing wrong? Why be uncomfortable if it's something the doctor can fix?"

"Hell Rainie, I'm 93! I've got to expect some discomfort. Look, if I go to the doctor he'll probably put me on more medication for something or other, and it probably will prolong my life. But why? Just breathing and eating doesn't qualify as life. Or at least, it shouldn't. I'm not asking to be euthanized, I just want Nature to be allowed to run its course."

I had called and talked to Bob's son Daryl about it. He reluctantly agreed that his father, still mentally competent, had a right to choose how much or little medical care he wanted to receive.

I finished my first cup of coffee and went to check on George, my iguana. He would have to stay in his cage while I was gone but I wanted to be sure his water and kibble was fresh. George is two-feet long, but his cage takes up one whole wall of my living room. Staying in his cage wasn't exactly torture.

I refilled his drinking water and noted that his swimming pool needed to be cleaned soon. Half of his cage was devoted to a long, low glass tank filled with filtered water for him to soak in. Iguanas like that kind of thing.

I refilled my coffee mug and took it into the bathroom to keep me company while I got ready to go. Until I've had my third cup I don't like to be too far away from it. Yes, I've heard the studies about all the bacteria floating around in a bathroom, but hey, it was my bacteria. Besides, I brewed my coffee strong enough to kill most anything that happened to fall into it.

I showered, brushed my teeth and dried my hair. One side of my bangs kept sticking straight up no matter what I did. What was the deal? I'm not much for messing with my hair beyond washing and drying it, but I tried a little mousse and water to no avail. Finally I found an old bottle of hairspray under the sink and held the offending lock down while I sprayed the heck out of it.

The results were not pretty, but I didn't have all day to spend on my hair. Maybe Bob had an old fedora I could borrow.

By then my second cup of coffee was down to the dregs so I went back to the kitchen for a refill. It was already seven thirty so I poured it into a travel mug and stepped out on the porch for a smoke. I only smoke about a pack every two or three days, but I've been giving serious thought to giving them up. Not only are they ridiculously expensive now - over six bucks a pack in Michigan - but the shortness of breath worried me a little. It wasn't like I was gasping for air all the time, and in fact riding my bike hardly bothered me at all. It was when I was working with Jack that it worried me. Too often I found myself in a sprint for my life, and one of these times I was going to run out of air before the bad guys did.

My good old Escort started right up, not the least bit intimidated by the cold and dreary wet. It was banged up and full of rust and bullet holes and had a bit of a bad smell, but it ran like a champ and got good gas mileage. Oh, and it was paid for. That went a long way in my frugal book.

My friends wonder why I'm willing to put up with a car with so many quirks, but the truth is it's been a gradual process, and it's quite possible that I'm in denial.

For instance, one morning I opened the car door and the overhead light didn't come on. When I went to change it, I discovered the cover wouldn't come off, even with the aid of a screwdriver jammed into strategic places. Okay, it's a bit of a pain not to have that light, but I keep a little flashlight in the glove box that works just as well. I got used to it.

So then one of the back door latches jammed, and now the door can't be opened from the inside. I don't carry many passengers, but when I do someone has to let them out. Again, it's a bit of a pain, but I got used to it. Now, the transmission is giving me a little trouble; about half the time it won't go into reverse gear. Oh, and the parking brake is shot, meaning I have to park it in first gear or it will roll away.

The thing is I manage to get used to one quirk before another one crops up. It's happened so slowly that it's not really that noticeable. Kind of like the one pound a year American's gain after the age of forty. People don't really notice until one day they're sixty years old and realize that they weigh twenty pounds more than they did two decades ago. Maybe they decide enough is enough, and go on a diet.

I suppose some day I'm going to look at my little escort and decide enough is enough, the car is a piece of shit and I need a new one. But not today. I really *like* the old thing. It's comfortable, like a pair of old shoes.

I stopped at a gas station downtown and filled my tank, trying not to wince at the almost four dollars a gallon price, glad that I didn't drive the extended-cab, extended-bed, extended-everything pick-up truck like the guy at the next pump. I watched the driver out of the corner of my eye, trying not to be too obvious, and speculated whether he was a farmer who needed that big truck or a man using a big truck to distract people from his own shortcomings.

He was wearing a baseball cap and brown insulated coveralls, so common on Buchanan men in winter that it could almost be a uniform. They were practical for everything from snow-blowing to hunting to just walking out to get the mail on particularly cold days, so they didn't really tell me much.

I looked down at his boots: heavy, well-worn work boots with bits of mud and other icky stuff stuck to them. Ah, a farmer.

I finished pumping my gas, satisfied that I had figured it out. I know, who cares, right? But I was a curious kind of girl, and I just liked to know these things. Besides, what else did I have to think about while I stood in the cold holding the gas nozzle? I know I could have been working on a plan to end world hunger, but that might require some real concentration, and I'm pretty sure I'm supposed to be at least peripherally aware of the gas pump when I'm filling the tank. Something about sparks and huge explosions, although I've never seen it happen.

I got back in my car, and by the time I got to Bob's I'd finished my third cup of coffee and my mood had kicked up a notch. See, who needs antidepressants when we have caffeine and nicotine?

I was pleased to find Bob sitting in the kitchen, using a page-sized magnifier I'd brought him to work the crossword in the paper.

"How are you today?" I asked.

"Pretty good!" he answered. "In fact, I was hoping maybe we could bake some cookies today for the food pantry."

"Hey, that's great!"

Bob used to bake cookies for the local food pantry twice a month, a sweet supplement to the food baskets. He also donated money, for nutritional food, but he thought it every person's God-given right to have dessert, even if it was just a couple of cookies.

I had been helping him with the cookies since I started working for him, but he hadn't been up to doing it for quite a while. I took this as a good sign.

"Do we need to run to the store for anything?"

"No, I have everything I need. I thought we'd make chocolate chip and oatmeal raisin."

"Sounds good." Too good, really. It would be hard to resist those hot, chewy delights fresh from the oven, but I didn't dare eat any. The threat of obesity was like a dark shadow hanging over my head, and I had to be ever vigilant or it would consume me.

Bob set aside the paper and grabbed his walker. He came over to the counter and started pulling ingredients out. I stood close by in case he needed me, but I let him do his thing. That old cliché "move it or lose it" is true at any age, and it was important that my clients do as much for themselves as they safely could.

"Let's see...flour, sugar, brown sugar, oatmeal..." He reached up again and winced and grabbed his hip. I reached out to steady him until he got both hands back on his walker.

"Are you okay?"

"Damned hip!" Bob slowly turned and went back to the table, his left leg dragging a little. "It felt fine when I got up this morning!"

"You haven't fallen or anything?" I was only with him three mornings a week, and I suspected he sometimes overdid things when I wasn't around.

"Hell no. I hardly walk anymore, when do I have a chance to fall?" He dropped his head into his hands. "Guess I can't do the cookies after all."

"Don't be ridiculous, of course you can! There's no rule that says you have to stand up to bake cookies."

I gathered an armload of the supplies he'd already put on the counter and brought them to the table. "I'll be your legs." I went back and got his heavy Kitchenaid mixer, an ancient beast that had stirred thousands of batches of cookies, cakes and dough in its long life.

"You expect me to just *sit* here and do it?" Bob glared at me.

"Why not?" I plugged the mixer in behind the table and positioned it within his reach. "Come on now, tell me what else you need."

He glared at me for another second or two.

"Bob, just because you never did it this way before doesn't mean you can't do it this way now. What would you rather do, go sit in the living room and watch the traffic?"

He snorted a little laugh. "You mean the two cars that might drive down the street between now and five o' clock?"

"Exactly. What's it going to be?"

"Well, I'll need the raisins and the chocolate chips. Oh, and butter and eggs from the fridge…"

I hopped to it, and pretty soon we got down to some serious cookie baking.

By the time I left Bob the skies had started leaking a soaking, chill rain just a few degrees too warm to be snow. Yuk! Now I really wanted to crawl back into bed.

You folks that live down south or out west might think I'm being a sissy, but let me tell you, this is no spring rain. This stuff is cold, and the cold seeps right down into your bones until you're shivering from the inside out. I didn't want to *drink* another cup of hot coffee, I wanted it pumped in intravenously.

Of course I didn't go home to bed. First I had to deliver twelve dozen cookies, all neatly packaged in zip lock bags, to Redbud Area Ministries, a local charity that operated with the cooperation of a variety of churches. I left the bags with a smiling volunteer, along with an envelope that held a check from Bob.

After that I still had work to do, this time at B&E, the security and private investigations firm where I was a part-time private investigator's assistant. I ran data base checks and other dull tasks that the much-higher paid licensed P.I.'s didn't want to be bothered with. I also did background checks, which were a little more fun. They involved interviews with the people who gave written references, and you never knew for sure how those would go.

And then there were the times I got involved in Jack's stuff. I can't tell you how many times I've told myself to tell him no, to just walk away from his craziness. The truth is I can't. Jack is hot and scary at the same time and sometimes I'm just a little afraid to be alone with him. On the other hand, he's hot, and I *am* a single woman.

Well, mostly. I did just meet a new guy a few weeks ago, and he seems promising. His name is Michael, and my mom introduced us. He's an accountant and he's helping her with her taxes. Mom is being audited, and after her initial reaction that her income was none of the IRS's business, she realized she'd better do something or she might go to jail.

Michael is coming to my house for dinner tonight and I think I'm being a little disloyal thinking how hot Jack is, but it's not like anything is ever going to happen between me and Jack. He's so far out of my league I don't think we're even playing the same game.

I stopped to chat briefly with Belinda, Harry Baker's personal assistant. Today her hair was a gorgeous shade of red and she was wearing a short skirt that showed a lot of very nice leg. Belinda was a far different person than I was. She loved to dress for attention, while I tried to sort of fade into the background.

"Good morning!" I called cheerfully. I handed her a baggie filled with cookies. "Something for your coffee break." Bob had insisted I take some, but no way was I actually going to eat them.

"Yum, are these fresh baked?"

"Bob made them just this morning. Chocolate chip and oatmeal raisin. He uses fresh grated cinnamon in the oatmeal. You've never had anything like it."

"Forget waiting for the coffee break!" Belinda pulled out an oatmeal cookie and held the bag out for me. "Have one with me."

"No thanks, I had plenty while they were hot from the oven." Okay, that wasn't true, but it was just a tiny white lie and I hardly even blushed telling it. I've been practicing my P.I. skills, and telling a lie was one of them. I was getting better at it, but I didn't think I'd ever master it with people that I know. It was different with strangers, especially those I didn't expect to ever see again. It didn't really matter much if they caught me in a lie, but I wanted to be trusted by the people I knew, and once lied to, twice shy and all that.

Belinda was frowning at me. "Uh oh, you're not crash dieting again, are you?"

"No," I told her, but I couldn't hold her gaze and she shook her head.

"You've got to eat, Rainie. Starving yourself won't improve your waistline."

"I know, I know. I'm going to go have lunch in just a little while. Do you have anything for me?" I changed the subject. I didn't like talking about my weight. I struggled to remain a size twelve, and even at that I usually had a very small but noticeable roll of fat at the top of my jeans.

Belinda gave me a new file to work on and I wandered back to the computer room, where I already had several files in progress. The bulk of my time at B&E was spent doing the computer work for finding deadbeat dads or missing persons, or running credit and background checks on prospective employees. Now and then something interesting would pop up, but I've been a little cautious since last fall when I went way overboard on a simple case. I still shuddered with embarrassment over that one, even though I seem to be the only one who thinks I went too far.

At the moment I had two background checks to run, one for a prospective employer, the other with no explanation. Those were sometimes entertaining. It might be a woman checking out a guy she was dating, just to be sure he was all he said he was, or someone checking out their daughter's new boyfriend.

"Hey Rainie, what's up?"

"Hey Jack." I turned to look at him, always a pleasant sight. Tight denim and cotton wrapped around a tall muscular frame. Practically a piece of art.

"What are you up to today?"

"Background checks."

"Wow. Fun." He grinned to take the sting out of his sarcasm.

"So what about you?" I asked, genuinely interested. Jack was a licensed P.I. as well as a body guard and all around bad-ass, and he always seemed to be doing something interesting.

"Actually I could use some help if you're up for it."

"Uh oh. Why do I need to be up for it?"

"Hey, it's nothing that bad," Jack grinned. "I got a tip that a guy I need to talk to is staying with his sister. The problem is, he probably doesn't particularly want to talk to me, so *I* can't just walk up and ask for him. They'd see me coming and he'd be out the back before I made it up the sidewalk. I want you to go to the front door. People tend to trust a woman more, so they'll probably open up. Then you tell them you're from B&E, the guy will freak and run out the back, and I'll be there to snatch him up."

I shook my head, staring at Jack in disbelief. "Wow, you really believe this stuff is that easy, don't you?"

"Sure, why not?"

"Jack, none of these little ventures go as simply as you say they will. There are always people shooting or things blowing up."

"Not *always*." Jack had a whole repertoire of grins, from sweet to wet-your-pants scary. Now he favored me with that bad-boyish one, the one that said "gee, I was just playing around, I didn't know that cherry bomb would blow the toilet off the wall."

"But I guess if you're scared…"

"I'm not scared!" I lied. Of course I was scared. Anyone in their right mind *would* be. Then again, Jack wasn't, so that made him…

"You're getting that distant look again, Rainie. Am I losing you?"

"No, I was just thinking. What the hell, let's go find your guy."

"That's my girl!" Jack threw an arm around my shoulder and gave me a brief hug. It was a comrade-in-arms type of thing, and he let me go in a hurry. He was aware of my aversion to public displays of affection and respected that. On the other hand, I kind of liked physical contact with him. I'm fickle about some things.

Okay, maybe a lot of things.

Chapter Two

It was three o'clock, the sun was already well on its way to the western sky, and the temperature was dropping rapidly. The rain had changed over to snow as promised. It was falling in thick, heavy flakes that were already covering the road. Maybe not the best weather for a road trip, but hey, this was Michigan. If you wanted a good day for travel you'd pretty much have to stay home for three months.

Naturally we rode in Jack's truck, a shiny black Ford Ranger with every bell and whistle the engineers could dream up as well as a few add-ons that they hadn't. Jack turned down the stereo when we got in so we could talk, reducing the volume on B.B King. Jack's music tastes are almost as eclectic as mine, although he doesn't get how I can like bluegrass. Sometimes I don't get it either, so I don't try to explain it. Sometimes in life it's better to just tap your toes and go with it.

"So Belinda tells me you've got a new boyfriend."

"Don't you two have better things to do than gossip?"

"That isn't gossip," Jack tried to look offended. "That's just keeping up with the welfare of a friend."

"Oh, I can see the distinction now!" I laughed. "Anyway he isn't a boyfriend, just a guy I've gone out with a few times."

"An accountant?" Jack seemed to think that was pretty funny.

"Hey, he's smart and amusing and owns his own business. I could do worse."

"Does he wear pocket protectors?"

"No! Actually he's more of a jeans and tweed jacket kind of guy, and for your information he works out regularly. He's not some pale desk jockey in a bad suit."

"Hey, I didn't say there was anything wrong with accountants."

"Then why do I feel like you're making fun of me?"

"I'm not, I'm just curious to know what the flavor of the month is."

"Hey, that's kind of mean!"

Jack laughed. "I'm not trying to be mean, it's just that you don't have the greatest track record with men. Maybe you need to see Dr. Phil. I think you might have commitment issues."

He was right, I didn't seem to be able to hang on to a man. I was married once but it turned out my husband was gay. Tommy and I were good friends now, but that didn't really count as keeping a guy.

For a while I dated Brad, a local rich kid that had inexplicably taken a liking to me. We broke up after a fight about me working with Jack. Then I had dated Dan, a blues guitar player, but he had ditched me at a party when I'd had too much to drink, and although that had apparently just been a misunderstanding, our relationship never recovered. Oh well, maybe Michael would stick around a while.

"Hey, sorry if I offended you." Jack sounded genuinely contrite.

"You didn't." Well, maybe a little.

The guy we were looking for was supposedly in Berrien Springs, a smallish city north of Buchanan.

We were cruising along at a good clip down a two lane country road, Jack looking relaxed, driving with one hand at six 'o clock on the steering wheel. The road was snow covered and the white stuff hadn't let up in the least. I don't mind driving in these conditions, but I have to admit I'm a little nervous riding. It isn't that I don't trust Jack's driving skills, it's just that I prefer to have my own hands on the wheel. I guess I have control issues. I tried a little conversation to distract myself.

"So why exactly are you looking for this guy? Did he jump bail?" That was one of many services B&E Security provided, but not one I normally got involved in. Bail jumpers were for the ex-special forces or other bad-asses of the world, not for poet-caregiver-P.I. assistants.

"No, he violated his parole."

"So what are you going to do? You can't arrest anyone."

"He's a known fugitive. If I catch him I can turn him over to the cops."

"Isn't it the cop's job to catch him?"

"He's not a high priority for them. If they pick him up for something else, like a traffic stop, they'll take him in, but they aren't going to spend a lot of time looking for him."

"So why are you?"

"Because he has information we need. I just want to talk to him. If he cooperates, I'll let him go."

"Even though you know he's violated parole?"

"What do I care? That's his P.O.'s problem."

As so often happened, I was beginning to feel like I had missed a crucial point in this conversation. It seemed to be meandering in a big, sloppy circle.

"But you just said you could turn him over to the cops."

"I could, but I don't really want to. Lots of paperwork, and the cops don't appreciate private citizens interfering with their job."

"Even if it's to their benefit?"

"Vigilantes tend to get hurt, or worse, they violate the suspect's rights all over the place and the cases get thrown out on technicalities. And I for one don't plan to worry a lot about this guy's rights."

"Nice," I grimaced, and Jack laughed.

"I don't intend to be. Hey, the guy did time for domestic assault and home invasion. I don't have a lot of sympathy."

"What's his name?"

"Danny Finnegan. When we get there, just go up to the front door and knock. His sister will probably answer, because she's a stay at home mom. Ask her if she's seen Danny. Be aggressive about it, tell her you know he's in there."

"And what will you be doing?"

"Hanging around in back, waiting for him to run out the back door."

"What if he just hides in the basement?"

Jack gave me a sour look. "Don't you ever think positive?"

"Sure. I'm positive this is going to turn out ugly. It always does, no reason to think this time will be any different."

"You'll have the keys to my truck. If it gets ugly you can just take off."

It was my turn to give him a look. "Do you really think I'd just take off and leave you?"

He smiled. "Anyway, Danny isn't known to carry a weapon, so this isn't likely to get too ugly. No sweat, really."

"Really." I rolled my eyes, already sweating.

Danny Finnegan's sister lived in a working class neighborhood not far off the main thoroughfare in Berrien Springs. The houses were all of the three bedroom, one bath variety, with smallish but serviceable yards, narrow driveways, and one car garages without automatic door openers.

Narrow alleys ran between the streets, convenient for the garbage trucks, but also for sneaky P.I.'s and other types who didn't want to approach the front door. I dropped Jack off at the mouth of the alley and waited while he jogged past a few houses. He stopped and waved me off, and I drove around the corner.

Some of the houses had their numbers clearly displayed, usually near the front door, large black numbers: **409**, **411**, like that. Others were missing digits, like **4 2,** or just not there at all.

I was looking for 417, so I concentrated on the odd numbered side of the street, driving slowly while peering through the curtain of snow.

I've often wondered who decides what number a house gets. And why are there gaps in the numbering in so many neighborhoods? Like on this block, the odd side goes 409, 411, 415. So where is 413? The houses are only about twenty feet apart, so it's not like 413 used to be there and got torn down. I guess it's just one of the universe's great mysteries, right up there with dark matter and where the second sock goes when you put it in the dryer.

I found 417 right where it should be, next to 415. It was a single story with old rough green siding and white trimmed windows in need of paint. It didn't look like the sidewalk had been shoveled for several days.

I wasn't here to evaluate the house. I jumped out of the truck and slogged through the snow to the front door.

There was a tiny covered porch with a single plastic lawn chair and a tiny table with an ashtray. This was a common sight now as smokers were forced to move outside with their habit. It used to be people sat on their front porches to enjoy the weather or say hey to the neighbors when they walked by. Now it was more of a furtive thing, the smoker hunched apologetically over the ashtray, a pathetic loser who, unlike seemingly every other thinking person in the world, can't give up the smokes.

Yeah, I can say that, because I have an ashtray on my front porch, too.

The front door came equipped with a small window covered with a frilly curtain. I rang the bell, and after a few long moments I saw the curtain twitch to one side. A single eye peered out at me, although I assumed it was probably attached to someone. The eye shifted to the left and the curtain dropped back into place. I heard urgent whispering, but I couldn't make out the words.

Impatient, I rang the bell again, and followed it up with a short, hard knock. I hoped I seemed determined and confident, a woman who wouldn't take no for an answer, but inside I was a quivering bowl of poorly set gelatin that would likely melt to mush with the slightest application of heat.

The door opened slowly and a woman appeared in the opening. She held the door tightly, keeping it against her so I couldn't see into the house.

She was medium height and weight, with longish brown hair that hung past her shoulders. She was pale, as if she'd been sick and was just recovering, but there were bright flushes of color high on her cheeks and splotching her neck.

"May I help you?" The words were formal and stilted. It was clearly not a phrase that came naturally to her. She was blinking rapidly.

"Mrs. Rankin?"

"Yes, that's me." She stared at me as if the next words I uttered would reveal her ultimate fate.

"My name is Lovingston." I pulled out my cool little ID wallet that held my driver's license on one side and an employee ID card from B&E on the other. It gave me absolutely no authority - I wasn't even a licensed P.I., just a lowly assistant - but it looked official, and most people didn't actually bother to read past an official looking logo. Or so Jack claimed.

Apparently that was true of Mrs. Rankin, because her eyes widened momentarily before she resumed the rapid blinking.

"What can I do for you?"

"I'm looking for your brother, Danny Finnegan. Is he here?"

Her eyes flicked to the left and abruptly the blinking stopped.

"Um no...no, why would he be here?"

"We got a tip..." I stopped talking, because her lips were moving. Oddly, no sound was coming out. For just a second I was afraid I'd spontaneously gone deaf, maybe a sudden flashback reaction to that Aerosmith reunion tour I'd attended with my mother, the one where I was sitting two rows away from the room-sized speakers.

But no, I realized, she wasn't making any sounds. In fact, she was moving her lips in that exaggerated way people use so you can read their lips. Funny thing is, all that does is distort the message, like talking through thick glass.

I stared at her lips. What was that? It looked like she mouthed "Meg Ryan's here" but I doubted that was right. I mean, that would be a hell of a coincidence, Meg Ryan visiting Mrs. Rankin at the same time I was there looking for her brother.

"What was that? What kind of tip?" Mrs. Rankin prompted me, and I realized she wanted me to keep talking.

"We were told Danny is staying here…" I trailed off again, because I can't read lips and speak at the same time, and once again her lips were moving. In fact, now she was frantically rolling her eyes up and to the left over and over again, as if her eyeballs kept breaking free of their moorings and she had to continually re-anchor them. Then I realized what she was doing. She was indicating that someone was just beyond her shoulder. At the same time I got what her lips were trying to tell me: "He's right behind me!"

I nodded to let her know I got it, fearing that if she kept it up her eyes really would break loose and literally roll up into her head.

"If you have any information…"

"No, no, I have no idea where he is…" She broke off and silently mouthed: "Help me!"

Damn, why did I have to understand that one? *I* couldn't help her. I felt like holding my ID up again and pointing out to her that I was just a lowly P.I.'s assistant. Ask me to help a bedridden elder and I was all over it. I had the skills and empathy to get the job done and get it done right. Ask me to play poker, or write a poem, or grow vegetables. I had all those skills. But rescue a woman from her parolee brother who had apparently turned on her, a man who'd already been arrested for domestic assault?

The only thing I could think to do was to yell for Jack.

That, of course, would eliminate his advantage of surprise. On the other hand, Danny Finnegan was obviously not going to go running out the back door like Jack had hoped.

"Mommy, can I have a pudding?" The voice belonged to a little girl about five years old, who easily wormed her way past the blockade Mrs. Rankin was making with her body. The child pushed past so she could look up at her mom. What kid doesn't instinctively know that their mother has a much harder time saying no to their face?

I tried to take advantage of the distraction.

"Well, I can see you're busy..." I took a small step back. I would drive around and get Jack. He would know what to do.

Maybe I should have seen it coming, but I'm not a mom, and apparently I don't get just how a woman behaves when it comes to protecting their children.

Mrs. Rankin scooped up the little girl and shoved her into my arms.

"Take her! Run!"

Before I could react Mrs. Rankin was turning away from the door.

"You stupid bitch!" The owner of the disembodied voice had a big man's hand, and I saw it snatch Mrs. Rankin by the hair. My first instinct was to leap forward and help her; then I remembered the little girl. Her mother was willing to risk herself to get the kid to safety. Who was I to argue with that?

The door slammed shut and I turned and ran for the truck as fast as I could, making surprisingly good time for having to slog through a foot of crusty snow with a forty pound weight in my arms. As I ran I screamed for Jack.

"Jack! Help! In front!"

I had no idea if he could hear me. I didn't know for sure where he was. He might be right up at the back of the house, or he could be back in the alley. I also wasn't sure how well my voice was carrying. Not for the first time, and I'm sure not the last, I was reminded that even two or three packs of smokes a week was too many. Running in snow is almost as bad as trying to run in water, and I was gasping for air by the time I reached the truck.

I popped the door and tossed the kid inside, ignoring her screaming. I wasn't sure what to do next. Should I drive around back and look for Jack? Should I call the cops?

Yeah, that sounded like a good idea. I mean, we weren't really doing anything wrong here, so let them handle it. I was so used to being involved in questionable dealings when I was with Jack that calling 911 seemed counterintuitive.

I pulled out my phone, but suddenly the front door opened again and Mrs. Rankin came running out. A tall thin man with long hair and a scraggly beard was right on her heels, and by the time she made it off the porch the guy had snatched her again. He pulled her to the ground and was dragging her back to the house by her hair like a Neanderthal in a cartoon. That really pissed me off, and I forgot all about my phone. I jumped out of the truck and ran back across the snow.

She was screaming, grasping at his hands to relieve the pain and keep from having her hair all pulled out. I didn't even slow down. I ran into the guy full tilt, my shoulder low like a linebacker in the NFL - okay, maybe high school football - B team - but it was good enough to knock him on his ass. Mrs. Rankin screamed again, and I winced when I saw the thick strand of hair the guy had tangled in his fingers, but at least he'd let her go.

Sure he'd let her go, because now he was coming after me!

His foot lashed out and got me a good one high on the thigh. Either he knew just the right spot to hit or he got lucky, because instantly I was down on one knee, howling from the pain. He took advantage of my sudden disability and kicked out with his other leg, aiming for my head.

His boots looked heavy, and I think that blow would have done some serious damage if not for Mrs. Rankin, who with a shout of pure fury launched herself at the guy. The kick caught her halfway into its arc, an ineffectual half-strength blow that did little to slow her down. She was on the guy with nails and teeth like a wolverine just poked with a stick. Now it was his turn to yell, and he didn't sound nearly as cocky as he had a few seconds before.

I got to my feet and backed away, afraid I was going to take a random blow from flailing feet. I circled around, looking for an opening so I could give Mrs. Rankin a hand.

For a short time it looked like maybe she wouldn't need help. I'd heard stories of mother's defending their children who turned into something as vicious as a mama bear, and now I could tell one of my own. I wondered if I could kick ass like that if I ever settled down and gave birth.

The guy was bloodied, but unfortunately he outweighed Mrs. Rankin by a good forty pounds and he had a much longer reach. With a sudden arch of his back and flip of his hips he turned the tide and now *he* was on top, his own fists raining down on her.

I wasn't wearing big boots like he was, but at least I was wearing tennis shoes instead of sandals or bare feet. I kicked out with my good leg, aiming for his ear.

The connection was good. Much better, in fact, than I expected it to be. I've seen Chuck Norris kick people in the ear lots of times, and they just shake their heads and keep coming.

This guy grunted once and collapsed on Mrs. Rankin like a puppet whose strings were cut. Like a pole-axed steer. Like a sack of potatoes. Like a...well, you get the idea.

"Oh crap!" I leapt back, astonished. Had I just killed him?

"Help!" Mrs. Rankin was struggling to roll the guy off of her. I stared at them, for the moment unable to move. What had I done?

"Rainie? What the hell is going on?"

I gaped at Jack, who had come from around the back of the house. I finally managed to close my jaw and get three frantic words out: "I killed him!"

"Killed who?"

"Danny Finnegan!" I pointed at the guy I'd kicked. Jack reached over and grabbed the guy by the back of his shirt and flopped him over in the snow to get a look at his face, at the same time freeing Mrs. Rankin.

Jack shook his head.

"That's not Danny."

"Danny's probably long gone, and good riddance!" Mrs. Rankin got to her feet, wiping at her bloody nose with the back of her arm. "Where's Barbie?"

"Barbie?" I repeated stupidly, thinking "*with Ken, I suppose.*"

"My daughter! What did you do with her!"

Oh, that Barbie! "She's in the truck."

Mrs. Rankin took off running toward the truck and Jack took off running for the house in search of Danny. I stood there, staring at the guy I'd just killed. Admittedly he was a bad guy, but hey, I was far from perfect myself. In fact, now I was a murderer!

They would throw me in jail. If I didn't die from the claustrophobic panic of the cell door clanging shut I would spend the rest of my life with nothing to do but stare at a stone wall and think about what I'd done. I'd killed a man. Snuffed him out. Unquickened him. Okay, that's probably not a word, but whatever, I'd made him dead.

But then the guy moved.

He moaned and rolled his head to the side and opened one eye.

He wasn't dead! Thank god, I'm not a cold blooded killer! I won't have to go to jail and this guy can go on doing whatever it is he does.

With a speed I wouldn't have thought possible in a guy who'd been unconscious ten seconds before he reached out and grabbed my ankle. I reacted without thinking and kicked out with my other foot, catching him on his other ear.

He dropped back with a moan and I skipped out of the way.

"Hah! Serves you right!"

So much for my guilty conscience.

It only took Jack a couple of minutes to search the small house. He came back out, looking pissed off.

"He's gone."

"Hopefully you spooked him so he won't come back." Mrs. Rankin had managed to calm her daughter.

"Why were you hiding him in the first place?" I asked.

"I wasn't hiding him! He came in a couple days ago with that... that pig!" she pointed at the unconscious guy on the lawn. "He wouldn't let me send Barbie to school. He knew I wouldn't do anything as long as my daughter was here." Mrs. Rankin started to cry. "My own damned brother! He went to jail for treating his wife this way."

"I'm sorry, Mrs. Rankin." I was suddenly grateful for my own brother. Drunk or sober he'd never hurt anyone.

"Do you know where Danny is?"

"No. He left this morning, hasn't been back."

"Uh huh." Jack clearly didn't believe her, but he didn't argue. "Come on, Rainie. Let's go."

"Wait! What about him!" Mrs. Rankin pointed at the unconscious guy on her lawn.

"What about him? Call the cops and have him arrested."

"I can't do that. If I press charges on him I'll have to testify against my brother, too."

"So? After what he put you through he deserves to go back to jail."

"Of course he does, but I'm not going to put him there. He's my *brother*."

"And that's your daughter," I pointed out. "Do you really want to put her through this crap again?"

Mrs. Rankin tightened her hold on Barbie and stared at me for a few seconds. Finally she nodded.

"Come on, Barbie. We need to call the police."

"Will they make the bad man go away?"

"Yes, honey." Mrs. Rankin disappeared inside and we heard the deadbolt turn.

"Just to be sure." Jack pulled a long plastic zip tie out of his coat pocket and secured the scraggly guy's hands behind his back. He could get up and walk away if he woke up, but he probably couldn't break into a locked house without the use of his hands.

"Okay, we're out of here."

Chapter Three

Jack dropped me off at the office so I could pick up my car. I got home at five-thirty and let George out of his cage. I filled his bowl with bite sized pieces of fruits and veggies I kept pre-cut in the fridge and let him out to bask under his heat lamp.

Michael was coming at seven o'clock and I had promised to cook dinner. I was actually a pretty good cook, having learned from my mother how to prepare meals from fresh, organically grown ingredients. I didn't do it very often, and few people were aware of my hidden talent. It was simpler to just eat cereal or peanut butter, and doing so usually kept my weight down, but a couple of months ago I realized that strategy wasn't working any more.

I wasn't a waif to begin with, struggling mightily to keep my weight at one forty, but then I gained ten pounds while in recovery from a gunshot wound in my arm. The pain had made it easy to avoid regular exercise for a while, not to mention I seemed to be eating everything in sight. Jack thought that might be nerves, a minor case of post-traumatic stress. Whatever, I just knew I seemed to feel better when I was stuffing my face.

Of course, I didn't feel so good when I could no longer button my jeans.

I managed to lose five of those extra pounds, but they came right back

I complained about it to my friend Eddie, who was spending some time with me, teaching me self-defense techniques. He replied with what seemed a radical idea at the time: too many carbs, not enough protein and fat. What? Not enough fat? But I tried his plan, and sure enough in a couple of months the ten pounds were gone and I had more energy than ever.

Don't get me wrong, I still wasn't cooking much, and a lot of nights I just slathered some peanut butter on a celery stick or a spoon, but tonight Michael was getting bar-b-q chicken breast and broccoli with cheese sauce. I made my own bar-b-q sauce, a recipe my mother had created but that I had spiced up a bit. My cheese sauce, I had to admit, was a creamy smooth delight.

Michael arrived promptly at seven and sat at the kitchen counter drinking a beer while I put the finishing touches on dinner. I pulled the chicken out of the oven to rest while I steamed the broccoli and made the sauce. I browned flour in butter, then added some chicken broth and stirred it until it thickened. I added a bit of cream, a generous pinch of celery salt and pepper, and finally some freshly shredded cheddar cheese.

I plated everything and invited Michael to carry his own plate to the dining room.

I could have been more formal but I preferred to be cautious about such things. If you showed the ability to be properly domestic men tended to expect it all the time, and I didn't want Michael to get any ideas. I mean, what if this relationship actually went somewhere? I didn't want to get trapped into cooking and serving him meals all the time. Just because I *can* cook that doesn't mean I wanted to do it all the time, or even more than a couple of times a year.

Michael ate slowly and deliberately, every few bites raving about how good it was. I'm normally a pretty fast eater. I have issues with food and I prefer to just get it over with. I forced myself to eat at Michael's pace. I don't want him to think I'm an unrefined pig.

"So how are my mom's taxes going?" I asked just to make conversation and keep my mouth empty for a minute.

Michael smiled. He crooked up one side of his mouth and cocked his head to one side. It was kind of cute. Actually he was kind of cute all over. He had thick brown hair with a natural curl that he wore on the longish side, so it always looked a little tousled. He wasn't classically handsome, but he had nice features and expressive brown eyes. He really did work out regularly, like I'd told Jack, but he wasn't buff by any means. He was about 5' 10" and had a very minimal belly paunch, but he had nice forearms and great hands. I don't know what it is about a man's hands, but I sort of have a thing for them.

"Your mom has an interesting method of bookkeeping."

"Yeah?" I smiled back, knowing my mom well.

"She seems to live far beyond her means, but she can account for all her cash. It's the bartering we're having problems with."

"She does that a lot."

"I'll say. She housebroke some guy's dog in exchange for having her plumbing fixed, and another guy patched her roof in trade for some home-canned tomatoes."

"So what's the problem?"

"The IRS expects all of that to be accounted for."

"What?" I was stunned. "What business is all that to the IRS?"

"Bartering is considered income. Check your instructions. It's all there."

"That's ridiculous."

"I agree, and that's why she hired me." Michael grinned. "She's paying me in goat's milk and fresh eggs."

I laughed. "Are you going to claim it?"

"Hell no! And by the time I'm done your mom won't be claiming most of that stuff either. As far as the IRS will know Jedediah is just an amazing carpenter, plumber and all around fix it guy and they never have to hire anything done."

"That's somewhat true."

"Yeah, but it's still hard for the powers to be to believe that your folks live in that nice house on Jedediah's ten thousand dollars a year income from the co-op."

"Mom told me you think someone might have turned her in."

Michael shrugged. "I can't be sure, but the truth is the IRS doesn't usually go looking for people like your mom. Most of the laws were enacted against gangsters and drug dealers to give the feds a backdoor to arrest them."

"You mean like Al Capone going to jail for tax evasion."

"Right. It says right in the instruction booklet that you have to claim income from illegal activities."

"No way!"

"Sure. Like I said, it's their back door."

"Mom said she wasn't too happy about having to declare her 'caregiver' income."

Michael laughed. My mother had recently taken on several clients who were eligible to buy medical marijuana under Michigan's new law. She had been growing special herbs in her greenhouse for personal use for years, but now she could actually grow it legitimately.

"Yeah, she doesn't see why the government should get any proceeds from the growing and selling of a weed. In this case I disagree with her, though. Those people really need that stuff, and it's good that it's finally legal for them to have it."

"She has three cancer patients," I sighed. "She delivers to two of them, because they're too sick from chemo to come and get it."

"Your mom is a good person."

"I'm glad she found you. Not every accountant would help her like this."

"I'm glad she found me, too," he smiled again. "If she hadn't I wouldn't have met you."

"Probably not. I do my own taxes."

Yeah, I know. I gave a practical response when he was clearly trying to flirt. I don't know what my problem is. I see other women flirting effortlessly, always saying just the right thing. Belinda, even Thelma, make it sound so natural, but I always seem to say something stupid.

Michael went back to his food, obviously disappointed by my cold response. I swallowed a sigh and took another tiny bite of my chicken. At this rate it would be breakfast time before I finished dinner. I willed him to eat faster.

I was relieved when my home phone rang. I excused myself and stepped into the kitchen to grab it off the counter. Again, I know it was a little rude, but thanks to me dinner conversation had gotten awkward.

"Hello?"

"Hi Rainie, it's Gina."

"Hi Gina," I was surprised. Gina and I had been pretty good friends back in our younger days but we rarely ran into each other anymore. She was married with kids and the whole domestic routine, and I...well.

"I hope I'm not interrupting anything."

"No, not at all," I answered, and winced when I remembered Michael. I was glad he couldn't hear her side of the conversation.

"I'm calling to ask a favor. Actually the favor isn't for me, it's for Pam LaBell, remember her?"

"Sort of." I closed my eyes, trying to bring Pam to mind. I remembered the name, but not much else.

"She was the girl who was always trying to tag along with us to parties, the short girl who always drank whiskey?"

"Oh yeah," I laughed, suddenly remembering her. "Man, she could really put away the shots!"

"Not any more. Pam got religion years ago, hasn't touched a drop since."

"Wow, that's hard to believe."

"Her name is Pam Swanson now. She's a teacher and spends all her spare time doing charity work. She's really a terrific person. She'd do anything for you."

"Okay, so you've established *why* I want to do her a favor. Now tell me what the favor *is*." I had a feeling I wasn't going to like it.

"Not long after she found religion Pam also found a husband. They had a son who is about to turn eleven."

"Good for her." I turned to look through the archway at Michael, who was glancing my way now and then, not eating. Great, he'd decided to wait for me. I made a motion with my hand for him to go ahead without me but he just shook his head. There was another difference between me and Michael: he has good manners.

"That was good, but about two years after Davey was born her husband disappeared and hasn't been heard from since."

Uh oh. I could feel a freebie request coming on. I've been asked a couple of times to do free research since the word has gotten around that I work as a P.I.'s assistant. I turned down both requests, reminding the people that I worked for a company and their resources weren't free. I should have just told Gina no and not wasted her time, but I was a little curious. Like a cat, that stuff always gets me in trouble.

"Disappeared? Like packed his clothes and left or fell off a boat into Lake Michigan?"

"Like he went out one night to get diapers for little Davey and never came back. The store clerk at the pharmacy remembered him coming in and buying diapers, but no one saw him after that. He just disappeared."

"Weird. So by now they've declared him legally dead, right?"

"The point is Pam doesn't think he *is* dead, and she needs to find him."

"Why? If he just took off she's clearly better off without him."

"She is, but Davey is the issue." Gina paused for dramatic effect. "Rainie, he has leukemia. He needs a bone marrow transplant or he'll die."

Crap. Double crap. I glanced back at Michael, who was watching me. I wished I had his manners and had ignored the phone. I mean, I have an answering machine. It would have been a lot easier to ignore this request if it was on an impersonal tape recording.

"So she needs to find her husband because he might be a potential donor."

"Right. The problem is Pam doesn't have any money to hire a detective. Davey needs so much care she only works part time, just enough to keep her insurance."

"I don't know what you think I can do by myself. I'm not even a real detective, and this guy has been gone nine years. I doubt if even a full court press by B&E would turn him up after this much time."

"Real detective or not, you've pulled off some pretty amazing stuff. You caught those serial killer grannies and you busted that meth ring. You must know what you're doing."

"I just got lucky," I corrected her. Yeah, lucky I wasn't killed.

By now I realized it wouldn't have mattered if I had only heard this on the machine. I was hooked. I mean, who could listen to this sob story and not want to help? The problem was I really *didn't* have any investigative resources of my own. All the data bases were contracted by B&E and employees were expressly forbidden to access them for personal use.

Even so I found myself saying, "I'll see what I can do, Gina." Over her profuse thanks I interjected, "Wait! I'm not making any promises, I just said I'd try. Give me Pam's number and I'll give her a call."

"You don't know how much this will mean to her."

"I don't want to get her hopes up. The odds of me finding him are so close to nil I'd have to invent a new number to describe them."

"I know Rainie, but at least it will give Pam some hope, and let me tell you, she could use some. I don't know how she gets through her days, watching that poor little boy…" Gina broke off and I knew she was crying. That caused my own eyes to tear. Great, just what I needed, my date seeing me blubbering in the kitchen. Michael was never going to ask me out again.

I cleared my throat. "Give me the number."

Gina got control of herself and recited Pam's number. "That's at her parent's house. She lost her apartment a few months ago when Davey came out of remission."

"Okay," I said, just to say something. How much worse was this going to get? "I'll call her first thing tomorrow."

"Tomorrow? Can't you call her now?"

"Look Gina, I kind of have company over for dinner."

"Oh... Oh! You mean like a date company?"

"Yeah, like that."

"I'm sorry Rainie! Is it that hot guy you run around with? What's his name, Jack?"

"No, it's not. Look, I've got to go."

"Okay. Call me sometime, we'll go out for coffee or something."

"Sure, okay. Bye."

I hung up and turned to look at Michael again, who was looking at me with some concern.

"Is everything all right?"

"Sure!" I injected too much false cheer in my tone and tried to take it down a notch. "Just work stuff, sorry." I went back to the table. "Do you want me to warm this up?"

"No, it's fine." Michael took a bite of his broccoli and smiled to prove it. I looked at my own. The cheese sauce was beginning to congeal, and it didn't look fine to me at all. It didn't surprise me that cold food wouldn't bother Michael; at the pace he ate he probably hadn't had a hot meal since his mother's breast milk.

"I think I'll just pop mine in the microwave for a minute." I picked up my plate. "You sure yours is okay?"

"It's wonderful." He took a bite of cold chicken

Hm, I couldn't quite decide. Was this a good quality or an annoying quirk?

Too soon to tell.

Another point in Michael's favor was the fact that he was also a fan of Jeopardy, so after dinner we sat and watched it together.

I know that might sound pretty lame, but it's actually a pretty good way to gauge potential compatibility. You get a chance to figure out what your prospective partner knows. Or doesn't know.

Michael and I were pretty evenly matched as far as how many questions we answered, but it was obvious that his strong suits were geography and politics - neither my forte by any means - and mine are literary and science. If we could have played Jeopardy as a team we would have cleaned up.

Satisfied with his performance, I walked him to the door a short time later. He stopped and turned to me, and I realized we were about to have our First Kiss.

Now, this was a big deal. Kissing is an integral part of the mating ritual. I've often wondered if human beings picked up kissing from watching nature, in particular birds. I watch the cardinals at my bird feeder, the male feeding the female from his own mouth, convincing her he will be there with the chow when the babies come along and she's stuck back in the nest. I wonder if, subconsciously, that's what human kissing is all about: a promise of sustenance.

That being said, for me a first kiss tells me a lot about the relationship to come. Is he too aggressive, trying to shove his tongue down my throat in the first five seconds? (That of course reminded me of Jack. The one and only time he kissed me that's exactly what he did, but then, we were both high on adrenalin and I wasn't sure that counted.) In normal circumstances such aggression says to me that the guy is in too big a hurry to consider my needs, or worse, he's a control freak. I already hold that position over myself, and I don't plan to relinquish it to *any*one.

On the other hand, is he too passive, giving me a bare peck, maybe even on the cheek? In that case he might be waiting for me to make a move. Since I'm pretty backward when it comes to sexual encounters our relationship would probably remain forever platonic.

And then there's the third possibility, which is what I got from Michael: just right. No tongue, prolonged just long enough to let me know he was interested, not so long that it got awkward. Even better, I felt a little tingly. Not full blown fireworks, but maybe a sparkler.

Not bad for a start.

Chapter Four

On Tuesday morning I woke up to find Pam foremost in my thoughts. I know there are a lot of people out there suffering hardships, especially with the economy being what it is, but Pam's problem had been dumped right into my lap. It wasn't something I could just donate my change to or join a march for. It was a real problem for a real person and I had been asked to come up with a real solution.

I would do my best, but this morning I had somewhere else to be.

Tuesdays and Thursdays are my days with Thelma, my best friend as well as my client. She's seventy-six years young and has more money than ways to spend it, so she pays my regular wages so I'm able to spend time with her. The thing is, she really doesn't need a caregiver. She has a chauffeur to drive her where she wants to go on days I'm not there, although Morty was in his nineties and his eyesight and reflexes were failing. As it was Thelma only had him drive her around in town limits, where the speed limit was twenty-five miles per hour and there wasn't much traffic. She kept him on because he needed the money to supplement his inadequate social security, and because he had a great sense of humor. Mostly dirty old man humor, but he made Thelma laugh, and that was important to her.

Thelma did her own cooking when she felt like it and walked down four blocks to the Hilltop Diner when she didn't. That was okay. The Hilltop served pretty good "home cooked" meals. Thelma also had someone who came in to clean once a week and she paid a kid down the street to do her heavy yard work and shoveling. She still did minor home repairs herself, and in fact had taught me a little bit about plumbing and simple electrical tasks.

Recently she had invested a lot of money opening a store in downtown Buchanan with my sister Brenda. It was a resale shop called "Next To You," specializing in high-end used clothing and small household items, and it was doing surprisingly well. My sister had already gone down to part time hours at her regular job so she could run the store on Tuesdays, Thursdays and Saturdays. Thelma ran it Monday, Wednesday and Friday, and if nothing else it was becoming a popular hangout for the livelier senior citizens in town.

I walked out my front door to find the world blurred by lake effect snow. It was coming down heavy, maybe as much as an inch an hour, but fortunately there was no wind to drift it. It was doing a nice job of covering those ugly piles of dirty old snow, kind of like putting a fresh coat of paint on the world. Or so I told myself as I kicked snow off my shoes and climbed into my cold car.

I arrived at eight o'clock to find Thelma on a stepladder changing the light bulb in the foyer. I steadied the ladder while she climbed down.

"I think I'm going to have to change that fixture," Thelma complained. "That's the second bulb it blew this month."

"Seems a shame. That's an original fixture, isn't it?"

Thelma squinted at me.

"Uh oh, what's wrong?"

"What makes you think something's wrong?"

"You didn't scold me for being on the stepladder, which you always do even though you know it doesn't do any good. And you have your blouse on inside out."

"What?" I looked down and sure enough I could see the seams on my shirt. "How the heck did I manage that?"

"Distracted most likely. I do that sort of thing when I'm in a hurry or in a funk, and you don't look like you're in a hurry. Go fix it and come into the kitchen. We'll have some coffee and you can tell me what the problem is."

Thelma folded up her ladder and headed for the kitchen and I went into the little bathroom off the hall to turn my shirt right side out. I'm glad I was wearing a coat. I had stopped for a pack of smokes on the way, and I'd be too embarrassed to ever go back into the corner gas station if they'd seen me with my shirt seams showing.

I sat at the table with Thelma and told her about my conversation with Gina.

"That's really sad. So how long do you think it will take you to find the guy?"

"It's not that simple! For one thing he's probably long dead. Even if he's not, law enforcement hasn't been able to find him in all this time, what prayer do I have?"

"Law enforcement probably hasn't wasted a minute looking for him since the first week he went missing. If he was a kid or a battered woman, maybe, but a healthy adult male?" Thelma shook her head. "They have better things to do."

"I suppose you're right. Still, if he's dead it won't do much good if I do figure out where he went."

"So when are you going to get started?"

"I'm going to call her tonight and set up a time to meet with her. After I get more details I hope I'll have an idea where to start."

"Why don't you call her now?"

"This is our time."

"We don't have any special plans. Maybe I can go with you to see her."

That made me hesitate. I love Thelma, but she has impulse issues. Getting her involved with any aspect of my P.I. work is a potential problem. Then again, I was doing this on my own time, and I was only going to talk to Pam. What could it hurt?

"All right, I'll call her."

Pam was more than willing to see me immediately, and she had no problem with Thelma coming along. She didn't really care who knew about the situation as long as she could find her long-lost husband.

Pam had moved in with her parents in Niles. By the time we arrived the snow had piled up three new inches on the roads and the plows had yet to come anywhere near the side street they lived on.

The house was narrow, crammed in between two other narrow houses that had been converted to apartments. The house was in need of a coat of paint and a section of the porch railing was missing.

Thelma and I walked up to the door. I managed to stay a half pace behind Thelma, just in case she slipped. My job as her caregiver might be just a façade, but that didn't mean I couldn't watch out for her welfare.

I knocked and we waited a long two minutes before the door was finally opened by a middle aged woman with lank, dull brown hair, her face a study in exhaustion. She was thin enough to be featured in a commercial for famine and her skin had an unhealthy pallor, as if she hadn't been out in the sun for years.

"Hi Rainie. Boy, you sure look good!"

With a jolt of shock I realized this was Pam. She was a year or two younger than me, putting her at maybe thirty, but she looked like a hard-fought fifty. The dark circles under her eyes were pronounced enough to be stage makeup, but the haggard look of her testified that they were genuine.

"Pam!" I did a poor job of hiding my surprise. She smiled wanly.

"Yeah, so much for the party girl, huh? Come on in."

Thelma and I stepped into the house. It was as shabby inside as out, the furniture lumpy and worn, the carpet threadbare, the walls in need of paint. An older woman wearing a faded, old fashioned housecoat stood just outside the kitchen door, wringing her hands nervously.

"Is this the detective?"

"Yes, mama." Pam introduced us. "This is my mother, Greta LaBell. Mama, this is Rainie."

"And this is Thelma," I added.

"I think we've met," Thelma said to Mrs. LaBell. "Didn't you volunteer at the senior center for a while?"

"Oh, yes," Mrs. LaBell nodded nervously. "That was before my husband Gus got his stroke."

"Gus had a stroke?" Now Thelma looked shocked. I was inwardly groaning. Just how much bad luck could be visited on one family?

"Yes, six months ago." Mrs. LaBell glanced toward a hallway that must have led to the bedrooms. "He's sleeping right now or I'd invite you to say hello."

Pam ran a hand through her hair in a gesture that looked more like a habit than a need to push it out of her face. "Mama, can you listen for Davey for a few minutes while I talk to Rainie?"

"Of course, dear." Mrs. LaBell reached into her housecoat and pulled out a pack of cigarettes. "Here, have one of mine."

"Thank you, mama."

Pam took the cigarettes and looked at me, a little guilty maybe.

"I know I shouldn't, but sometimes…anyway, we only smoke in the garage. The smoke isn't good for Davey or Dad. Do you mind?"

"Of course not. I'm a smoker, too."

"Really?" She smiled wanly. "Sometimes I think me and Mamma are the last of the hold outs."

"I'm glad you didn't say 'the last of a dying breed.'" I quipped. That brought a short bark of a laugh from Pam, and she looked startled by her own response.

"I had forgotten about your sense of humor. You always could make me laugh."

We followed her through the kitchen and a cluttered breezeway to a little one-car garage that seemed to have everything in it but a car. There was some furniture and appliances and at least ten boxes piled in one corner, probably the remains of Pam's apartment life.

Pam flicked on a little electric space heater and indicated several plastic lawn chairs that surrounded it.

"I'm sorry it's not more comfortable, but I need to take a break while Davey and Dad are both asleep."

"No problem."

Pam lit a cigarette, her hands shaking, and drew deeply.

"So Gina told you the problem, right?" She ran a hand through her hair again and this time it came away with several strands hooked in the webbing between her fingers. At this rate she would be as bald as Jack in no time.

"Yes, but I was hoping to get more details." I pulled my notebook and pen out of my bag. "My understanding is your husband was last seen at the drugstore, right?"

"Yeah, he went in and got diapers for Davey. Then poof! He was gone."

"Did they ever find his car?"

"No, nothing. If they had they might have suspected foul play and looked a little harder, but as it was they assumed he just took off voluntarily."

"Is that what you think?"

Pam grimaced and shrugged. "I guess so. We were pretty young, you know? It was a lot of pressure, and David didn't handle stress very well." Young was right. She couldn't have been much more than nineteen when she had little Davey.

"How so?"

Pam drew on her smoke again, clearly stalling while she decided what to say.

"I think maybe he was drinking or doing drugs."

"Why do you think that?"

"I don't know, he was just acting odd for a couple of months before he left."

"Odd?" I had to keep prompting her. She stopped after every statement for a drag on her cigarette, and I could tell she didn't want to say what was on her mind.

She sighed, exhaling a long stream of smoke, and apparently decided to get it over with.

"He would sometimes just stand and stare out the window. I mean for hours, not moving. I'd try to talk to him but it was like he wasn't really there, like he was a cardboard cutout or something.

"And then he started yelling at the TV, especially like when the news was on. He'd be yelling and cursing at the newscaster as if he thought the guy was speaking right to him." Pam took another puff. "It was kind of creepy."

Sure sounded creepy to me, but I wasn't thinking drugs or alcohol. That sounded like full-blown mental illness to me.

"Did you tell the police this?"

"Yeah...well, sort of. I mean, I didn't tell them how bad it was. I was afraid if they thought he was a druggie they wouldn't bother to look for him at all, you know?"

"Did it ever occur to you that there might be something else wrong with him?"

"Something else?" Pam looked genuinely puzzled. "Like what?"

Hm, schizophrenia, dissociative disorder...I wasn't a psychiatrist but I dealt with all kinds of things as a caregiver that might account for his behavior.

"I don't know," I shrugged. "I'm just trying to get a clear picture here. So did he say or do anything just before he left that worried you?"

"Not really." Pam shook her head and lit another cigarette off the butt of the first one, soaking up as much nicotine as she could before she returned to the sad reality waiting for her inside the house. I didn't blame her. In her situation I might be tempted to nip at the bottle or maybe even go for stronger remedies.

"He hadn't been sleeping well for a few days. He was up pacing half the night. But this was about eight o'clock in the evening. He changed Davey's diaper - he was real good with the baby." Tears sprang into her eyes again. "That's another thing. He loved that boy. I mean absolutely *doted* on him! Why would he just walk away without a word?"

"I'm hoping we'll figure that out." I patted her knee and she nodded.

"So anyway he changed the diaper and said we were almost out so he would go get some more. We actually had four or five left, more than enough to wait until morning, but I could tell David was restless and just needed to get out for a while, you know? So he went to get them and never came back."

Pam raised a hand to her head again and I was tempted to reach up and stop her, fearing for her fragile hair, but I didn't. She pulled out a couple more strands and sucked on the cigarette again. "I called the police in the morning when I got up and saw he wasn't back, but they made me wait until the next day to take a report!" Pam sobbed, just once. She took a deep breath and visibly took hold of her emotions. "I can't help wondering, if they'd looked right away, if they might have found him."

"Maybe, but if he left voluntarily they wouldn't have been able to do much anyway."

"Maybe not, but at least I would know! Now I keep thinking that maybe he's out there, remarried, new kids, living a fine life, not even knowing or caring that his little boy is lying in there dying!"

Now Pam did lose it, and I let her cry it out for a while. She sobbed, her head hanging almost into her lap, the dull curtain of her hair too thin to completely obscure her grief. I looked at Thelma, fearing I might cry myself. Thelma was staring back at me, shaking her head. I couldn't quite tell what she was thinking.

Finally Pam finished crying and lit another cigarette around her last few hiccupping sobs.

"I'm sorry," she whispered hoarsely.

"Don't be. I can't imagine how you're managing to hold it together at all," I answered honestly.

"I need to get back inside. Mama can only do so much. She can't do any heavy lifting, she has degenerative arthritis in her back."

Of course she did. I wanted to scream at someone for visiting all this misfortune on this little family, but I didn't know where to direct my anger. If there was a supreme being, could he really be allowing this? Was he sitting back like some Roman nobleman at the Coliseum, watching the Christians get eaten by the lions? Or had he turned his so-called omniscient mind to other, loftier pursuits and forgotten the little people he'd created down below? Or maybe he wasn't anywhere at all.

I didn't have any answers. All I could do was help Pam in whatever way my inferior mortal self could manage.

"Okay, I just need some general information, like his social security number and birthday, stuff like that."

Pam nodded and went over to a box on top of the stack. She pulled up a flap and took out a folder that must have been lying right on top. It was one of those cheap folders I always saw for sale during the back to school sales, the kind that had three little clasps in the middle to hold notebook paper and a pocket on each side for loose stuff. This one was stuffed full to bulging. Pam handed it to me.

"This is everything I have on him. I got it together a couple of years ago, when Davey first got sick." Pam stubbed out her smoke. "I thought I could do a little search myself, but..." she ran a hand through her hair again. "It's just too much."

"I can see that. Now, you understand I can't promise anything, right? I just do this part time, and I don't have the resources I need to really do a thorough job."

"I understand," Pam was staring at the floor, blinking rapidly. "I know it's a lot to ask of someone I just partied with back in the day. I'm just so desperate…"

"Don't worry about that. I'll do what I can, I just don't want you to get your hopes up."

"Well, it's okay if I hope a little, isn't it?" She looked at me and smiled wanly, a ghost of the party girl I remembered.

"You can hope more than a little," Thelma spoke up. "Rainie's pretty good at this stuff. If nothing else she'll probably find something for the cops to go on."

"Anything you can do." Pam turned to lead us back through the house. We said good bye to Mrs. LaBell, who was standing at the stove dispiritedly stirring a pot of soup. Pam handed her the pack of cigarettes and hurried off down the hall to check on her son.

Thelma and I left, a bit dispirited ourselves.

We drove most of the way back to Buchanan in silence, contemplating Pam's situation. I was thinking that Pam needed a break before she collapsed from exhaustion, but I couldn't figure out what to do about it.

Just as we reached the edge of town Thelma spoke up.

"Forget it, Rainie. You don't have time to be a caregiver for them."

"What?" I was startled; it was as if Thelma had read my mind.

"I know what you're thinking, but you're already working full time, and now you're taking on finding Pam's husband in your free time."

"How do you know what I'm thinking?"

Thelma rolled her eyes. "I know you, Rainie. Always trying to save the world."

"Not the whole world," I protested. "Just my little corner of it."

"Hah!" Thelma shook her head. "Do you know any other good caregivers that could help out?"

"A couple, but I don't think Pam can afford it."

"I know, but I can. I'm thinking maybe two days a week. Do you think that would give her enough of a break?"

"*You're* going to pay someone to help her?"

"Why not?" Thelma sounded offended. "You don't think I was affected by that tragic story?"

"But Thelma, that would cost..."

"Two hundred forty bucks for two eight hour shifts. I know, I can do the math. So what?"

"Oh yeah, I keep forgetting you're loaded." I laughed, and it felt pretty good.

"That's just one of the things I love about you: you aren't after my cash." Thelma grinned. "So, do you know anyone?"

"I think I know the perfect person, and as far as I know she isn't working right now."

"Great. You call her, set it up."

"Um, don't you think we should okay it with Pam?"

Thelma frowned. "Why would she object?"

"I don't know, pride?"

"Honey, you're right, pride might just be the last thing she's got going for herself, but I think we'll be able to work it out."

We stopped by "Next to You" to see how my sister was doing at the store. I hadn't seen her for a few weeks, but that wasn't unusual. We were better at being siblings if we conducted most of our relationship from a distance.

I was surprised to see several people browsing the well-stocked racks.

"Business looks good."

"It's great." My sister seemed happier than I'd seen her for a long time. She had some problems with depression, but this new venture had done more for her than any drug the doctors had prescribed. "We're thinking about adding a line of new shoes and handbags."

"Really?" I looked at Thelma.

"Just talking, so far. Maybe this summer, when the Chicago people come back around."

Quite a few people from Chicago kept summer homes in or near Buchanan. It was, for them at least, a relatively short commute, only a couple of hours if you took 94, and well worth it for those who wanted a little time out of the city.

"Keep it up and you'll need a bigger space."

"Oh, not for a while." But Brenda's eyes scanned the store, as if already calculating where the new merchandise would go. "So, have you been shot at lately?" Brenda smiled when she said it, but there was an undertone there, a little something that I couldn't quite define but that was often present when my sister spoke to me. It was just a little bit mean, like a suggestion of sarcasm or a thickly veiled touch of disapproval, but not so open that I could justify getting pissed off.

"Nope." I answered with a thin smile of my own. "How is it with you? Been shopping lately?" That was my own little dig back. My sister had obsessive-compulsive tendencies. Until a few months ago she had an entire room devoted to the clothes and shoes she had hoarded, much of which she'd never even worn. That room had been the first shipment of goods that started this store, but that didn't mean my sister was cured. Normally I wouldn't give her a hard time about it, since I knew I had some odd quirks of my own, but hey, *she* had started it!

"At least my shopping doesn't get people maimed or killed." She retorted.

"I..."

A customer stepped up to the counter with a question and saved me from getting mean.

"See you later." I mumbled, and Thelma and I slipped out the door.

We went for a late lunch at The Tavern and then headed back to Thelma's place. She wanted me to call Heidi, the caregiver that I had in mind to help Pam. We were standing in the kitchen discussing the details when Thelma's phone rang. She waved at me to answer it, since I was closer.

"Hello?"

"Who's this?" A rather brusque female voice demanded.

"No, who is *this*?" I replied in a tone just short of rude. "You're the one who called here."

"I'm calling for Thelma. Is she there?"

"May I tell her who is calling?"

"It's Candy, her *niece*," the woman shot back.

"Just a moment," I covered the mouthpiece and said to Thelma. "It's Candy, your *niece*."

Thelma rolled her eyes in that way she had but came over and took the phone from me. I listened unabashedly to her side of the conversation. I was well aware that Thelma didn't think much of her only living relative.

"Hello Candy...that was Rainie, my caregiver...no, everything is fine...no, I didn't fall...nope, no heart attack either. Why, were you hoping?" Thelma snorted a little laugh. "Candy, I'm fine, still kicking. Why are you calling again, anyway? You already called on my birthday last month...yes, I know I'm getting older, hence the birthday...I don't know why I'm so sarcastic, maybe it's old age...look, I'm kind of in the middle of something, could you call back another time?"

"*Like never*," Thelma whispered to me with her hand over the mouthpiece. I grinned and Thelma went back to the conversation.

"Yes, with Rainie...no, I don't even have a doctor...oh no! Something's boiling over on the stove, gotta go, bye bye!" Thelma hung up the phone.

"That girl drives me crazy."

"What was all that about heart attacks and doctors?"

"I guess I shouldn't have told her you were my caregiver. Now she thinks I'm suddenly frail and in need of assistance. Like I'd ever let *her* take care of me! She'd probably hold me under water in the bathtub so she could claim her inheritance earlier."

"Thelma! That's an awful thing to say."

"That's all right, she's not getting anything, anyway. Well, that's not strictly true. I've set aside enough money to reimburse her for long distance charges from her calls to me and the postage on the Christmas and birthday cards she sends." Thelma laughed, almost a cackle of delight. "Sure wish I could be there when she hears them read *that* codicil in the will!"

"Thelma, you're awful." But I laughed with her. I had never met Candy, who lived in Florida, but that was saying something right there. In the two and a half years I'd been with Thelma her niece had never come to visit, and until recently she only called or sent a card twice a year. Hardly a loving niece.

I called Heidi. She was a studious twenty five year old working her way through nursing school. She was quiet and competent, a calming influence on any situation. I thought she would be a perfect fit for Pam.

I explained the situation to her, including the fact that Thelma was hiring her. She was silent for a long moment while she considered that.

"Okay, so are you going to take me over and introduce me or should I just show up?"

"I'll take you over, but I want to talk to Pam first. How about we tentatively say Thursday?"

"That's fine. Call and give me an exact time."

"All right. Thanks, Heidi."

"She'll do it?" Thelma asked when I hung up.

"No problem. You're sure you want to do this?"

"Rainie, how many times do I have to explain this stuff to you?"

"I know," I grinned. "You don't want to give it to some charity so the CEO can air condition his dog houses, you don't want to give it to your gold digger niece, and you for *sure* don't want to leave it for the government to get their hands on it."

"Exactly. I prefer to spend it now, so I can choose where it goes. Although I seem to be having some difficulty getting rid of it. My investments are all going up even while most stocks are dropping, and even the new business is already paying back my investment. I'll never run out at this rate."

"Poor Thelma," I laughed. "Maybe you should get a cat, and you can leave all your money to Fluffy in your will."

"That might be fun, except I'm allergic to cats."

"That is a drawback."

"But hey, I could pay someone else to take care of it..."

I rolled my eyes. I wish my biggest problem was figuring how to get rid of my money.

I went straight home from Thelma's, fed George and let him out, and settled at the kitchen table with a big chef's salad and the folder Pam had given me.

Pam had done a good job compiling information. She had included a copy of his birth certificate and a couple of good photos and his vital statistics as of the day he'd disappeared.

She listed his social security number and the names and phone numbers of his only living relatives: a mother and a brother who both lived in Plymouth, Indiana. That was a smallish city about an hour and a half's drive from Buchanan, not too far for a weekend visit.

There was also a copy of the police report, which didn't tell me anything more than Pam had, and a few notes on the investigation. Basically they didn't find anything, not even his car, a blue 1989 Cutlass Oldsmobile. They had put out a BOLO for it (cop talk for "be on the lookout") but no one had ever reported seeing it. Likely no one would ever notice it unless David was pulled over for a traffic violation or abandoned the car in a public place.

I had never tried to find anyone who had been missing for so long, but I assumed I should start where I always did: the databases. I could look for his name on credit or arrest reports, search local newspapers for mention of his name, check tax records to see if he had any property listed in his name anywhere in the country, and the DMV to see if he'd ever bought a new car or re-plated the Olds in another state. I could also check to see if there was an obituary listed for him.

Of course, I could do all that if I had access to all the services B&E contracted with. I had signed an agreement when I went to work for them stating that, among other things, I wouldn't use their contracted services for personal use. I guess it was a temptation among P.I.'s assistants to look up dirt on their loved ones or something.

The thing was, I also knew that B&E rarely checked on who was doing what on the databases. They seemed to trust us. But was it so wrong to break the rules if it was for a good cause?

I debated the issue with myself all evening and the next morning, but in the end I couldn't find it in myself to be so dishonest. It's not that I'm all that moral. It was more a matter that I really liked my job at B&E and I didn't want to get fired. I would just have to talk to Harry Baker about it.

Chapter Five

When I got to Bob's the next morning he was sitting at the kitchen table with his son, Daryl. They had a pile of papers between them.

"Good morning!" Bob greeted me cheerfully. Daryl's greeting was a bit more subdued.

"Dad wants me to go over this with you." Daryl turned the top page so I could see it, and I wasn't terribly surprised to see it was a DNR. No, not a form from the Department of Natural Resources; it meant Do Not Resuscitate.

"I'm sure you already know what this is."

"I do." I looked at Bob. "Did you at least ease him into it, or did you just shove the paper into his hand?"

Bob smiled. "I'm afraid I shoved. I was worried I wouldn't get it done in time."

"I really hate this," Daryl mumbled. "How can you be so casual about it?"

"You'll be casual about dying when you hit your nineties, too," Bob assured him. "Come on, it's not like I'm going to kick off right away just because I signed it. This is just to be sure they don't take any extraordinary measures to save my life. If my heart stops then so be it. Is that so unreasonable?"

Daryl stared at Bob, tears in his eyes. "And I want you to live forever. Is that so unreasonable?"

Bob chuckled. "Yes, as a matter of fact, it is."

Daryl finally smiled back, a wan attempt to lighten up.

"All right, so I guess we need to keep a copy of this handy in case anything happens." Daryl cocked his head at me. "So if he has a heart attack or something, do we still call 911?"

"Sure. This just means they won't try to bring him back if he codes. They'll still provide all comfort measures."

"Okay." Daryl stood and hugged his dad. "I've got to get to work. I'll see you later, okay?"

After he left Bob had me hang a copy of the DNR on the fridge where it could be easily found.

"I don't want any mistakes."

The whole situation should have cast a pall over the day, but actually Bob was more cheerful than he'd been in weeks.

"I want you to take me to the mall." He told me. "I want to buy a few things for the grandkids."

"Like what?"

"Expensive things," Bob grinned. "I want to spend their inheritance on them."

"What?" I had to admit that threw me a little.

"Think about it; don't you hate giving gift cards on Christmas or birthdays?"

"Yeah, I do. It makes it seem like you don't know the person well enough to choose an appropriate gift."

"Exactly. Well, inheriting money is like the ultimate gift card, isn't it? But I know my grandkids. They'll all just invest it or put it in a savings account, so I want to go buy a few things that I know the kids want but would never buy for themselves."

"Like a going away present?"

"Yes!" Bob laughed. "Although I promise, I'm not planning on croaking off tonight."

"That's good news." I smiled, not quite able to laugh about it. "All right, let's go shopping."

Bob and I shopped until almost one o'clock, putting a nice dent in the grandkids' inheritance. He purchased two lap top computers and a flat screen TV with surround sound. I was surprised at how much fun it was. I doubt I'll ever be in a position to spend that much money all in one day, and it was kind of a vicarious thrill.

I dropped him off and helped him carry everything in. Once he was settled I headed to B&E, an hour behind schedule. It was a good thing my hours there were flexible.

As soon as I got to the B&E offices I went to Belinda and asked to see Harry Baker.

"Uh oh, what's up?"

"What's with all the uh oh's lately? Does everyone I know think they can read my mind?"

"I don't know what you're talking about. I just know you've never voluntarily spoken to Harry Baker since your initial interview. Frankly, I thought you were a little afraid of him."

"Afraid of Harry?" I laughed, but the truth was he did intimidate me. He was like Jack but with a business degree and the power to fire me.

"Okay, whatever you say." Belinda glanced at her computer screen and gave it a couple clicks. "He has a free half hour at two o'clock. You want me to put you in?"

"Not really," the cowardly voice inside me said, but out loud I answered "yes." She clicked a couple more times.

"All right, I've got you scheduled."

"Thanks, Belinda." I turned to go but Belinda called me back.

"Hey, just a minute, I've got something else for you." She held out a slip of paper. "This is Greg Hopper's number. He needs some help with a case, wants you to give him a call."

"Yeah?" Greg Hopper was an older, experienced private investigator I'd worked with before. He was the most inanimate person I'd ever met. He rarely smiled, frowned, or showed any kind of emotion at all. The first time I'd met him I'd wondered if he were drugged into near insensibility, but I had since learned that it was his normal personality. If you could call it that. On the other hand, he was by all accounts a very effective P.I., and who was I to judge?

"You mean help like Jack wants help, or help like data base checks?"

"I think something in between. Harry has him working on a contract with an insurance company, investigating possible fraud."

"I thought insurance companies had their own investigators."

"Most do, but some prefer to contract this sort of thing out. More cost effective, I guess. Anyway, give Hop a call and he'll explain it."

"All right. See you later."

I went back to the computer room, and while the first data base site was loading I called Hopper. I waited through four rings, thinking I'd probably get voicemail, when suddenly he answered.

"Hopper." His tone was so flat it sounded like a computer generated voice, and I hesitated for a second, expecting a beep so I could leave a message. When none was forthcoming, I realized I was actually speaking to him.

"Hi, this is Rainie Lovingston. Belinda said I should call you."

"Yeah, great. So listen, I've got this possible insurance fraud case I'm working. This guy has been on disability for almost a year, says he's in too much pain to work, but the doctors aren't seeing much wrong with him. They say it might be a soft tissue injury, mostly involving the nerves, and there's no way to really prove he's not in pain. The guy's going for permanent disability, but before the insurance company pays out the big bucks they want to be sure."

"Okay, so where do I come in?"

"I sent his file to your email. Read up on him, get familiar with the case. I've been staking him out, but I have to go out of town for a few days. I want to get together with you, show you my routine, maybe have you spend a couple hours a day keeping an eye on him while I'm gone."

"Why are you staking him out?"

"So I can catch him doing something he claims he can't do," Hopper answered, and I thought I detected a slight note of impatience. "You know, working on his roof, having rough sex in his hot tub, whatever."

Eww! I thought, but didn't say. I sure hoped it wouldn't be the sex thing.

"How injured is he supposed to be?"

"Bad enough he can barely walk with the aid of a walker. Can't lift or bend or stand for any length of time."

"Okay, when do you want to do this?"

"As soon as possible. When are you available?"

"I have a meeting at two o'clock, but I should be done by three."

"I'll pick you up at the front of the building at three o'clock."

"Okay.　　　　See　　　　you　　　　then."

Promptly at two o'clock Belinda announced me to Harry Baker and left me alone in his big office.

Harry sat behind an immense desk cluttered with all kinds of important looking folders and papers. He had his suit coat hanging behind him, but his shirt was perfectly pressed and his tie properly knotted. He didn't always look this put together, but I wasn't sure which style made him seem more intimidating.

He was looking at me expectantly, a pen in his hand poised over a sheet of paper he'd obviously been writing on.

"Miss Lovingston!" He pushed the paper a few inches to the left. "What can I do for you today?" His voice probably would have been booming if not for the thick carpet and heavy paneling on the walls that seemed to absorb all but the most piercing sounds.

"I want to ask a favor."

"What was that?" Harry gestured for me to come closer. I cleared my throat and took a couple of steps across the carpet and tried again in a louder voice.

"I said, 'I want to ask a favor.'"

"All right, sit down." He indicated the deep-cushioned guest chairs in front of his desk. I perched on the edge of one, knowing from past experience that otherwise I would sink down into the depths until I looked like a little kid in the principal's office. I wondered if he had chosen these chairs for just that reason.

"So what's the favor?" Harry offered me a quirk of his lips that might have been a smile if I used my imagination. Because I wanted him to be friendly, I decided to pretend that's what it was. It made me feel braver.

"Well, I have this friend. Well, an acquaintance really, I mean I hadn't even spoken to her for more than ten years but I guess we were friends back then…"

"Hold on, Miss Lovingston," Harry raised a hand to cut off my babbling. "Let's cut to the chase. Does this friend want a job or free services?"

"What?" I was startled into monosyllables, a frequent habit of mine. Now Harry did smile.

"I've heard this opening before, although usually the speaker is a bit more eloquent. It's usually one of those two things, so which is it?"

"Um, the second one. Free services I mean."

"And you considered just using the databases and hoping I didn't catch you, but you felt too guilty."

I stared at him, wide eyed. "No! I mean…"

Harry laughed. "Don't worry about it. Most of my part-timers have considered it at one time or another, but in the end they always come and ask. This is a sweet job for the pay. I know it, you all know it. I also do thorough background checks on all of you, and I don't worry a lot about being cheated. But that's beside the point. Tell me why this person should get my very expensive services for nothing."

I took a deep breath and let the whole story out, not forgetting the part about her dad having a stroke and her mom's degenerative bone disease. "So anyway I thought I'd look into it on my own time, but to have any hope of success I have to have access to the databases. I just wondered if I can do that…on my own time, I mean."

Harry sat back in his chair, staring at me solemnly.

"You're not making this up, are you?" He shook his head. "No, no one would make up a story like that unless they were trying to sell a soap opera script. Christ, this woman can't catch a break, can she?"

"I guess not. So you can see why I want to help her if I can."

He tapped his pen on the desk a couple of times, and nodded.

"All right, so here's what we're going to do. You can do this on company time, but keep track of the hours separately so I can write it off. I'll have Belinda assign a P.I. to it just in case you need someone to flash a license for some reason, but otherwise this is all on you, okay?"

"I...wow. Yeah, of course it's okay!"

Harry nodded and pulled his papers back in front of him, a clear sign of dismissal. I stood up, thanking him profusely, and headed for the door.

"Oh, one more thing, Rainie."

I stopped and looked back, surprised by his use of my first name.

"What's that?"

He grinned. "Try not to let the guy shoot you when you find him, okay?"

I smiled back. "I'll try to remember to duck."

My meeting with Harry only took fifteen minutes, so I had a little time to kill before I had to meet Hopper. I went back to the computer room.

I pulled out my informal file on David Swanson and started searching for signs of him on the internet.

I found plenty of David Swansons, but none that matched his social security number. If he was still alive he was going by another name, or somehow so far off the grid that even the billions of fingers possessed by the internet couldn't touch him.

I searched for his mother and brother. The only information Pam had on them was their names and the fact that they lived in Plymouth. Pam had warned me that they were both a little odd, especially John, the brother. They hadn't wanted anything to do with her or little Davey after David disappeared. She was pretty sure they believed she had killed him.

I suppose I shouldn't expect a warm welcome.

A quick search showed that John, the brother, still owned the house Pam had provided the address for. The mother's house, on the other hand, was listed in the tax rolls as belonging to Joseph Stanislavski. I could still go there, see if Mr. Stanislavski had any idea where the woman had moved to. I could also hopefully talk to the brother.

I was going to be busy with Hopper today, and tomorrow I was with with Thelma, so it would have to wait for Friday.

I sighed. It wasn't unusual for it to take a few weeks to get these things done, and normally there wasn't a big rush. In this case, I didn't know how much time little Davey had left. Maybe I should call Thelma and tell her I couldn't make it tomorrow. It would only be the second day I'd missed in two and a half years, and the first one was because I got shot. I thought she'd understand.

She didn't.

"Why can't I go with you?"

"Because I'm charging the hours to B&E. That makes this official business."

"So? Don't charge them. I'll be paying you anyway, since it's Thursday."

"That isn't the point…"

"Why don't you want me to go?"

"It isn't that. Look Thelma, the line between my two jobs gets blurred often enough. I need to keep this stuff separate."

"Oh, so now I'm just a job to you?"

Ouch, that hurt.

"Thelma…"

She must have heard weakness in my tone because she quickly pounced. "I'll wait in the car. I just like the idea of going for a drive."

"You can't wait in the car. My parking brake is broken and I have to park the car in first gear. Can't leave it running unless the clutch is in." That's the thing with manual transmissions. I remember when I was a kid I turned the key in my mom's car without using the clutch while it was parked in gear. It jumped forward and took out the garage door. It scared the crap out of me and took my stepdad a whole weekend to fix it, but at least I knew better than to do that again.

"It won't be that cold out. I'll be fine."

"Wait, we can't do it tomorrow, anyway. We're supposed to meet Heidi at Pam's house at three o'clock."

"We'll be back in plenty of time. Come on, what else do we have to do tomorrow?"

I sighed. What harm could there be in letting her come along? And it *was* a long drive to Plymouth. I wouldn't mind having company.

"All right, you can come. But you have to wait in the car!"

"I'll bring a book to read. See you at eight?"

"Yep, see you then."

I hung up, suddenly remembering the email Hopper said he was sending. I opened it up and scanned it quickly. The guy in question was Bart Gibson. Hopper had done a lot of legwork on him, and had come up with quite a bit of information, unfortunately little of it substantiated.

According to numerous people Hopper had interviewed, Gibson had been running scams since his teen years, starting with stealing people's pets, then waiting for the lost and found ads to come out so he could "find" the precious dog or cat and return it, usually claiming a reward. He had never been convicted of anything, but his old neighbors remembered that he had an unusual knack for finding lost animals.

He had been on disability one time before, in his twenties, after a car accident. He'd milked the insurance company for six months on a claim of whiplash, finally dropping it when the insurance company had started pushing for him to seek a second, possibly even a third opinion.

In his early thirties he had been arrested, but not convicted, of fraud. That case involved him selling home repairs to various people - most of them senior citizens – collecting a ten percent down payment for supplies before work started. Problem was, he didn't have a home improvement company, didn't even own a hammer that the police could find. Even so, the case was dropped for lack of evidence and a reluctance on the part of the scammed victims to testify.

Huh. Great guy. Couldn't wait to meet him.

I stepped out the front door of B&E at five minutes to three to find Hopper already waiting. I climbed into his SUV, a gray Chevy of some kind. It was outfitted with a complicated looking dashboard complete with satellite radio and GPS, and reminded me a lot of Jack's truck. I wondered if it was a guy thing, having all the gadgets, or if women succumbed to the siren call of cool stuff, too. I was fascinated by the *idea* of technology, and all the stuff it could do, but I had never felt the need to own the latest thing.

"So, did you read the file?"

"Yeah. Kind of scummy, isn't he?"

"Yep, that pretty much sums it up." Hopper smiled briefly, an unfamiliar expression for him, and I half expected to hear his lips creak with the effort. Almost immediately he went back to his usual deadpan expression.

"So, I'm going to drive you past his house, show you the neighborhood, show you the best places to watch from. You still have that old Ford clunker?"

"It's an Escort," I corrected, mildly offended. "And it runs great!"

"Sure, that's what people tell you when they want to sell you a car with no transmission. Anyway, the car is perfect for this. His neighborhood is a bit rundown, too. Your car will fit right in."

He drove north on Eleventh Street and turned down Smith Street.

The houses were mostly small, a couple of bedrooms and one bathroom, with small, struggling lawns and a lot of kid's toys in evidence. A realtor would probably call them "starter homes." The truth was, most of these people were here for the duration.

Hopper was right, the cars parked on the street were almost all aged, rust and dents far more prevalent than custom paint jobs.

"Isn't this SUV a little obvious?" I pointed out.

"That's why I don't drive it when I stake out Gibson. I borrow my sister's old Buick. We're just driving by this time, so no one will think much of it." He pointed at a small, gray shingled house on the left. "That's Gibson's place. Most people on this street work, but it seems like half the cars don't run, so there's always a lot of cars parked on the street."

"So I just park here and watch the house?"

"You can for a while, if you open a map maybe, or talk on your phone. Watch the other houses too, make sure no one is paying you any undue attention. You see someone watching you, drive away. Park around the corner, stroll back. You got a dog by chance?"

"No, an iguana."

"An iguana." He looked at me, deadpan.

"Yep, George. He's my bud."

"Of course he is." Delivered in Hopper's dry tone, I couldn't decide if he was making fun of me or actually agreeing that an iguana could be a good pet.

"An iguana won't work. Borrow a dog if you can, walk up and down the street a couple of times."

"So I just hang out all day and try to catch him doing something physical?"

"Not all day, just a couple hours at a time, max. More than that he'd be on to you for sure. He usually goes out in the afternoon, drives a green Astrovan. If you can, follow him. You ever followed anyone before?"

"A few times," I exaggerated. I actually only remembered following someone once, and that time the guy had stopped and shot at me. "Does this guy carry a gun?" I asked casually.

"Not that I know of, why?"

"Gee, I don't know. Because I don't want to get shot at?"

"Yeah, that kind of sucks." Hopper nodded agreeably. "I don't think you have to worry about that. Anyway, you don't have to spend too much time on this, I just thought a new face wouldn't hurt while I'm out of town. Besides, Jack tells me you're kind of lucky."

"Lucky?"

"Yeah, he says things tend to happen when you're around, and they usually work out pretty good."

Really? Things happen when *I'm* around? And since when does getting beat up, shot at and kidnapped count as working out pretty good?

"Yeah, well Jack has a pretty skewed view of the world."

"He's a good guy. He likes you well enough."

"Yeah, I guess. Look, I've got another case I just picked up, so I won't have a lot of time to devote to this."

"No problem, I don't expect you to solve it while I'm gone, just thought maybe you'd pick something up."

"Because I'm lucky."

"Right." He pointed at the glove compartment. "There's a camera in there. Keep it with you. If you see him doing anything that might be outside the range of what he's supposed to be able to do, get a movie of it."

I pulled the camera out of the glove box and smiled.

"Pink?" And not just *kind* of pink. It was hot pink, the kind of thing every thirteen year old girly-girl just *had* to have.

"Yeah, damn Harry. He ordered on line and got a whole case of the stupid things, didn't want to go through the hassle of sending them back. Personally, I think he did it on purpose. That's the sort of thing he'd think is funny, sending professionals out to do a job with what looks like a kids toy."

I was looking the camera over. It was a lot more complicated than my little point and shoot; I would have to spend some time getting familiar with it.

"So, you got it?"

We were already pulling back into the lot at B&E.

"Yep, no problem. So when will you be back?"

"I don't know, I've got this family thing in Ohio. A few days, at least. Just send the reports to my email."

"Good enough." I waved goodbye and walked to my own car, beat up old wreck that it was. I gave it an affectionate pat on the hood as I walked around it. To hell with Hopper, what did he know about good cars?

Chapter Six

The sun was shining when Thelma and I hit the bypass for the first leg of our trip south. The roads were clear and Thelma had brought a cassette tape of Queen's Greatest Hits, which we had blasting from the Escorts speakers. Yes, I said cassette tape. Riley upgraded my car speakers last year when he had bought new ones for his car, but I couldn't afford to change the stereo, so I still had the stock AM/FM cassette tape unit that came with the car fifteen years ago. I didn't have any tapes, but Thelma had quite a collection.

We turned south off the bypass and had clear sailing down US 31 until we reached the small town of Lakeville. We drove under a cloud bank and suddenly we were in heavy snow, the roads already covered and slick. That's the way it was in the Midwest. I'm sure you've heard the old thing about how if you don't like the weather just wait five minutes, it will change. Around here it can also be that if you don't like the weather just *drive* five miles and it will change.

I slowed down accordingly but kept going. Thelma changed the tape to Grand Funk Railroad. I was familiar with all this music thanks to my mother, and I kind of liked it. It was mostly upbeat, good driving music. Thelma liked to sing along, and fortunately she had a pretty decent voice.

I had been to Plymouth a couple of times. They had a Blueberry Festival over Labor Day weekend that ended with a fireworks display that could knock your socks off, and my mother had brought me here for a bluegrass festival once. None of this was enough to give me a working knowledge of the streets, so I stopped at the first mini-mart I found to ask for directions.

The girl behind the counter popped her gum at me a couple of times and then started chewing vigorously while she stared off in the middle distance. At first I thought she was deliberately ignoring my request, but after a moment or two she blinked and looked back at me.

"Guess I don't know." She grinned, as if that was pretty funny. In a way I guess it was, especially the part where she ground her gum in an effort to jump start her brain. "Let me get Ned. He used to deliver the newspaper so he'll probably know."

She stepped from behind the counter and walked a couple of steps before hollering toward the back of the store. "Hey Ned! There's a lady here needs directions!"

A long moment passed while the girl gnawed on her gum and I stood impatiently, trying not to fidget. Finally a door marked "EMPLOYEES ONLY" opened and an immensely fat man waddled out. His belly was so huge his pants were all the way down where his hips would have been if they hadn't been swallowed by yet more fat. I didn't know what was holding them up; maybe they were sandwiched tightly between rolls. He was wearing a uniform shirt with the company logo on it. The shirt was long, but not quite long enough, and it revealed a thin strip of hairy belly. Worse, it was stained with grease and two huge half-moons of sweat under the arms. There was a fresh stain that looked like a mixture of ketchup, mustard, and chunks of pickle.

I'm trying not to judge. After all, I've had a lifelong struggle with my own weight, and I know how easy it is to let it get out of hand. But couldn't he at least keep himself clean?

He wheezed up to me, his breath chugging like a cold diesel engine, his body swaying back and forth as he walked like a city bus on rough pavement. When he stopped, still a few feet away, I noticed he also smelled somewhat like a city bus.

"What are you looking for?" He didn't sound particularly happy to be of service, and he was glaring at me as if I'd just called his mamma a dirty name.

"I'm trying to find Prairie Lane," I told him in my most pleasant voice. My charm didn't win him over.

"It's right off the main drag," he explained in a tone that implied even the village idiot knew where Prairie Lane was. "Go down about a half mile. There's a grocery store on the corner. Can't miss it." But the look in his eyes said he thought I was probably dumb enough to do just that.

"Thanks." I answered with a big smile, although I was thinking that this was the kind of guy who gave fat people a bad name. No matter what had caused him to be so overweight, whether it was a thyroid problem or just serious overeating, he could still take a shower now and then and use a napkin when he ate.

I didn't voice my opinion, since it didn't matter to anyone but me, and besides, I was mostly just ticked off by his rudeness. As if to balance it out, the ditzy gum chewer gave me a big smile and a "have a nice day!" from behind the counter.

The snow had stopped again, making it easier to find the address on Prairie Lane, the former home of

Mrs. Betty Swanson, the current home of Joseph Stanislavski. It was a nice little house on a block of nice little houses, all with the same basic architectural style. I was guessing this was another one of those tracts thrown up after World War Two, when so many soldiers came back looking to move away from the old family home.

I parked out front and put the car into first gear before killing the engine and releasing the clutch. "You're sure you'll be warm enough?"

"I'll be fine." Thelma held up a copy of "Atlas Shrugged" by Ayn Rand. Her bookmark was about at the half-way mark. "The book is just getting good."

"So who *is* John Galt?" I asked with a grin. I'd read the book myself some years ago, and I had recommended it to her.

"I don't know yet, and you'd best not tell me!" Thelma tried to glare at me, but she wasn't very good at it. She was just a naturally easy-going, happy person.

"I won't. It's worth getting through all thousand plus pages to find out for yourself."

"And the politics?"

"Finish it first, then we'll argue it."

"So go, let me read."

I walked up the narrow but neatly shoveled walk to the front door. The house was painted white with green shutters. It had a small concrete porch with a low iron railing; no little table with an ashtray, though.

I rang the bell and immediately heard a little dog yapping, as if the doorbell was set to bark instead of ring.

"Hush now. No bark!" I heard a woman's voice through the door, and she sounded firm enough, but the little dog paid no attention. She opened the inside door and the little black and white dog, a terrier of some kind, started leaping at the glass on the screen door, yapping even louder. The woman was on the young side, with shiny brown hair held back by an elastic headband and no discernable makeup. She was wearing jeans and a cardigan sweater rolled up to the elbows. She tried again to quiet the dog, but then gave up and turned her attention to me.

"May I help you?" I had to admire the woman's powers of concentration. She was looking at me with a small smile, speaking over the barking like it was no more than a little finch's sweet call.

"Mrs. Stanislavski?" I guessed.

"Yes?"

"I'm an assistant investigator from B&E Security and I'm looking for the former owner of this house, a Mrs. Swanson?" I tried to speak loudly, but apparently it did no good, because the woman just shook her head.

"Trixie! Stop that right now!" She yelled at the little dog, pointing a warning finger, and the dog stopped jumping but kept yapping. The woman rolled her eyes and slipped carefully out the screen door, closing it firmly behind her. Trixie went nearly mad leaping at the door, but the woman studiously ignored her and looked at me, rolling her sweater sleeves down against the cold.

"What was that?"

"I'm sorry to bother you, but I'm looking for the woman who used to live here, Betty Swanson?"

Mrs. Stanislavski grimaced. "Hm, old Betty the cat lady? What do you want with her?"

"Actually I'm looking for her son, and I'm hoping she can provide some information."

"Wouldn't count on it." She shook her head. "Old Betty is crazier than those feral cats she was always feeding. Don't get me wrong, she was nice enough, just a little soft in the head, you know?"

"I've never met her."

"Well, take my word for it. She was a hoarder, you know." The woman shuddered and glanced back at the house. "It took them two weeks just to haul all the stuff out of here. Nothing but tiny aisles to walk down between stacks of junk, you know, like they show on TV. And among it all there were a couple dozen feral cats. I don't think she even knew they were all in there. She always fed them out the back door, and I think they just snuck in and made themselves at home. They peed and crapped on any handy pile of papers, and let me tell you, there were plenty of those."

"Sounds awful." I spoke just to let her know I was interested, but I'm not sure it mattered. She was one of those people who obviously loved to gossip, and even though I wasn't a fan of idle gossip myself, in my line of work those were the best kind of folks to run into.

"Yeah, that's how they found out about the hoarding. The neighbors complained to the city about the smell. They thought they might have to demolish the whole place, but instead they just gutted it, put in all new wallboards and floors. Now me, I just keep my little Trixie, and she's housebroken, I can tell you."

"That's good."

"Still, like I said, old Betty was nice enough. I mean, you can't really fault a lonely woman for feeding stray cats, and her being soft-headed and all, well, you can't hold that kind of thing against a person, right?"

"No, you really can't. So do you know where Betty is now?"

"Sure, she's at that nursing home just east of here... um, let's see... Sunnyview, that's it."

"I'm sorry, I'm not from around here. Can you tell me how to get there?"

"Sure. Go back to Main Street, take a left and go about six blocks and turn right on Frappe Road. That's the road runs right next to the tracks. Go about a half mile and you'll see Sunnyview on the left. It's a long brick building with a big lawn."

"That's great. Thank you, you've been a big help."

"No problem." She shivered and reached for the door. Trixie had finally stopped barking, but as soon as the door opened she started up again. The woman smiled indulgently at the dog.

"Silly old thing." She went in without another word and I went back to my car.

"Are you sure you're warm enough out here?" I asked Thelma when I parked in the nursing home lot.

"Sure, I'm fine."

"I might be a while this time."

"That's fine. If I get too cold I'll go sit in the lobby for a few minutes. Don't worry about me."

It was silly to worry about her getting too cold. She was quite capable of watching out for herself. I certainly had plenty of other things to worry about with Thelma, like her propensity for climbing ladders and crawling under things to fix them, or the fact that she had a brand new gun under the cash register at the store. No doubt, when I looked at it from that perspective, waiting in a cold car might be the safest place for her.

I went up to the front door and was greeted with a big sign that read:
RING BELL
WAIT FOR BUZZER
OPEN DOOR

Next to the sign was a giant red button. This wasn't unusual for a nursing home. Most of them had confused patients, and the doors were kept locked and alarmed to prevent any of them from wandering away through the snow in their pajamas.

I pushed the button and waited for several long moments. I was just about to hit it again when I heard a loud, obnoxious buzzing noise. It startled me so much I almost forgot what I was supposed to do, but fortunately there was that big sign to remind me to OPEN DOOR.

I pulled it open and mercifully the buzzing stopped. I stepped into a clean but somewhat shabby lobby. There was a tall counter to the left, and behind it was the woman who had likely buzzed me in. She was short and plump, with graying hair coiffed in a complicated hair-do that must have involved a lot of curlers, teasing and hairspray. Her nametag read "Harriet Fromm." She smiled with what looked like genuine welcome.

"I'm so sorry to keep you waiting, I just ran a file to the back office. May I help you?"

"I hope so. I'm looking for Betty Swanson."

"Oh, how nice! She gets so few visitors. Are you a relative?"

Now, here's where I should have said who I was and why I was there, but I hated to disappoint Harriet. I mean, she seemed so pleased that Mrs. Swanson had a visitor. So I did the kind thing - really, it was out of kindness, not shear duplicity - and I lied.

"I'm a friend of the family. I'm just in town for the day, so I thought I'd pop in and see her."

"That's lovely!" Harriet beamed. "She's in room two-oh-two. That's just down this hall," Harriet leaned over the counter to point, a difficult task since the counter came almost to her shoulders. "Go all the way to the end, go to the left, and two-oh-two will be on the right hand side."

"Thank you."

"Oh, wait," Harriet stopped me. "Would you please sign the register?" She pointed at a thick book lying open on a pedestal near the door. It looked like an old-fashioned hotel registry. There were lines for the date, the time in and out, my name and who I was there to see.

Harriet must have seen me hesitate, the attached pen poised over the page.

"The insurance companies require that. I guess it's in case of a fire or some such, so they know who is in the building."

"Oh. Makes sense, I guess." Except that if there was a fire this book would probably be one of the first things to burn up. Oh well, I wasn't doing anything wrong, so I signed the book.

I moved in the direction Harriet pointed.

I was saddened by the odors that assailed me as I moved deeper into the facility. There was the lingering odor of cabbage, maybe from last night's supper, and worse, the clear, sharp scent of urine. It wasn't coming from any particular room. It seemed to hang in the hallway, like an invisible miasma clinging to everything.

While it's true that now and then you might smell urine in a place where there were likely numerous incontinent people, when the smell was that invasive it meant that the residents were not being properly cared for. That smell meant wet undergarments and sheets, and dirty laundry left too long in the hallway. In turn that meant rashes and bedsores and generally miserable people.

I was saddened because even the best nursing homes were hard-pressed to keep up with the demands of their residents when the state codes dictated how many caregivers were needed per patient, numbers that made it almost impossible to give excellent care. But this place was obviously not one of the best, and I felt sorry that Mrs. Swanson had to end her years in this shabby, stinking place. Never mind that she had apparently lived in even worse conditions before she came here. This was a skilled-care facility, and she deserved better.

No one questioned me as I made my way down the hall. I wove around several residents in the hall, all in wheelchairs. Some of them just stared dully as I walked by. Two of them reached out for me, and I stopped and held their hands for a few minutes, although neither one said anything to me.

I passed a med cart, locked but unattended. At the intersection of the two hallways there was a nurse's station. A thin woman in scrubs sat behind the desk, writing in a spiral notebook. She didn't look up as I walked by.

I made the turn and there was another lady in a wheelchair. She saw me and her face broke into a wide grin.

"Elizabeth, is that you?" She held out her arms for a hug. I took one of her frail old hands and shook my head.

"No, I'm sorry, I'm not Elizabeth," I answered gently. "Is that your daughter?"

"Oh, that's right." Her face crumpled like an old wad of tissue and she started to cry. "I forgot, my Elizabeth is dead. Dead twenty years now."

"Oh, I'm sorry." I squatted next to her chair, still holding her hand.

"You look so much like her, for a minute I thought..." she trailed off and cried softly for a minute. I held her hand and didn't say anything.

"Well." She gave a final sniff and wiped her nose with a delicate looking handkerchief embroidered with tiny pink flowers on the edge. "So sweet of you to comfort an old lady." She patted my hand. "No one seems to have much time for that around here."

"I just wish I could do more," I told her sincerely, but her eyes already had that faraway look so many elders got when their minds spent more time floating in the past than sailing in the clear waters of today. I patted her on the shoulder and went on to room two-oh-two.

There were two names listed under the room number. The second bed, which should be by the window, was designated for Betty Swanson. The door was open, so I tapped on the doorframe to announce my presence and leaned in and took a peek.

The bed nearest the door was unoccupied. The sheets were askew and there was a soiled nightgown draped across the foot. The second bed was neatly made, and occupied by a little blue stuffed cat with a bright red ribbon around its neck. Near the window was a woman in a wheelchair.

"Mrs. Swanson?" I called out hopefully. The woman turned to me and smiled, revealing yellowing false teeth.

"Yes?"

"Hello, Mrs. Swanson." I stepped across the small room and held out my hand. "My name is Rainie. How are you today?"

"Rainy? Like the weather is rainy?"

Before I could answer the question - which I'd been asked countless times in my life – she went on.

"It's not rainy at all today. Snowy. Lots of snow." She shook her head and looked out the window. Her view was of a courtyard, knee deep in snow. About fifty feet away I could see another wing of the facility jutting off from the main building.

"Yes, there has been a lot of snow," I agreed.

"Well, snow is prettier than rain, don't you think?" She peered at me, her eyes bright behind a pair of large plastic eyeglasses. "No, you just said you like the rain, didn't you?"

"No, not particularly." I smiled and tried not to lose all hope, but it was clear that Mrs. Swanson was dealing with some cognitive issues. I doubted she would be any help in my search for David, but I valiantly pressed on.

"I'm looking for your son, David."

"David? Have you looked in his room?"

"He doesn't live here anymore, Mrs. Swanson. He's all grown, up, remember?"

She sighed and looked back out the window. "Oh yes, that's right. My little Davey, all grown up." She fell silent.

"Have you seen him lately?"

"Sure, I see him whenever he comes." She smiled. "Such a good boy. And oh, how he loves Halloween! He always comes up with the best costumes!" She was focusing back on me, her voice excited and proud.

"I would make them, of course, but they were always his ideas. Like the time he dressed as a television. We cut out a box to make it look like he was on TV, like those talking heads that do the news. Then he had a bigger box on his body to look like a cabinet. Painted it all himself. It was so clever!"

"So what was he wearing last Halloween?"

"Hm, let me think," She stared out the window a minute. "I guess he was a janitor. Yep, that's it. He was dressed up like a janitor."

"And when was that?" I was thinking 1990, but she looked at me as if I was stupid.

"In October, of course! When else would he dress for Halloween? Are you trying to confuse me?"

"No, of course not, I just misunderstood. So he was here last Halloween?"

"He brought me candy." She pointed at a chipped candy dish shaped like a jack-o-lantern. It looked old; I was disappointed. She was definitely thinking of a time long past. Even so I thought I'd keep asking questions as long as she was answering. Maybe I'd pick up something useful.

"Did he say where he was living?"

"He lives in Niles…at least, he always has." She peered at me with some concern. "Are you saying he moved?"

"No, I was just asking. Do you have an address for him?"

"Oh, I don't remember things like that anymore." She went back to gazing out the window, but before I could form another question she spoke up again.

"Is it lunchtime? I'm very hungry."

"It's almost eleven o'clock. I suppose they'll serve lunch soon."

"I hope we're having meatloaf. I like meatloaf."

"So do I."

"They put ketchup on top and bake it right in. It's good."

"Mrs. Swanson, do you remember anything else about David?"

"David, that's my son."

"I know. We've been talking about him."

"That isn't very nice. We shouldn't talk behind his back."

"We're not…" I took a deep breath and sat back for a minute, needing to regroup.

"Does David ever send you letters? Maybe cards on your birthday?"

"Oh yes, he's such a good boy. He draws the sweetest little cards, colors them all in...I always hang them on the refrigerator door."

"That's sweet. Have you gotten one lately?"

She frowned. "Now that you mention it, I haven't. I wonder if he's all right? My David was always...oh, not fragile, exactly, but too sensitive, if you see what I mean?" She stared out the window again, and I had just about decided I was wasting my time. She was a nice old lady, but obviously the Alzheimer's was taking over. Then she spoke again.

"Well, he's probably just fine, living with the eagles."

"The eagles?"

"Yes, when he was here last Halloween - you remember, I told you he brought me candy?" She pointed at the chipped candy dish again and I nodded. "He told me he was living with the eagles, and he seemed so happy."

The eagles? Wasn't that a band my mom listened to? Or did she mean the Fraternal Order of Eagles? I think there was a chapter in Niles. Or maybe she was just a little nutty.

She wheeled her chair over to the dresser and picked up the candy dish. She set it on her lap and wheeled back to me.

"You see? He remembered how I love Halloween. He's such a good boy."

She held the dish out for me and I took it, admiring it as sincerely as I could manage. It clearly meant a lot to her.

It was about the size of a softball, the top of the jack-o-lantern cut away to accommodate candy. I realized that at one time it had probably had a lid. I turned it over. On the bottom there was a little white sticker that said Goodwill Store. It had cost twenty-five cents. It occurred to me that the sticker looked pretty new. It was still bright white, the edges smooth, the printing not faded at all. Hm, could he have really been here just a few months ago?

"It's very nice." I handed it back to her.

"My dear David." She clutched the dish to her bosom. "He would come more often, but he can't be caught outside." She leaned toward me and lowered her voice. "They might find him, you see, and then he couldn't live with the eagles anymore."

"Who might find him?"

"The government people, of course!" She sat back suddenly, looking alarmed. "Is that why you're here? Oh my, he said there might be people asking questions, looking for him..."

"No, no, I'm not from the government..."

But it was far too late for denials. Mrs. Swanson started screaming bloody murder.

"You get out! Get out now! Help me! Someone! Help me! Get her out of here!"

"Mrs. Swanson, please..." I tried to comfort her, but when I leaned closer her screams got louder.

I left quickly. I hadn't meant to get her so upset, but someone else would have to try to calm her. At this point my continued presence was just making things worse. Besides, I didn't want someone to come running, thinking I'd done something to her.

There was no need to worry about that. No one was even paying attention to her screams. Well, one lady did. She was sleeping in her wheelchair in the hall, but Mrs.Swanson's screams woke her up and she joined the chorus: "Help me! Help me!"

I approached the nurse's station, where a different young woman in scrubs sat writing notes in the log. She could have been a nurse, an aid or a doctor; everyone in health care wore scrubs nowadays, even to the grocery store. There was no way to know who was who.

I waited for her to look up and acknowledge me, but she seemed engrossed in her work. Behind me Mrs. Swanson and her sympathizer were still going full throttle, but apparently blood-curdling screams were not enough to distract this woman from her clerical duties.

After a couple of minutes I cleared my throat and said, "Excuse me."

Finally the woman looked up at me with an annoyed frown.

"Can I help you?"

"I was just visiting Mrs. Swanson."

"Yeah?"

"She misunderstood something I said, and she's very upset." I paused, letting the screams for help fill the gap. "I thought maybe someone should look in on her."

The woman glanced at a display on the wall. The room numbers were listed there, each with a tiny LED bulb above it.

"Her call light isn't on."

"She's very upset. I don't think she thought to push the button."

"If she needs help she should turn her call light on."

I clenched my teeth to bite back a very nasty word. "I just told you, I don't think she's thinking that clearly."

"None of them are. That's why they're in the Veggie Ward." She smirked and I clamped on to the desk, wondering how much jail time I was going to get after I smashed this smug little bitch's head into the floor.

"You need to go check on her. Right. Now."

The woman's eyes widened and she pushed her chair back, getting a little distance from me.

Apparently my urge to kill was showing in my eyes. Jack tells me I have "a look." This time it must have been the kind of look that says I'm about three seconds from making *you* into a veggie, because the woman got to her feet.

"Okay, I'll check on her."

"Now." I didn't trust myself to say any more. I can tolerate a lot of things in my fellow human beings. I try not to judge, knowing that I am a long, long way from perfect. The one thing I can't tolerate is someone deliberately ignoring the well being of another person, especially when they are supposed to be caregivers.

The woman came out from behind the desk and edged away from me, down the hall in the direction of Mrs. Swanson's room. I watched her until she stopped to say a few words to the lady screaming in the hall. Whatever she said, the woman stopped screaming. With a glance back at me she moved on to Mrs. Swanson's room.

Barely satisfied, I got the hell out of there. I didn't bother to sign out in the book. If there was a fire, good luck finding my burned body in the wreckage. I'd had enough nursing home for one day.

Chapter Seven

"Whoa!" Thelma said when I got in the car and slammed the door. "Who pissed on your cornflakes?"

"Thelma!" I couldn't help but laugh. She never failed to shock me. "What kind of language is that?"

"Pretty funny, huh? I heard someone say that in a movie a couple of months ago and I've just been waiting for a chance to use it. I didn't think I'd get to use it on you, though. You never get mad!"

"Really?" That was funny. It seemed like I got mad all the time. Then again, I hated to hurt people's feelings, so I probably didn't show it all that much. "Anyway, I'm just ticked off at the nursing home. They didn't seem particularly compassionate in there."

"All of them? Or one in particular?"

"Well, I only spoke to two employees, and one was nice. So I guess just half of them."

"Did you get any new information on your missing man?"

"Afraid not. Mrs. Swanson is suffering from dementia. Maybe we'll have better luck with the brother."

"Do you know where he lives?"

"I have an address." I sighed. "I guess I'll have to ask for directions again."

"We'll pass that same station going back."

I thought about having to haul ol' diesel breath back out of his lair so he could be rude to me again, and shook my head. "I saw a pizza delivery place on Main Street. I'll ask there. Pizza drivers know where *everything* is."

"Yep, they're just like a mailman, only with cornier uniforms, less pay and no benefits."

I laughed. "Yep, just like 'em."

By the time I pulled into the lot of the pizza place the snow had started again, and I groaned inwardly. It was coming down heavy enough to obscure the street signs, which was going to make finding the brother just that much harder.

I caught one of the pizza drivers heading back into the store from a delivery, and called out to ask for directions.

He was a young kid with long hair in a ponytail and a smile that belonged in a toothpaste commercial. He leaned on the roof of my car.

"What's the address?"

"Six -twelve east Chippewa."

"Okay, I know right where that is." He gave me clear directions to Chippewa. "Once you make that last turn the house will be on the right hand side, and six-twelve should be about mid-way down the block."

"Thank you," I told him when I was sure I had it.

"No problem." He showed me another flash of dazzling teeth and went back to work.

"He was a real cutie!" Thelma commented as I drove away.

"Thelma, he's young enough to be your grandson."

She snorted. "More like my great-grandson, but so what? I can still appreciate cute, can't I?"

"Sure, I suppose you can."

"So, do you think the brother will know where David is?"

"I don't know. Pam said she tried to call him a couple of years ago, when Davey first got sick, but she only got the answering machine and he never returned any of her calls."

"You suppose he really thinks Pam killed David?"

"I hope not, because that would mean he hasn't seen David. Pam said the guy is kind of odd, so we'll see."

We were closer to downtown, and traffic was picking up. At the same time the snow was falling faster and thicker, which was slowing everything down. That was just as well, though, as we had to be practically right on top of a street sign before we could read it.

"There!" Thelma suddenly cried out. "There's Maple Avenue. You're supposed to turn left."

"Crap." Because of course, I was in the right lane, trying to get close enough to read the stupid sign. I worked my way over in the line of traffic and turned into a shopping center, got turned around and crawled back to Maple Avenue.

"Okay," I said once I'd made the turn. "Now we're looking for Chippewa Street. The kid said there's a big blue house with a giant blow-up Santa on the lawn on the corner."

"I'm not sure I could see Santa through all this even if he was riding Rudolph," Thelma complained, peering through the thick curtain of snow. "Maybe my niece has the right of it. Maybe I should move to Florida."

"Come on, Thelma. Don't wimp out on me now."

"I know, I know. It just seems we've had so damned *much* snow this year... hey wait, I think I see something big and red right over there."

I followed the line of her pointing finger, and sure enough, I could just barely make out a ten-foot tall Santa swaying among the snow flakes.

"Good eyes, Thelma." I took the turn slowly, but even so the back end of my car slewed way over to the left and back to the right before it finally righted itself. No snowplows had been on these side streets for a while, and there was a good four or five inches piled up already. In spots it was already up to the bumper in my little car. I hoped they got the plows out here soon.

I crept slowly down the road, fruitlessly trying to read house numbers.

"It's no use, the snow is too thick. I'll have to get out and look." I found an empty spot at the curb about half-way down the block, hoping the kid had been right about that part. "I'll be right back."

I got out and slogged up a driveway to the sidewalk, thinking once again that I really ought to buy a pair of boots. My tennis shoes were filling with snow and my feet were freezing. Oh well, spring would get here eventually, and then I'd be back to bare feet anyway.

As I came up the driveway I saw a woman brushing snow off a huge SUV, the tailpipe putting out little puffs of white smoke in the cold air. She glanced at me, but saw that I was turning down the sidewalk and not coming to see her. She went back to cleaning off her vehicle, a difficult task with the snow coming down so hard.

The sidewalks had been shoveled, but the new snowfall today had already piled up, making the walk a difficult one. Fortunately I didn't have to go very far. The next house had the numbers "612" displayed on a fence post.

The fence was a six foot high chain-link, an unusual sight in what seemed to be a quiet neighborhood. There was a gate with a big padlock, the mailbox attached outside the fence so the mailman wouldn't have to approach the house.

Uh oh. I was sensing that David's brother John might be just a little bit of a recluse. Maybe even paranoid.

I peered at the house through the snow. There were black shutters, all closed. Huh, that was weird. I'd never seen shutters closed before. I had assumed they were all decorative, but apparently not. I walked along the fence and followed it up a driveway that led to an unattached garage. I detected the slightest indent of footprints under the new snow, leading away from the house. Someone had come out recently.

The fence continued all the way around the back yard, blocking access to the house and the garage. There was another gate back here, also padlocked, but the footprints continued beyond it to a back door.

Using my amazing skills of deduction, I guessed that John had gone somewhere on foot, probably in the last hour or so. I didn't think he'd go very far in this weather, so odds were he'd be back soon.

I walked back to the sidewalk. I was getting soaked from snow melting in my hair, but I didn't think I should wait in the car. Once he got through that locked gate I didn't think he'd be willing to let me in.

I stood there, indecisive. The woman next door had gone into the house, leaving her SUV running. That annoyed me. I wasn't fond of SUV's. Not only were they gas guzzlers, but they always seemed to be blocking my view when I was trying to pull out of some place in my little car. And sure it was snowing heavily, but it wasn't all that cold. Did she really need to warm the car for fifteen minutes before she drove away? Every little puff coming out of the exhaust pipe was competing with the oxygen we pretty much needed in our atmosphere.

I was just getting wound up on my little inner rant when I saw a shape coming toward me down the block. I could just make out through the falling snow that it was a man. Good, that was probably John. I could talk to him before he scurried away behind his big fence.

The woman next door came out carrying a couple of packages and put them on the back seat of the SUV. She closed the door and paused to look at me.

"Can I help you with something?"

"No, thank you," I answered politely. I realized she was probably suspicious of me lurking here on the sidewalk. "I'm just waiting to speak to your neighbor."

"John Swanson?" She frowned. "Are you a friend of his?"

By now the man-shape was right in front of her house, and I could see it was a tall, thick set man wearing a parka and heavy boots, a canvas grocery bag dangling from one hand. When the woman said "John Swanson" the man froze in his tracks, and he was staring at me, probably waiting for an answer. Damn the woman for her nosiness. Couldn't a person lurk in a snowstorm for five minutes without being disturbed?

"I just want to ask him a few questions," I answered her, but I was looking at the man, hoping he could see that I was harmless.

No such luck.

He dropped the grocery bag and started running, but not away. Instead he headed straight for the woman standing next to her SUV. He barreled up the driveway and shoved her aside and jumped into the vehicle.

"Wait! I just want to talk to you!"

But it was too late. He already had the car in reverse and moving down the driveway. I leaped out of the way as the vehicle rolled past.

"No! Stop!" The woman had fallen on her butt when he shoved her, and now she was scrambling to get up. "Please! My mom is in the car! Stop!"

"Your mom?" Suddenly I understood why she had kept the engine running so long. I pictured her mother, probably old and frail, expecting a slow trip to the doctor's office through the snow, instead about to be taken on a high speed run with a crazy man at the wheel.

I reacted quickly and ran for my own car, shouting over my shoulder. "Call 911! I'll try to keep him in sight!"

I jumped into my car and started it up.

"What's going on?" Thelma started rapid firing questions at me. "Was that the guy you're looking for? Why did he take off?"

"He freaked and stole the neighbor's car and her mother is in there!" I was already pulling away from the curb, my tires spinning in the thick snow, finally getting a grip. The SUV was already at the first intersection, moving way too fast for conditions. I didn't dare get involved in a high speed chase with the guy. The old lady would be killed for sure.

"Go get him, Rainie!"

"I can't, Thelma. I just hope to keep him in sight, but I'll have to stay way back and not panic him. Call the cops, tell them what's going on."

Thelma pulled out her cell phone. I passed the first intersection, just barely able to make out the taillights of the SUV a block ahead. I saw it start to turn right, but suddenly the lights tilted crazily.

"I think he rolled!" I shouted to Thelma, my adrenaline in high gear.

"Should I still call?" She was holding the phone, staring ahead, trying to see what has happening.

I got to the corner and sure enough, there was the SUV, on its side, the front end crumpled against a tree.

"Yes! Call! They'll need to send an ambulance!"

I stopped the car and jumped out, running over to offer what assistance I could. The SUV had landed on the driver's side. As I approached I saw a head pop out the passenger side window, which was now the top of the vehicle.

It was John, and in spite of his size he apparently had the agility of a monkey. He levered himself out the open window, took one look at me and leaped off the truck. He landed in a crouch, righted himself and took off running.

I wanted to chase him down, but he would have to wait. First I had to see if the old lady was all right.

I ran around to the windshield and peered through, but I couldn't see her. She must have been in the back seat, and now she must be lying against the door. I hoped she'd been wearing a seatbelt, but even so I was picturing fragile bones shattered and delicate skin shredded.

I ran around to the underside of the car, trying to figure out how to climb up and through the open window. I could smell gasoline, and I wondered if it was leaking onto something hot. Did cars really catch fire that easily, or was it just in the movies so they could show off their spectacular special effects?

Thelma was standing next to my car, and she shouted and held up her phone.

"I'm on the line with 911. They want to know how many injured?"

"I think just one!" I shouted back. "The driver took off."

Thelma put the phone back to her ear and I went back to my examination of the SUV.

There were plenty of foot and handholds under there, but they were all metal and hot, steam rising off them as the snow hit and instantly melted. I had left my gloves in my car, so I hurried back to get them.

"They're sending an ambulance." Thelma informed me.

"Good. I'm going to try to get in, see if I can do anything to help her while we're waiting." I grabbed my good leather gloves and pulled them on as I ran back to the accident. Even with lights and sirens an ambulance was going to take awhile with all this snow.

The smell of gas was stronger, and I felt a moment's hesitation, once again fearing a fire. Well, if it was going to happen, that was all the more reason to hurry up and get the helpless old lady out of there.

I stood on the passenger side tire and got a grip on the bracket holding the driver's side tire on. I was sure there was a technical name for it, but right now I didn't need a mechanic's knowledge, I needed a rock climber's. The SUV was only as tall as my shoulders lying on its side, but it was harder than it sounded to climb up the underside. I got my foot on something (the driveshaft? I wasn't sure) and managed to pull myself up. I flopped awkwardly over the top and sat up on the door.

So far, so good. I scooted over to the window and dangled my feet through, then scooted a little more and got a grip on either side of the window frame. I peered into the backseat, but between the tinted windows and the fresh coating of snow there wasn't enough light for me to see the injured woman.

"Hello, can you hear me?" I waited a minute, but didn't hear anything, not even a moan of pain. Terrific, she wasn't even conscious. I had to get in to her.

I thought about lowering myself through the window, but I wasn't sure how to do that. I wasn't a weakling, but then again I didn't spend a lot of time doing pushups. I was afraid that half-way down my arms would give out and I would fall and stick my foot through the steering wheel. I could almost feel a leg breaking, and shuddered. Nope, I wasn't going in that way.

Instead I flopped over on my stomach, my legs still inside, and scooted myself backward. I felt around with one foot until I found the edge of the bucket seat, then scooted the rest of the way in, lowering myself until I was standing on the inside of the driver's door. It might not have been pretty to watch, but it worked.

I ducked my head in and twisted around to see into the back seat.

No one was there.

"Hello?" I called out, not sure why. Certainly she hadn't been riding in the cargo compartment, and I didn't think the impact had been hard enough to knock her over the back seat. Maybe she had crawled there, disoriented.

I squirmed my upper body between the bucket seats, an awkward maneuver that required a lot of contortion on my part. There was nothing in the back seat but the packages I'd seen the woman loading. I couldn't get back far enough to peer into the cargo area.

"Hello, are you in here?"

I still didn't hear anything. If she had been conscious enough to crawl in back, surely she could answer me.

There wasn't anything else I could do from here. Belatedly it occurred to me that I should have tried the back hatch, first. It would have been a lot easier to get in. I gave myself a mental head-slap and squeezed back through the seats. I grasped the window frame and got my foot back on the edge of the seat and levered myself back up.

I had just gotten my butt on the edge when the owner of the SUV came running up, her eyes wide and frantic, her cheeks stained red from exertion and cold.

"Did you get my mother? Oh, you have to hurry, what if the car catches on fire?"

My thoughts, exactly.

"I looked, she's not in there."

"Of course she is! I put her there myself, just before he took off!"

"And I'm telling you I was just in there, and there's no one in the car!"

"She's in the back! In a white box marked 'Gloria Bentwood.'"

"In a box?" For just a second my mind conjured a picture of a white coffin in the cargo area that I'd somehow overlooked, but I immediately rejected the idea. That was impossible unless her mother was a midget.

Then I suddenly got it.

A box. Small enough to be on the back seat.

"Are you talking about your mother's *ashes*?"

"Of course!" The woman looked at me like I was too dumb to breathe. "What did you think I was talking about?"

I wanted to laugh. I wanted to cry. I wanted to smack this woman for making me think there was a live person in danger of being dead.

"You said your mother was in the car." I said instead.

"She *is*! At least, all I have left of her." The woman started to sob. "Please, get her out before the car catches fire!"

I almost pointed out that that wouldn't hurt her. She was, after all, already reduced to ashes. I didn't say it though. The woman was clearly distraught enough. Still, did I want to risk my life for a box of remains?

"The police will be here soon…"

"No! It can't wait!" The woman suddenly came closer. "Get out of the way!" She sobbed. "I'll get her!" She started to climb up, but immediately recoiled when her bare hand touched the hot metal underside.

"Hang on!" I told her. "I'm already up here. I'll get her."

I flopped back over on my stomach and got back into the SUV. I squished myself between the seats again and looked for the white box.

Yep, there it was. Unfortunately it had fallen open, and much of the cremains had spilled out.

I stared at the pile of ashes for a long ten seconds. Should I just scoop up as much as I could and not mention this? Or was it kinder to let the woman know that some of mom would be imbedded in the SUV's upholstery for all eternity?

"Hurry!" I heard the woman urging from outside. "I smell gas!"

Oh yeah, I had forgotten about that. No more time for considering the right and wrong of it. I hurriedly scraped up as much of her mom as I could and stuck the lid back on the box. There was still quite a bit of residue left on the door. I swiped at it with my gloved hand and managed to brush most of it away. Good enough. If they repaired the vehicle they would probably give it a good vacuuming anyway. She would probably never have to know that not all of mom made it back to the box.

The SUV never did catch fire. The cops and the ambulance finally arrived, and I had to explain how the person I thought was trapped in the car turned out to be a box of ashes. The cop listened, nodding his head, trying to look appropriately solemn, but I could see he was struggling not to laugh. I imagined this was going to be a fun story to tell back in the locker room at shift change.

Once I'd given a statement and the cops were convinced that I hadn't actually been involved in or caused the accident - at least not directly – Thelma and I were free to go.

By now the snow had stopped again, but there was nearly five inches piled up on the roads where the snowplows hadn't yet been. It was going to be a long, slow trip home. I only hoped the band of snow hadn't moved north, and that it was still clear once we passed Lakeville.

"So what about talking to John Swanson?" Thelma asked.

"Forget it. I don't know what his problem is, but I've dealt with enough nut cases for one day. He probably wouldn't have told me much, anyway."

"Boy, that was something, wasn't it? A car chase in a snowstorm, and you climbing in that car, all set to rescue some poor old lady..."

"There was no car chase." I corrected her firmly. "I told you, I was just going to try to keep him in sight. It was all his fault he was driving too fast."

"Sure, sure. It wasn't your fault."

"And I had no way of knowing there wasn't a live person in there. She said her *mom* was in there, not just her *remains*!"

Thelma laughed. "I wonder where in the world she was taking those ashes in all this snow, anyway? Do you think her mom just liked to go for rides?"

"Thelma, that's not funny!"

But I laughed, because it really was, in a morbid kind of way.

We made it back to Niles in plenty of time to meet Heidi at Pam's house. We got there early, and Pam let us in.

"I still don't know what to say to you." She told Thelma. "You don't even know me. I don't understand why you're being so generous."

"Like Rainie told you on the phone, I've got a lot more money than I need. My husband was one hell of a shrewd investor. I don't want to leave my money to charity, because most of it would just go to pay some CEO's big salary, and I sure don't think my niece would make good use of it."

"I just hate to take charity." Pam said quietly.

Thelma grinned. "Don't think of it as charity. Think of it as redistributing wealth."

Pam answered with a tiny smile.

"I appreciate you redistributing it in my direction."

Heidi showed up ten minutes early, a habit good caregivers get into. If a client is receiving twenty-four hour care there needs to be an overlap so information can be exchanged between shifts.

I introduced her to Pam and Mrs. LaBell, and we all sat in the living room, taking some time to get acquainted.

Heidi was short and wiry, and deceptively strong. She was also one of the most compassionate people I've ever met.

That compassion is what makes her such an excellent caregiver. A caregiver needs to be able to empathize, to actually think about how the client feels, in order to give good care. For instance, everyone has probably experienced being a little short of breath after a sudden sprint, but what about a client suffering from Emphysema? They were short of breath all the time, and many will panic when experiencing "air hunger." It's important for a caregiver to understand that in order to be a calming influence. It's also important to keep in mind the feelings of the family, the stress and grief they're experiencing over their loved ones. I was confident Heidi could handle even this tough situation.

Pam took Heidi in to meet Gus and Davey in their respective rooms, and we came back out to the living room to discuss their needs. Pam and her mother went over the basics.

"Usually Davey likes to be out here most of the day, but Gus never wants to leave his room."

"He stays in bed all day?"

"For the last couple of weeks," Mrs. LaBell sighed. "The doctor says he should get up more, but he doesn't want to."

Heidi nodded. "Can I make a suggestion? Instead of me coming twice a week for eight hours, I think I should come four mornings a week for four hours. That way I can help Davey and Gus get out of bed."

"Gus won't." His wife sighed again.

"Sure he will." Heidi smiled. "I know it may seem strange, but more often than not people will do things for their caregivers that they won't do for the people they love."

"It's seems like for some people it's easier to say no to family," I put in. "I'm not sure why. Maybe because they know you don't want to put them through any extra pain, and they play on your sympathy, or maybe just because they see caregivers as 'medical authorities.'"

"Well, I *don't* want to cause him any extra pain!" Mrs. LaBell said.

"Of course not, neither do I. But how old is Gus?"

"Seventy three next month."

"He could easily live another twenty years. Do you want him to spend them all in that bed?"

"I'd rather have him out here with me, even if it's just to watch TV."

"Exactly. So we get him up every morning. At first he'll probably only stay up and hour or two, but as he gets stronger he can stay up longer. What sort of things does he like to do?"

"He used to like to read, but he can't anymore, since his eyes got so bad. He likes checkers…" she looked to Pam. "I can't think of much else."

"He *loves* to tell war stories! I used to try to talk him into writing them down, but he never would."

"Okay, so he can tell me some stories while we play checkers, and we could get him audio books from the library."

"That's such a great idea!" Pam shook her head. "Why didn't I think of audio books?"

"You've had a few other things on your mind," Heidi reminded her. "So, how well does Gus get around?"

"He hardly does at all anymore. They were hoping to get him back up using a walker, but he wouldn't do the exercises so the physical therapist stopped coming. He doesn't even want to use his bedside commode anymore."

"We'll work on that, too."

"You think you can get him to exercise?"

"Probably. I'll certainly try."

By the time we left Pam and Heidi had sized each other up and clearly determined they could work together. Heidi wanted to stay a while and get to know Gus and Davey a little bit, maybe help with dinner and clean up so she could get comfortable with their routine.

Pam hugged Thelma, then me, at the door, blinking back tears. "You're both angels."

"Hah, I haven't changed *that* much since our party days, Pam!" That made her laugh, and it was good to leave her with a smile.

Chapter Eight

On Friday it was sunny, the temperature climbing to an almost balmy thirty-two degrees. Well, balmy for January in Michigan, anyway. We hadn't gotten any of the snow we'd run into down in Plymouth, so the roads were clear.

Bob was feeling pretty clear himself, so we spent most of the morning playing Scrabble. I made potato soup and hot ham and cheese sandwiches for lunch, cleaned up afterwards and went to B&E to put in some computer time.

I did a search for "eagles" in Niles. I found several mentions of the Fraternal Order of Eagles, and a few articles about a pair of bald eagles that had been sighted near the St. Joseph River, but that was it. I supposed it wouldn't hurt to ask around at the FOE. Maybe David was a member, or at least had been at one time. I didn't think the bald eagles would reveal much in an interview, but could David have told his mom he had been down there and saw them?

That, of course, was assuming that he really had brought the dish to her last October, and not ten years ago. I was having a lot of trouble believing he was still in the area after all this time and had never tried to contact his kid.

I wondered if the nursing home kept records of visitors. Suddenly I remembered the book.

"You big dummy," I muttered to myself. I should have taken the time to peruse it before I huffed out of there. Then again, searching line by line would have taken a long time, and I doubted if Harriet would have approved. Besides, Halloween was almost three months ago. How often did they have to start a new book? Would they keep the old ones?

I called Pete Jennings, the P.I. Harry had assigned to help if I needed it, but his phone went straight to voicemail so I left a message.

I didn't have a lot else going on, so I drove up to Smith Street to try my hand at staking out Bart Gibson.

I parked behind a pickup truck, hoping it might obscure Gibson's view of me, but I had a pretty decent line of sight that included the front and side of his house, as well as a slice of his backyard.

I stared at the house for a while. Well, maybe three minutes. The shades were drawn, and no one was out and about. I was already bored to tears.

I looked around for something to do. I had a book in the back seat, an old copy of "Don't Know Much About History." The problem was, if I got into that, I would probably miss it if Gibson *did* do something.

Crap. I drummed my fingers on the dashboard. I got my brush out and brushed my hair and put it up in a ponytail. Another three minutes gone. Still nothing at Gibson's house.

So P.I.s did this stuff all the time? No wonder Hopper never smiled. A few days of this and I'd need some serious antidepressants. Or maybe some mild hallucinogenics. Yeah, that would probably make the time go faster. Of course, I wouldn't remember what the hell I was doing here, or who I was supposed to watch, or probably even my own name.

I sighed and fidgeted and looked back at the house, *willing* Gibson to come out and *do* something. Anything! I wish I could be visited by some of that luck Hopper thinks I have.

Somehow I managed to sit there for a whole hour without chewing off my own foot. By that time people were coming home from work, and I think more than a few of them took an extra long, suspicious look at me.

Or so I told myself, because that meant I should get moving.

I headed home for a shower. I was supposed to meet Michael at my mother's house for dinner tonight. As usual Mom hadn't set any particular time, but Michael and I had agreed on seven o'clock. We simply weren't as good at living without the benefit of clocks and time schedules as my mother was.

Dinner at my mom's was fun. Jason came with his kids, Audrey and Alec. Audrey was a precocious and adorable eight year old, and Alec, at the age of five, already seemed confident enough to take over the world.

Jedediah, my mom's long-time live-in boyfriend, tended to stay to himself a lot, and rarely had much to say to anyone outside the family. He had taken a liking to Michael, though, and the dinner conversation was pretty lively. Jedediah was very animated when you got him going on some on his favorite topics, which ranged from the humane raising of chickens and dairy cows to government conspiracies to such things as what made the sky blue. He had been a great step-father, always willing to answer endless questions, even if it meant taking a trip to the library or calling a local university to find an answer.

After dinner we moved to the living room, planning on playing some cards, but the conversation kept going and we never got around to dealing them out.

Michael's opinions surprised me several times. He was pretty liberal, and surprisingly anti-government. No wonder he got along so well with my mom and Jedediah.

They were in a rather heated discussion about the events currently playing out in the Middle East when Jason leaned toward me.

"Do you remember all those stories I used to tell when we were kids?"

"Sure! Lots of adventure stuff, with Captain Black and his intrepid sailors. And the locked room mysteries! I loved those!"

My brother used to get a group of kids together and concoct a mystery story for us, using a G.I. Joe doll as the murder victim. He would lay out the facts of the case and we'd try to figure out whodunit. Sort of a childish version of mystery dinner theater.

"I still do a little writing." He said it as if it were an embarrassing admission.

"Really? I haven't heard you mention writing since high school."

"That's because I never figured I'd take it anywhere. I figured it would always just be a dumb hobby that no one would care about. But..." he hesitated, as if suddenly shy.

"But what?" I prompted.

"Well, I sort of wrote a book."

"Sort of?"

"Okay, I did." He reached under his chair and pulled out a thick yellow envelope.

"Is this it?" I snatched the envelope eagerly. "What's it about? Can I read it?"

"It's a mystery, and yeah, I was hoping you'd read it and give me an opinion on it."

"This is so cool!" I undid the little metal clasps and slid the thick sheaf of printed pages out. The title was "One More for the Road."

"I want your honest opinion."

"Of course! Are you going to try to publish it?"

"I'd like to, but I don't know. Getting a publisher to even look at a new writer's work is damned near impossible. I've been researching it, and it seems you have to know someone, or *be* someone, before they'll even look at the first page."

"You'll still try though, right?"

"I want you to read it first. That's why it's so important that you give me an honest opinion. If it needs work, tell me so. I don't want to waste my time sending it around if it isn't ready."

"I can't wait!" I slid the pages back into the envelope. "I'll get started on it as soon as I can."

"No hurry," he lied. Of course there was a hurry. I know how anxious I was when I handed my poetry over to someone, waiting for an opinion.

"Keep it under wraps, okay?" He glanced at mom. "I don't want Mom to be hurt that I didn't ask her first."

"No problem." I tucked the envelope under my chair, out of sight.

At ten o'clock we said good night and Michael walked me to my car. I turned to him, eager for a kiss. I really like this guy. Maybe this relationship will actually go somewhere.

I've always wanted what my mom and Jedediah have, a long term partnership based on love and mutual respect. It was way too soon to think about the long term with Michael, but so far it looked promising.

I drove home, blissfully thinking of how life might be if we eventually moved in together. Of course, I haven't asked him yet how he feels about George. He seems okay with him, but if he wants the iguana to move out of the living room there is going to be serious problems. After all, George was there first.

It occurred to me that I hadn't heard back from Pete Jennings about the nursing home records, and I pulled my phone out of my pocket to see if I'd somehow missed his call. Nope. I guess I hadn't really said that my question was urgent, but I had thought he'd call me back in a reasonable amount of time.

Would he wait until Monday? I hated to waste that much time. Little Davey's situation wasn't going to be improved by any delay in finding his father – if, that is, his father was anywhere to be found.

I suppose Jack would be able to answer my question, and ten o'clock on a Friday night was definitely not too late to be calling him. I pulled up his number and hit send.

The phone rang once, twice...then, oddly, a third time. That had never happened before. When I called Jack he always answered on the first or second ring, or if he was in the middle of something he would turn off his phone and I got the immediate message that he was unavailable.

Now it rang a fourth time, and it clicked over to voicemail. I heard Jack's voice say "leave a message." I was so startled I didn't say a word, just hung up.

A moment later I was shaking my head and grinning. So I got his voicemail, what's the big deal? Just because he *usually* took my calls so quick that didn't mean he was required to. I mean, he had a life, right? I would just have to wait until tomorrow.

But that wasn't necessary after all. Five minutes later, Jack called me back.

"Hey!" I answered in my most chipper tone.

"Rainie. You saved my life!" Jack's voice was a breathless croak. He sounded like he had a serious case of bronchitis and pneumonia, with maybe a strain of strep throat thrown in for good measure.

"Jack, are you all right?"

"My house is burning down. Goddamn, I was sleeping..." he stopped to cough, a deep, scary sound. He gasped and said again, "You saved my life."

"Your house? Jack, are you all right?" I heard sirens in the distance over his phone. When I came to an intersection I turned east, toward Niles.

"Yeah..." He started coughing again, and this time it sounded like he wasn't going to stop.

"I'm on my way!" I told him over the noise.

He disconnected, and I took that as an acknowledgement.

I could see the light from the flames long before I turned on to his road. A police car was already blocking the way a quarter mile from his house, and the cop didn't care that I was a friend. I dumped the Escort on the shoulder of the road and took off running.

Jack's house was on a side road, a hundred yards from its nearest neighbor, so the road hadn't been plowed very well. I slipped and ran, slipped and ran, and it seemed to take forever to cover the distance.

I could feel the heat before I reached his extended driveway, which was filled with fire trucks, ambulances and police cars. I dodged around them, calling Jack's name.

It wasn't until I saw him, sitting on the back bumper of an ambulance with a blanket over his shoulders and an oxygen mask over his face, that I realized just how scared I'd been.

"Jack!" I called his name again as I ran across the churned up snow. He tossed the mask aside and stood up and threw his arms around me.

"Hey." He croaked, and I let loose a little snort of laughter that was half sob.

"Hey yourself." My face was buried in his shoulder, and the smell of smoke was enough to make my eyes tear. I mean, I'm sure it was the smoke, right? Jack didn't mean all that much to me, did he?

Jack started to cough again and the EMT interrupted our reunion.

"Get the mask on, man."

I reluctantly let him go, and Jack dropped back on the bumper, gasping into the mask. He was covered in soot, his feet shoved into an over-sized pair of boots, maybe borrowed from a fireman. I didn't see any visible burns, and breathed a sigh of relief.

I finally glanced over at the house, and my knees went weak. No wonder I could feel the heat from the road. The structure was fully engulfed, the flames shooting toward the sky from nearly every window.

"Oh my god! How is it burning so fast?"

"Maybe suspicious origins," the EMT answered for him. "He's lucky to be alive."

"You..." Jack had removed the mask again, but that single word got him coughing. The EMT pushed the mask back toward his face.

"Let me tell her." The paramedic looked at me. "I assume you're Rainie?"

When I nodded, he went on. "Okay, so Jack here says he was sleeping on the couch, he fell asleep reading. His cell phone rang and it woke him up, but by that time the whole house was filled with smoke and he barely managed to crawl out to the back door."

"You called..." Jack held out his phone.

"Keep the mask on!" the EMT admonished him. He looked back at me. "He needs to be transported to the hospital, but he won't go."

"Jack, if he thinks you should go..." But Jack was already shaking his head and pointing toward the inferno where he used to live.

"How bad is he?" I asked the paramedic.

"Don't know without x rays. He took in a lot of smoke. Probably needs breathing treatments, definitely needs that oxygen for a while."

"Jack..."

"No!" He spoke without removing the mask this time, and I shrugged helplessly. Even through the muffling plastic I recognized that tone. I'd used it enough myself to know that nothing was going to budge Jack from this yard short of a major explosion. At that thought I glanced back at the house, thinking of gas lines and such, but I assumed that by now the fire department had that taken care of or we'd all be evacuated.

I sat down next to Jack and we silently watched the house burn. I suddenly understood why neighbors gathered at fires and gawked while a family's home went up in smoke and flames: it was an awesome sight, a vision of destructive power that humbled you, that made you realize that in spite of your ability to reason and your opposable thumbs you were still just a fragile human being, one spark away from losing everything you'd built in a lifetime, and maybe even life itself.

At some point Jack reached over and took hold of my hand. Now and then, when a piece of roof would collapse or a window shattered, he would squeeze my hand, as if each new wound on the house was causing him physical pain. Maybe it was. This was his home, his sanctuary, the place where he could putter around in his garden without having to worry about damaging his macho image.

There was a sudden burst of shouting and the firemen all seemed to move back from the fire as a group. Seconds later, with a great crash, the remainder of the roof collapsed. Jack's grip on my hand tightened until I almost cried out.

"I'm sorry, Jack." It seemed inadequate, but I felt like I had to say something.

He dropped the mask and gave me his crooked grin, but this one didn't reach his eyes. "At least I won't have to paint the den now." His attempt at humor earned him another coughing jag. I smiled back, but my heart wasn't in it. I suppose it didn't reach my eyes, either.

I don't know how long we sat there watching the firemen doing their thing. I know hours passed. Jack was taking the oxygen mask off more and more, but he still couldn't do much talking. The EMT had gone to help his counterparts, treating (thankfully) minor wounds among the firemen.

Eventually a great bear of a man, made even bigger by the bulk of his firefighting equipment, came over to us, his helmet in his hand. A reflective tape on his chest proclaimed him to be "Ness." Jack stood and dropped my hand and the oxygen mask at the same time. I saw his jaw firm up and his eyes go cold, and suddenly the wounded, vulnerable Jack was gone as if he'd never been. It was almost as if he'd put up an invisible barrier around himself, and I actually took a step away. Standing in his personal space was no longer comfortable. This was the Jack that scared me.

"I'm Chief Ness." The fireman introduced himself, and I admit I was surprised. There was no insignia on his suit to identify him as anything but another fireman, and the layer of soot testified to his active involvement in battling the blaze. I had always thought the chiefs just sat in big red SUVs in their dress uniforms giving orders over the radio.

"Jack Jones," Jack answered, his voice less like a croak but still deep and rough.

The chief nodded acknowledgement.

"You say you were asleep when this started?"

Jack nodded. "On the couch."

"House insured?"

"Down to the last book on the shelf. Full replacement cost." Jack said it defiantly, as if it were a challenge. The fire chief nodded.

"The forensic guys will need your clothes, maybe swab your hands."

Jack nodded again. "So it's arson?"

"Can't say for sure, not until it cools down, but I'm fairly certain there was accelerant involved. You got any enemies?"

Jack laughed, a short, ugly sound cut off by a cough that he made some effort to suppress. "I'll give you a list."

The fire chief grimaced. "That's kind of what the Sherriff told me. You don't always operate within the parameters of the law."

"I don't have a record."

"I know that, too. But just being good enough to not get caught doesn't make you a model citizen."

"I pay my taxes and buy American. What more do you want?"

The chief smiled. "I guess that does put you up on a lot of folks." He turned and waved at a man standing a short distance away, a large hard-sided case at his feet.

"We need to get those samples."

"You want me to strip here? Can I at least keep my underwear?"

"Naw, you ride into the station with Hank, he'll give you something to put on."

"Am I under arrest?"

"Of course not."

"Then I'm not going anywhere. Bring me something to put on and you can have my clothes."

The chief sighed a long-suffering sigh. "It's been a long night. Do you really need to bust my balls over this?"

"I appreciate what you've been through," Jack glanced meaningfully at the smoldering wreckage behind them, "But I've had a bit of a rough night myself."

The chief nodded and turned to the new guy, who stood expectantly, case in hand. "Do what you need to do. I'm going to call for some clothes."

The new guy, who wore a jacket with FORENSICS in blazing yellow across the back and JEETERS in smaller letters on the front, set his case down. "I've got a couple of coveralls in the truck. He could wear one of those."

"Perfect," the chief acknowledged, and Jeeters left his case and moved off at a trot into the maze of emergency vehicles. It looked almost like a carnival with all the flashing lights and the milling crowd. It seems sometimes that our fun and our disasters have more elements in common than not.

Ten minutes later Jack emerged from the back of the ambulance in a navy blue coverall marked FORENSICS. Jeeters had accompanied him to preserve the chain of evidence, and he was carefully packing the soot covered clothing in large clear plastic bags. He'd already rubbed swabs over Jack's hands and packed those carefully away

I couldn't believe they actually thought Jack might have torched his own house. Could they not see how devastated he was by the loss? But looking at Jack, I supposed they couldn't. He still had the stolid mask on, the macho visage of I-don't give-a-shit-nothing-bothers-me. If I didn't have the memory of him clinging to my hand for the last several hours *I* might even believe he didn't care.

"When will you have a definite answer on the cause of the fire?" Jack didn't seem to be asking the fire chief, but instead demanding an answer.

The fire chief looked at him sourly. "It'll be a couple of days before we know for sure, but I'll have a preliminary answer tomorrow. Where can I find you?"

Jack shrugged. "At the end of this, I suppose." He held up his cell phone. "You want the number?"

"I'd like an address. A hotel maybe?"

"My place." I spoke up almost before I realized I was thinking it. Jack looked at me, clearly surprised. "I mean, if you want." Suddenly I was blushing furiously. I suppose I should have asked him first. Then I realized I should clarify another point. "I have a futon...in the spare room. If you want." I finished lamely, and Jack grinned.

"All right then, I'll be at Rainie's."

I gave the fire chief my address and he wrote it down in a notebook he pulled from an inside pocket. He'd unhooked his fire suit and the top half hung down the back of his legs. He wasn't wearing a uniform under it, but instead a flannel shirt. I suppose the fire alarm had caught him at home, probably relaxing in front of the TV.

"All right, I'll be in touch."

He walked away, Jeeters following in his wake.

I turned to Jack, suddenly shy and uncomfortable. What the hell had I been thinking, inviting him home? His temporary vulnerability had lulled me into believing he was just another guy in need, and like the soft-hearted sap I was I opened my mouth to offer help before my brain could engage and remind me what an idiot I was. When I was much younger that tendency had resulted in an endless stream of dogs, cats, birds, squirrels, mice and once even a catfish brought home to be nursed back to health with the competent supervision of my mother.

But my mother wasn't going to supervise this mess. I was going to be sleeping under the same roof as Jack, who I sometimes suspected was missing the gene that made most men consider the consequences before they acted. And what if he thought I was just making a veiled offer to share my bed? What if he thought the futon was just a ruse to hide my sluttiness from the fire chief?

He looked at me, his face expressionless. "You ready?"

"I guess." I glanced around, suddenly remembering his truck. My eyes settled on the wreckage and I realized there was an attached garage. My heart sank, and I looked back at Jack, who must have followed my train of thought because he nodded grimly.

"It was parked in the garage. I'll see about a rental tomorrow." Then he glanced at his watch. "Today, I mean."

"What time is it?" It just occurred to me to wonder.

"Four a.m, and I need a shower. Can we go?"

"Sure." I turned and started for my car. A shower. And meals. And a hundred other domestic and decidedly personal activities that Jack would be performing under my roof. For how long? I'd sort of left that open-ended, and it occurred to me, belatedly, that it could be months before he was able to rebuild.

I thought of the catfish I'd brought home that summer afternoon so many years ago. A man fishing had caught it and given it to me for reasons unknown. I'd carried it home in an old bucket and dumped it in my little plastic kiddie pool, where it swam round and round in circles, discontent to be confined. The next day my mother had scooped it back into the bucket and we'd taken it down to the St. Joseph River and released it. It had swum away without a backward glance, happy to be back to its own devices.

I only hope Jack will go as willingly when the time comes.

The drive back to my house was mostly silent, broken by Jack's periodic coughing. I agreed with the EMT that he needed to be treated for smoke inhalation, but I was too tired to argue with him.

I showed him where the towels were and he went off to take a shower. I grabbed a set of sheets and went to make up the futon. I added an extra blanket and was just turning away from my task when Jack appeared in the doorway, wearing only a towel around his hips.

"Hey, you didn't have to do that," he said, pointing at the newly made up bed. "I appreciate the place to stay, but I don't want you to wait on me."

"Don't worry, I won't." I was trying to find some place to rest my eyes, but they kept wanting to drift back to his naked torso. I could feel the heat in my face and wondered just how badly I was blushing. I needed to get out of there, but he was blocking the door.

"Um, excuse me." I took one step toward him, hoping he'd take the hint and move. He grinned and stepped aside, clearly enjoying my discomfort. This was the mean side of him that I didn't like. It was getting ever clearer that he was well aware of the effect he had on me, and he thought it was funny.

Once I was safely past him I stopped, annoyed. "I hope you aren't planning to run around like that on a regular basis. I prefer my house guests clothed."

"Hey, I'm sorry, but all I had was that coverall the forensics guy gave me and it smells like smoke. I was hoping you'd let me throw it in the washer."

"Oh." Great, once again, I was being the bitch. Of course he didn't have any clothes. Didn't I just watch them burn up? "Okay, I'll go throw them in for you."

I started to walk away when a thought occurred to me. "Hey, I still have those sweat pants you loaned me last summer after...um, the party." It still embarrassed me to remember that little fiasco, when I'd gotten so drunk I couldn't drive and I woke up in Jack's bed. "I'll get them for you."

I hurried off to my room to dig out the sweat pants. I don't know why I still had them. I guess I just hadn't gotten around to giving them back.

I brought him the pants, and satisfied that he wouldn't be wandering around naked I informed him that I was going to bed.

"The coveralls can wait until morning...or later, anyway. I think we both need some sleep."

"Agreed." Jack yawned. "I'll see you around noon?"

I nodded and went off to sleep.

Chapter Nine

I slept restlessly until 10:30. At that point I gave up and rolled out of bed. It isn't all that easy to just readjust your body's clock, and mine was insisting that it was day time and I needed to get moving.

I stumbled bleary eyed to the kitchen to find Jack already there, sitting at the counter with a mug of coffee and reading the morning paper. I poured a cup for myself and sat down.

"Want some of the paper?" He sounded ridiculously alert, in spite of the roughness of his voice. I suppose guys with his training were used to sleeping at whatever odd hours they could manage. I just nodded and took the front page.

"Eddie will be over in a few minutes."

"Why?" I sipped my coffee, wishing he wouldn't make conversation until I'd managed to get the first cup in me.

"He's bringing me some clothes, for one thing."

"Good." I know I sounded rude, but frankly I found it disturbing to sit next to him in his current state of undress. He was wearing the sweatpants, but there was still that naked torso to contend with. I swear I could feel the heat emanating from him, and even in my grogginess my body was responding. It was disgusting.

Jack was silent for a minute. Relieved, I drank more coffee and started reading an article about the Niles dam. It had fallen into disuse some years before, but apparently there was talk of revitalizing it.

"When Eddie gets here I'll ask him if I can stay with him for a couple of days."

That was a great idea! But no, my mouth opened and words poured out before it got the message from my brain.

"Eddie only has one bedroom, you'd be tripping all over each other. I said you can stay here, and I meant it. I'm sorry I'm a little crabby this morning."

"You aren't much of a morning person, are you?"

"Actually, I am, it's just that I don't consider it morning until I've finished my first cup of coffee."

"Fair enough." Jack went back to reading the paper and didn't say anything else until I got up to refill my coffee cup. He held his out for a warm up and I offered him a little smile.

"Good morning."

He smiled back. "Good morning."

"So when is Eddie going to be here?"

"He said a little after eleven. He's going to take me over to the office so I can get some paperwork."

"For what?"

Jack suddenly started coughing, and he turned away and bent over. I watched him, alarmed. The coughing seemed to involve his whole body, wracking him with explosive barks, his inhales wheezing and strained. I wanted to ask if there was anything I could do, but I didn't want to make him talk. He clearly needed all the air he could suck in right now.

Finally it subsided, and he sat silently for a half-minute or so, letting his breathing return to normal. He turned back to me and continued our conversation as if nothing had ever happened.

"I'm going to need copies of documents they have on file."

"Jack, are you really going to try to ignore that cough? You need to see a doctor."

He pretended he hadn't heard me. "My wallet went with the house. I don't have any ID, no credit cards, nothing. Otherwise I could go rent a hotel room."

"Oh. I hadn't thought about that." I gave up on the doctor thing. For now.

"I can't even rent a car until I get that straightened out. Hopefully by Tuesday I'll at least have my license. I'll get out of your hair then."

"Okay, but really, you can stay as long as you need to." I said it sincerely, but a little voice in the back of my brain was threatening to cut my tongue out if I didn't shut up.

"I really appreciate this. I'll try not to get in the way."

I was saved the need to answer by a knock on the door. Jack went to let Eddie in.

"Hey, Rainie."

"Hey, Eddie. How's it going?"

"Better for me than Jack. I hear you're his new hero."

"Hardly! All I did was call him."

"Oh yeah, I forgot all about that," Jack interrupted. He was carrying an armload of clothes that Eddie must have brought for him. "Why *did* you call me?"

"I just had a question about that missing person case I'm working, and Pete Jennings never called me back." Come to think of it, he still hadn't.

"Okay, what's the question?"

I explained about the nursing home and their visitor's log.

"If it was me, I'd just go ask the lady at the front desk. If you explain that whole tragic story, how can she say no?"

"I suppose, if it's the same woman that was there when I went the other day. She seemed sympathetic enough."

"Well, there you go."

I sighed. That meant another long haul to Plymouth.

"I'd better go get dressed." Jack went back to the spare room.

"He needs to see a doctor," I told Eddie as soon as Jack's door closed. "I thought he was going to suffocate this morning, he was coughing so hard."

"I'll get him to go."

"Really? He wouldn't even discuss it with me."

Eddie smiled. "That's because you didn't twist his arm hard enough."

"You mean that literally, don't you?"

"If necessary."

"It probably will be."

Eddie smiled briefly.

"Hey, on another subject, have you met Riley's new girlfriend?" Eddie asked me.

"No, he hasn't brought her around. Doesn't talk much about her, either."

"I've noticed. Kind of strange, don't you think?"

I shrugged. "A little. Maybe she's shy."

"I don't know. I saw him with her the other day. I passed them going the other way down in South Bend. From what I saw, she's pretty hot."

"Not surprising. Riley has always pretty much had his pick of women."

"But he doesn't normally try to hide them."

"I don't think he's trying to hide her." But I wasn't really so sure. Riley *had* been acting pretty odd lately, not coming to group gatherings, even missing poker. He'd never let a girlfriend come before poker before. "Maybe he's in love," I grinned.

131

Eddie laughed. "Right. And the Pope is Presbyterian this week."

Jack came back, dressed in Eddie's clothes. Eddie was a little bulkier than Jack, and the clothes fit him loosely. It was odd to see him wearing anything other than skin tight jeans. He still looked pretty good, though.

"We'll see you later, Rainie. You want me to bring dinner back with me?"

"I don't know, like what?"

"I could swing by Hilltop Café and get a box of their carry out chicken."

My tummy gave me a little rumble of pleasure at the thought of that.

"Okay, you get the chicken and I'll make a salad."

"See you around six."

I watched them leave, thinking how domestic that exchange had seemed. Was it possible I might even get used to having him around?

Nope. Not going to happen.

I called long-distance information and got the phone number for Sunnyview Extended Care in Plymouth. I called and asked for Harriet Fromm.

"She's not in today," the woman who answered said rather shortly. "Try on Monday."

I thanked her, but I think she had already hung up. I definitely wasn't going to try to sweet talk *that* lady, so I would have to put off my quest until Monday. That left the rest of today and all of Sunday with no particular plans.

I stepped out on the porch for a smoke. The sun was up, and it was surprisingly warm out, probably nearing forty degrees. Snow was melting and dripping off the roofs, and the streets were turning slushy. The melt off would make a mess, but the warmer temperatures were welcome nonetheless.

I finished my smoke and decided I felt pretty good for having had only a few hours sleep. I supposed I might as well go see what Bart Gibson was up to.

So maybe Jack was right, and I did have a touch of luck.

I drove to Smith Street and managed to slip my car into the same plowed out spot behind the truck I'd parked behind before and settled in to watch Gibson's house. This time I had brought my checkbook, figuring I could balance it while I waited. I didn't use it much, preferring cash transactions, but I did use it for gas. I liked being able to swipe my card, pump my gas and get back on the road with minimum fuss.

I had hardly gotten my pen and checkbook out before I saw Gibson's garage door go up. Sure enough, he backed his green Astrovan out. Yay, me!

I followed him, staying well back, always keeping at least one car between us. It wasn't too difficult as long as he stayed on 933, a relatively busy four lane highway. I drove most of the way with my windshield wipers on, in spite of the sunshine. The cars around me were throwing up a constant spray of dirty slush from the melting snow, just as I was throwing it back at them. Washer fluid was a big seller in winter around here, as necessary as gasoline if you wanted to get anywhere.

Gibson seemed to be heading for the Indiana state line. That was common enough. He might be heading down to one of the bigger shopping areas, or maybe stopping at Stateline Road. Cigarettes were two dollars a pack cheaper in Indiana than they were in Michigan, and there was no deposit on beer. On the other hand, you couldn't buy beer in Indiana on Sundays, but you could in Michigan. The combination made major intersections along the state line a popular spot for smoke shops and liquor stores.

Sure enough, Bart turned right on Stateline Road, and I followed him, still two cars back. He passed the Mini-Mart and the Smokes-for-Less shop and both liquor stores, but the two cars between us turned in at a little rundown spot named, as far as I could tell from the available signage, "COLD BEER."

I hung back, but once we got past the string of businesses there wasn't any other traffic. Fortunately he didn't go very far. He went up and around a curve and pulled into the entrance to Madeline-Bertrand County Park.

I drove on past the entrance, turned around in someone's driveway, and went back, giving Bart time to get in and park.

I was familiar with the layout of the place. It was a good sized park, much of it wooded, with extensive trails for hiking and cross-country skiing, as well as an excellent disc golf course. There were pavilions to rent for picnicking and a large playground for the kids.

I also knew there were two main parking lots, both within sight of each other, but not so close together that he might notice every car pulling in.

I pulled in and paid the entrance fee and drove toward the lots. They were well-plowed and sanded, and all the paved paths had been shoveled and salted. Several people were walking around, a few carrying skis. I saw a couple of guys heading for the disc golf course. They kept a shortened course open even in the winter for die-hard players, and apparently plenty of them wanted to take advantage of the unusually warm day.

I saw Gibson's van in the lot to the right, so I parked to the left and sat there for a minute, watching.

Gibson climbed carefully out of his van, clinging to the open door while he remoted the sliding door open. A golden retriever jumped out, grinning happily like retrievers do, and Gibson had to move quick to grab the dog's leash. I heard him command the dog to sit, and it did, reluctantly, its whole furry body quivering with repressed energy.

Gibson looped the leash over his wrist and pulled out his aluminum walker. It was a standard model, with five inch wheels on the front and tennis balls cut and fitted over the back legs to allow it to move smoothly over the ground without rubbing off the little rubber stoppers. He carefully leaned against the van while he unfolded it and just as carefully leaned away from the van and on to the walker. So far, except for the fast move required to snatch the leash, Gibson was giving every impression that he was a man with a serious handicap. He tied a plastic bag to the front of the walker. I couldn't tell what was in it, but it looked a little bulky.

The dog was surprisingly well behaved, only pulling a little now and then as Gibson led him to a paved path that led back into the trees. Gibson moved slowly and deliberately, carefully pushing the walker a bit out in front before he took a step, but staying within the aluminum frame. It was textbook use of a walker, the method physical therapists tried to teach but patients rarely achieved.

I waited until Gibson was out of sight, then, digital camera in hand, I followed him. I stayed back, assuming he wouldn't leave the paved path, since the woods on either side were knee deep in snow and hardly suited for a walker

I quickly lost sight of him when the path took a wide curve to the left, then another to the right. Ahead I could see that the trees opened up to something, and the paved path ended. I couldn't see Gibson.

Moving more slowly now, I continued to the end of the path, wishing I'd worn a lighter coat. The temperature had soared to a near tropical forty-five degrees, and with no leaves to block it the sun was warm even back here in the trees.

I got to the end of the path and stopped. I saw Gibson's walker, but not Gibson. Hmm. I seriously doubted if he'd been beamed up by aliens, so odds were he was somewhere nearby.

The path ended at a big field, a clearing in the forest, the grass left unmowed in the fall so that here and there a stubborn stalk poked up out of the snow. It looked like the county had cleared this space to use for something, maybe a baseball field or another pavilion/picnic area, but had never gotten around to doing anything with it.

Gibson was off to my right, a good twenty feet from his walker. The plastic bag was at his feet, lying open on top of the snow. I could see that it held several bright yellow tennis balls.

He had another tennis ball in his hand, and he called to the dog.

"Here it goes, Sparky! Go get it!" He leaned back and threw the ball, stepping forward for the follow through, and the ball sailed high and away across the field. The retriever barked joyfully and romped off after it, not bothered in the least by the deep snow.

I hurriedly brought up the power on my digital camera, set it to movie mode and started filming Gibson's amazing recovery. Look at that balance! And the way he could shift his weight from one leg to the other with no problem. It was a freaking miracle!

Sparky came bounding back, and Gibson gave him a rub and a few enthusiastic "good boys." Sparky was leaping for the ball and Gibson was holding it high over his head, teasing the dog, urging him to jump for it. Gibson laughed and stepped back a few feet, lifting his knees high to get over the snow, and wound up and threw the ball again. I watched it all through the little screen on the back of the camera while I filmed it. Hah! So much for permanent disability!

I don't know what attracted Gibson's attention to me. I didn't make any sudden movements, but maybe the sun flashed off the camera lens. Whatever, through the view screen I saw him suddenly turn toward me, and at the same time heard him yell.

"Hey! What the hell are you doing?"

I probably should have turned and ran right then, but I was feeling a little cocky. Hadn't I just proven in two days of following him what the insurance company hadn't been able to verify in nearly a year? I mean, damn I'm good!

I was still holding the camera up, getting Gibson's anger in 10.1 megapixel clarity, when he wound up with another tennis ball, and with accuracy that the Chicago Cubs could have benefitted from fired a fast ball right at me.

The ball hit the camera dead on. If it had been a baseball it probably would have broken my fingers, but as it was it just broke the camera and knocked it out of my hand.

It took me only a couple of seconds to react, but Sparky didn't have the disadvantage of surprise. He had taken off at a dead run as soon as Gibson threw the ball, but instead of going after it, he was attracted to the bright pink camera. He bounded over and snatched it out of the snow.

"No! Bad dog!" I shouted. "Drop it!" I reached for it, but Sparky grinned his slobbery grin and ran a couple of circles around me, happy with a game of keep-away. In the meantime Gibson was on his way, closing the gap between us with remarkable speed for a man with severe soft tissue damage to his back.

I don't own a dog, but I've had some experience with them, especially big dumb playful ones. I snatched up the abandoned tennis ball.

"Here, Sparky!" I waved the ball in front of the dog's face, and then threw it as hard as I could. "Go get it!"

Well trained to fetching the familiar ball, Sparky dropped the camera and took off after the ball just as Gibson arrived. We both dove for the camera at the same time, but I got my hands on it first. Unfortunately Gibson was a lot bigger than me, and in spite of nearly a year hobbling around like the fake cripple he was, he was still a lot stronger. He landed on my back and pinned me to the ground, my hands, still holding the camera, trapped under me.

"Get off me!" I wheezed more than shouted, my breath in short supply. This jerk was really heavy.

"Give me the camera!" He reached under me, groping around in search of the camera.

The snow gave me more room to work than solid ground would have, and I managed to take in a good breath. "Help! Rape!" I screamed. Immediately his hand withdrew.

"Shut up! I'm not doing *that*, I just want the camera."

"Get off and I'll give it to you." I wasn't lying. I had a new plan. I was fumbling with the camera, trying to find the finger hold for the little sliding door to access the SD card. What the hell, the camera was broken anyway, and all I needed was the card. Unfortunately my fingers were wet and slippery and stiffening from the cold, making the task a lot harder than it normally would have been.

"How do I know you won't just take off with it?" He hadn't moved, and the weight of our bodies was making it hard to do much of anything underneath, but I finally found the sliding door and worked it open.

"Just get off of me!"

Finally he got up, but he got a hold on the back of my coat and dragged me up with him. "I'm not letting you go until you give me that camera."

"All right already! I get it!" Actually, I should have said "I got it," because right about then I managed to pop the tiny SD card out of the camera. I palmed it as he reached around for the camera.

He snatched the camera away. "Now get the hell out of here!"

"Fine. Okay." I started backing away, trying to look defeated. "You win, I'm going." As soon as I got a safe distance away I turned and headed down the path, but I threw a few more empty threats over my shoulder at him, like a ten year old who had just lost a playground fight.

"I'm going, but I'll be back! You just wait 'til next time..."

I went around a curve in the path, and as soon as I was out of sight I slipped the little card into the pocket of my jeans, feeling pretty pleased with myself. Okay, so I'd trashed a brand new and probably expensive camera, but I'd gotten what I needed...

"Hey! You!"

Uh oh. I looked behind me and there was Gibson, pushing his walker ahead of himself but moving at a pretty good clip, Sparky romping along beside him. I wondered how he'd trained the dog not to chase the tennis balls attached to the walker?

"Give me that memory card!"

Well, what had I expected? Bart Gibson had been scamming individuals and companies for most of his life from what I'd gathered, and rather successfully. It took a pretty smart person to get away with that sort of thing. Naturally he knew how a digital camera worked, and had thought to check the compartment for the SD card - which, now that I thought about it, in my hurry I hadn't even closed.

I walked a little faster, but didn't want to do anything so undignified as to run away from a guy with a walker, even if I did know he was a fake.

He sped up, the little wheels clattering and banging over the asphalt. They weren't built for any kind of speed.

"I said stop!" Gibson shouted, but of course I ignored him. I was gaining ground, easily outpacing him.

"Damn you!" Gibson swore, and I glanced back to see he had finally lifted his walker and was running with it, like a woman lifting her skirts for a full out sprint. The image was really funny, but I figured I'd better laugh later. He looked really pissed!

I took off at a full run, Gibson and his happy dog right behind me. He probably would have caught me if he'd just ditched the walker, but for some reason he kept it, holding it high while he pounded away behind me.

I came out of the woods into the main part of the park and left the path, running across the snow in a direct line to my car. I heard Gibson swear again.

"Shit!" He yelled, and I turned just in time to see him fall in a crazy tangle with his walker.

140

He went down hard, one foot caught between the bracket that supported the front and back legs, and I actually heard the *snap!* when his leg broke.

He rolled onto his back, screaming, and the walker fell on top of him, the front crossbar hitting him across the nose.

I automatically turned back to help him, my caregiver instincts kicking into high gear. I heard a couple of people shouting, and saw two teenagers drop their disc golf bags to come running over.

"Whoa, what happened?" One of them had long red hair pulled into a ponytail and numerous facial piercings, including a large silver peg protruding from his lower lip. He wasn't wearing a coat, and his over-sized t shirt advertised some rock band named "Death Pennies." (I might lie awake tonight, trying to figure out how they came up with that name). He leaned over Gibson.

"Dude!" he said. "I don't think you're supposed to run with one of these things." He indicated the walker.

"Don't move him, man!" The other one, short haired and geeky looking in little round wire-framed glasses, said. His coat was hanging open, and he was wearing a t shirt under it that said "Talk nerdy to me." They were an odd pair, and I wondered how they'd ever met, let alone become friends.

"Maybe we should get the park ranger?" Death Pennies was looking down at Gibson's leg. There was a considerable amount of blood soaking through his pants and dotting the snow, and I felt a little queasy. It wasn't the sight of blood that got to me, it was knowing what was likely causing the bleeding: a serious compound fracture, the jagged bone piercing the skin from the inside out. I had already pulled my cell phone out, but I would prefer to have the ranger call 911 so I could get the hell out of here.

"Yeah, the ranger," I agreed. "Run up to the office..."

"He's already coming." Nerdy pointed at the little brick building that housed the park ranger's office. Sure enough, a youngish guy in a brown uniform was sprinting across the snow.

No one had tried to move the walker off of Gibson, and I decided I wasn't going to offer. It was lightweight aluminum, not all that heavy (although it had hit hard enough to give him a serious bloody nose) so it wasn't restricting his breathing. On the other hand, that shattered leg was still between the bars, and I sure wasn't going to move his leg to free him.

"What's going on?" the ranger arrived, a little breathless. I don't think his job here in this quiet park required a lot of sprinting. Maybe not too much thinking either; if I came up on a scene like this, with a bloody man screaming like a banshee giving birth to Godzilla, I think I could have figured out the highlights of the story.

"This dude was, like, running..." Death Pennies started.

"Yeah, carrying that...what do you call it?" Nerdy looked to his friend for the word.

"It's a walker," I supplied.

"Yeah, only not like in Star Wars..."

"No, but that would be *so* cool! No one would feel crippled if they had one of those bad boys under them..." they went off on a sci-fi tangent and the ranger rolled his eyes and looked at me.

"Did you see what happened?"

"Shouldn't you call 911? Or do you want me to?" I held up my phone, and the ranger blushed, embarrassed to need reminding to do his job.

"Oh yeah, right, right!" He pulled out a phone of his own and hurriedly dialed the emergency number.

"You!" Gibson stopped screaming long enough to point a shaky finger at me. "You bitch! You did this!"

"Hey now," I kept my voice mild, but only because I was talking through clenched teeth. I really *hated* being called a bitch! I knelt down next to him and put a hand on his shoulder. I leaned close and spoke in a soothing tone, just a concerned, comforting little caregiver. "You nasty, ugly little man," I said softly, my smile and sweet tone belying my words. I was pretty sure the others wouldn't hear anything but the tone of voice. "You got what you deserved. You're a sucking little leach on the ass of the world, but now at least you'll really need that walker!"

I patted him on the shoulder, stood up and walked away.

My job here was done.

I no sooner got to my car when my cell phone chirped. I looked at the readout and smiled when I pushed the talk button.

"Hi Michael!"

"Hi, Rainie. How are things?"

"Not bad." Really? I had just sat up all night watching Jack's house burn down, and now he was living with me. I had been chased by a crazy guy in a walker and watched him break his leg. Had I really just summed that all up with "not bad"?

"Cool. I was wondering if you're going to be busy tomorrow?"

"I don't have any plans."

"I was thinking about taking a run up to the Museum of Science and Industry in Chicago tomorrow. You wanna go?"

"I had a feeling you might. Jedediah was pretty high on that molecular science display, wasn't he?"

"Yeah, it sounds pretty cool."

"Sounds like fun to me. What time do you want to go?"

"I'd like to get moving kind of early. How about if I pick you up at eight o'clock?"

"Sounds good. I'll see you then."

I didn't even have time to put my phone back in my pocket before Belinda called with an errand for me to run.

"Hopper needs some paperwork picked up at the county courthouse down in South Bend. How does your schedule look on Monday?"

"I'm hoping to make a run down to Plymouth in the afternoon on that missing person's case, but I could hit South Bend on my way."

"Great! Just go to the records division and ask for Mary Beth. She'll have a folder waiting."

"No problem. See you Monday."

Eddie dropped Jack off at six o'clock, and he came in with the promised chicken. I loaded up my plate with salad and took one small chicken thigh, carefully peeling off all the yummy breaded and deep-fried skin and setting it aside.

We sat at the counter to eat, Jack sipping a bottle of water between bites while I indulged in some unsweetened iced tea. He looked at my plate.

"Is that all you're going to eat?"

"It's plenty."

"Not by half. You need some calcium and…"

"Hey!" I slapped my fork down on the counter. "Are you seriously going to lecture me about my unhealthy habits when you're sitting there, your lungs likely filled with pneumonia?"

Jack reached into his pocket and pulled out a tiny yellow envelope and slapped it on the counter next to my fork. "Antibiotics. Eddie made me go to the clinic this afternoon."

"Oh." I picked up my fork. "Anyway, I've been munching all day. I'm not that hungry." I didn't look at him when I told the lie, but I think he recognized the untruth anyway. I hurriedly changed the subject.

"Michael is picking me up in the morning. We're going to Chicago."

"Yeah?" Jack looked interested. "What are you going to do?"

"We're going to the Museum of Science and Industry."

"Huh. I haven't been there since I was a kid."

"It's one of my favorite places. I was happy to hear Michael likes it to."

"You've been seeing him a lot."

"He's a great guy. He's smart and funny and good looking and he doesn't complain about George. What more could I ask for?"

"So you think he's the one?"

"The one? You mean like marriage? No... I mean, I'm not in love with him yet or anything."

"Yet? So you think the potential is there."

"Yeah...I mean, maybe. I don't know! Why all the questions?"

"Just curious." Jack shrugged. "Making conversation."

"It doesn't feel like conversation. It feels like I'm being grilled."

"Sorry." Jack grinned, not looking very sorry at all

"I was wondering though," I got back to the point. "I haven't actually told Michael about you staying here yet, so could you maybe stay in your room until we're gone?"

Jack's lip quirked in a little half smile. "Secrets, Rainie? Not a good way to start a relationship."

"Not a secret," I blushed and hated myself for it. "I just didn't want to blurt the whole story out over the phone. I'll tell him tomorrow."

"Okay." Jack shrugged again. "But it's no big deal, is it? Me being here is totally innocent, right?" He gave me a sideways glance that almost made me choke on my chicken.

"Right." I managed. "But still…"

"Yeah, yeah. I'll stay in my room like a good boy."

Jack, a good boy. Not in this lifetime.

Chapter Ten

On Monday morning I woke up ready to conquer the world. Or at least, Harriet Fromm.

I was a little worn out from walking around the museum for eight hours with Michael, but it was a good worn out. We'd had a great time, mostly agreeing on which sections to spend the most time in. No doubt, Michael and I were very compatible. There had been a lot of hand holding and nuzzling and sweet stolen kisses. Our relationship had definitely moved up a level, and I was pretty damned happy about it.

Somehow, I never got around to mentioning Jack's house fire, or the fact that he was currently living with me. Fortunately when Michael dropped me off Jack wasn't home, and I begged off inviting him in, saying it was kind of late and I had to work the next day.

All true, but still a bit of a deception, nonetheless. Probably not a good way to start what I was hoping would turn into a long-term relationship, but the fact was Jack might be a little hard to explain.

I flipped the TV on long enough to check the weather report. It isn't as if the reports are all that accurate, but at least they sometimes give you an idea of what to expect.

Today they were predicting freezing rain. Oh, joy. I hit the off button and went for a refill on my coffee.

Rachel came by to pick Jack up at seven a.m., as bad-assed perky with the sunrise as she was in the evenings.

"So, how are the new roommates getting along?" There might have been a little hint of something in her tone, something not-nice, but I chose to ignore it.

"It's fine. Neither one of us is here much, anyway."

"Just at night." There, that was definitely a *tone*.

"Come on, let's hit the road." Jack sounded a little annoyed, but I wasn't sure why. Again I chose to ignore it. I had more important things to worry about.

I called Sunnyview when I left Bob for the day, and the phone was answered in a chipper tone: "You've reached Sunnyview. This is Harriet. How may I direct your call?"

"Oops, wrong number," I lied, trying to use a slightly higher voice than normal so she wouldn't recognize me.

"No problem, hon. Have a nice day!"

So, Harriet was working, and she sounded like she was in a good mood. I still had to stop by the courthouse for Hopper's paperwork, but hopefully I could make it to Plymouth before the pervasive atmosphere of grouchiness that seemed to infect the other employees of Sunnyview got to her.

It was cloudy in Michigan, but overall the weather wasn't bad until just after I hit the Indiana state line. That was when the promised freezing rain started.

I cranked up the heat in my car, setting it all to blow on my windshield. The wipers did an effective job of keeping the view clear, although a little scrim of ice started building up around the edges.

By the time I got to South Bend it was coming down pretty hard. I slowed down accordingly, as did everyone around me, and we continued on our merry way.

I made my slow way to Main Street in downtown South Bend, by then wondering if the freezing rain would follow me all the way to Plymouth.

I was singing along to "Crazy Little Thing Called Love," grooving with Freddy Mercury and the gang. All was right with the world.

The next minute my car was spinning like a hockey puck gone wild, and I was treated to a 360 degree view of first the road, then the river that ran next to the road, before my car hitched up against a snow bank.

It was the ice, I suppose. The freezing rain was coating trees, buildings...roads. But what the hell, it was January in southern Michigan, and slippery stuff fell from the sky most of the month. I didn't see a need to be overly concerned.

But now here I was, hitched up against a snow bank. The snow bank, in turn, was piled up against the guard rail separating the road from the river. For the moment, I was grateful for all that snow. The words grateful and snow don't occur in the same sentence too often unless you own a ski resort or a snow plow, but the St. Joseph River happens to be pretty deep and fast flowing, so yeah, I was grateful for the snow bank.

I was not, however, grateful to whoever had hit me in the first place. The initial surprise was wearing off and I was getting pissed; it so happens that I *love* my car.

I opened my car door and got out to assess the damage, setting my feet carefully on the shiny street. There was a good quarter inch of ice on the street; no wonder my car had done such an excellent job of mimicking Peggy Fleming. Nonetheless, unless the person who hit me was fresh off the jet from California, there was no excuse for hitting me. I mean, it's not as if it were cats and dogs or shoes and socks falling from the sky. Any of those things might be a distraction, obstacles to be reckoned with. But come on! This was just ice...in January...in southern Michigan. It was no big deal!

I was no sooner out of my car than I heard someone yelling frantically. "Oh man! Are you okay? Man, I'm sorry, I was hitting my brakes, but like the car just kept going...are you okay?"

I turned toward the frantic voice. It belonged to a teenager. He was tall, skinny and black, wearing an oversized T-shirt under an oversized coat that didn't hide his oversized pants. Of course, I knew the kid probably wasn't wearing hand-me-downs from the Chicago Bear's defensive line; he would fit right in at any high school.

My temper had already deserted me. The kid had endeared himself to me right away with that "are you okay" business, and besides, now I *knew* what kind of idiot had hit me. A teenaged driver, very likely sliding through his first Midwest winter, naively believing he could control his car like he did his snowboard.

Besides, I could already see that my precious car had miraculously not been damaged. It was so slick the car had given no resistance when the other vehicle had smacked into it. No harm, no foul.

"I'm really sorry, lady. Do I need to call the cops?"

"No!" Good god, this kid really was naïve! "If you file a report your insurance is going to go through the roof."

"Oh yeah...but your car..."

"It's not hurt. All this will cost you is to listen to a little advice."

"Yeah?" The kid looked at me suspiciously.

"First of all, on ice it's best to just let the car kind of stop itself; go slow, go light on the brakes, and allow about five times the normal time for stopping. Second of all...never admit guilt."

"Huh?"

"Look, I really appreciate you asking after my well being, but the part about how you couldn't stop...bad news, man. Never, *never* admit guilt. The insurance company will rip you up."

"Yeah?"

"Yeah."

Suddenly he grinned. "Hey, you're okay for a...I mean, thanks."

I suppose he was going to say "okay for an old lady." I was, after all, in my thirties, certainly old from his seventeen year old perspective. I figured this had been a decent encounter so far though, so I let it go.

"Look, if I were you I'd find a deserted parking lot somewhere and practice stopping. The only way to deal with this crap is experience."

He grinned. "Maybe I should go do some doughnuts in the old Safeway parking lot."

"That's not..." I shook my head. "Drive carefully." I slid back into my car, and he waved and moved back to his. My CD player had moved on to Tony Price, a bit more mellow than Queen. Okay, so maybe mellow wasn't a bad idea for an ice storm.

Harriet was still cheerful when I arrived at quarter to three, and she buzzed me in with a big smile.

"Hello! How can I help you?" She asked when I stepped up to the desk.

"I was here last Thursday, to visit Betty Swanson."

"Oh yes, I remember." Harriet's smile dropped a little wattage. "Didn't you say you were only in town for the day?"

Here's where it might get dicey. I put on what I hoped was an apologetic smile and confessed my duplicity.

"I really am from out of town. I live in Buchanan, Michigan. But I'm not really a friend of the family. I'm an assistant private investigator for B&E Security in Niles."

Now Harriet's smile was completely gone, replaced by a thin firm line that would have looked good on a particularly stern teacher. I rushed to explain what I wanted, and why, once again remembering to add the part about Mrs. LaBell's bad back and her husband's stroke. By the time I was done Harriet was shaking her head and clucking like a worried mother hen.

"Oh, that poor family! What tragedy!"

"I know. That's why I'm doing this. Harry Baker – he owns B&E – has even agreed to provide the company services for free." Of course, I was getting paid, but I had intended to do it on my own, so didn't that still count?

"It's so sweet of you to try to help. So what can I do?"

"When I spoke to Mrs. Swanson she said her son David was here to see her last Halloween. I'd just like to peek at the visitor's log to confirm that. It would help a lot to even have confirmation that he's alive and in the area."

"Well, I should say so!" Harriet tapped her lower lip with a manicured but unpainted nail. "You know, I think I remember someone... yes, it would have been about that time. A man came here, but he seemed really nervous. Looked over his shoulder all the time, like he thought someone was following him."

"When was this?"

"Oh, I'm not exactly sure, but it was definitely last fall sometime. Anyway, he didn't sign the book. He seemed almost... well, frightened by the idea. But he was polite, and he asked me if it was okay not to. I felt kind of sorry for him, so I told him it was okay to skip it."

"Who was he here to see?"

"He just said he was here to visit his mom. It was so sweet, he was carrying a little ceramic dish full of candy for her. It was chipped and looked kind of old, so I thought it might have been something from her house."

I felt a growing excitement. "A dish? Do you remember what it looked like?"

"Hmm," Harriet tapped her lip and thought about it. "No... but it was bright... maybe like an apple?"

"Or a pumpkin?" I prompted her, not wanting to cause her to form a false memory, but thinking I was probably on to something here.

"Yes!" Harriet cried triumphantly. "A jack-o-lantern, actually! I remember now, it was close to Halloween, because when I saw the dish I asked him if he'd been trick-or-treating. You know, just to put him at ease. I think talking to him just made him more nervous, though."

I couldn't believe it. Mrs. Swanson hadn't been relating a dream born of dementia. David really had been here. Unless it was his brother that had been here. I gave myself a mental head slap for not bringing the pictures Pam had given me. Even though they were ten years out of date, they might have been enough for a positive ID on David.

"Harriet, does Mrs. Swanson's other son come to visit very often?"

"John? Oh sure, every other Wednesday morning, just like clockwork. He always brings her a couple of those custard filled donuts. He's a bit odd, but he sure loves his mother."

Maybe, but John had probably been arrested for car theft, so I doubted he'd be around much in the near future. But it hadn't been John who came last October. I finally had my proof – at least, enough for me – that David was alive and well.

"I don't suppose you could describe this man for me?"

"Well, it's been a couple of months, but let me think." She closed her eyes, as if trying to form a picture of him on the back of her eyelids. "He was about six feet tall, and really thin. I remember thinking he could use a good home-cooked meal or two. He was clean shaven, but his skin looked all red and irritated, as if he'd just shaved. I can't remember much else. His hair might have been blonde... or maybe a little gray." She sighed. "I'm sorry, I just don't remember much else."

"You've been a great help, Harriet!" I told her sincerely. "I don't suppose you remember what he was wearing?" I was thinking about how Mrs. Swanson said he'd been dressed as a janitor.

"Let me think again... oh, something dark, that's all I remember. I'm sorry."

"Don't be sorry, this is the most information I've gotten yet. It may be that there's hope for little Davey after all."

"I'm glad I was able to do something, no matter how small, for those poor folks. I don't suppose they've set up an account somewhere for donations?"

"No, it isn't really a publicized thing."

"Well maybe they should. You know, you see it on the news all the time, people collecting money for others in need."

"I think finding David is the best thing we can do for her right now."

"Oh, of course. Well, if there's anything else I can do, you just call."

"I will."

I turned to go. Just as I reached for the door Harriet called out to me.

"Oh, I just thought of something else about that man."

"What's that?"

"I'm pretty sure someone brought him here. There was a white van sitting by the front door in the loading zone, and I was thinking I'd have to go tell them to move. But then once that man left the lobby, the van went and parked in the lot. So I think maybe whoever it was gave him a ride."

"Do you remember anything else about the van? Was it a big one, or a mini, like they use for taxis?"

"It was big, and it didn't have any windows on the side. Like a work van."

"Was there any writing on it?"

"I don't remember. I'm sorry."

I really wished she'd quit apologizing. "It's okay. Thanks again, Harriet."

"Good luck, dear, and God bless you."

I doubted that last part, but I just smiled and waved on my way out.

On the drive home, Michael called me.

"I had a great time yesterday," he said by way of greeting.

"So did I. I haven't been to the museum in a long time."

"Maybe next time we'll go to the Natural History Museum."

"Sounds great."

"So listen, there's a local band playing down at The Tavern Friday night. They play a lot of covers from the Eighties and Nineties, but they do some original stuff, too. You want to go?"

"Sure!"

"Great! We could go early and have dinner so we'd be sure of good seats."

"Sounds good to me. What time?"

"About seven? The band doesn't start until 9:30."

"Okay, I'll meet you there."

"I can pick you up."

"Okay." Sure. Great. Now would be a good time to tell him about Jack.

"I'll see you then."

"Okay." And the opportunity was lost when he hung up.

Maybe Jack would have made other living arrangements by Friday and I'd never have to explain him to Michael. Yeah, that would be good.

I stopped by the B&E offices on the way home to leave the file I had picked up for Hopper. I had already emailed him the incriminating movie of Bart Gibson and given him a rundown on the situation; the rest of this was his problem.

"Hi Rainie!" Belinda greeted me with a big grin. Today her hair was hanging loose around her shoulders, a bit of extra curl in it. She was wearing a tailored calf-length skirt that hugged her hips with a white ruffled blouse that would make a normal woman look like she'd just walked off the set of a low-budget pirate movie. Belinda, as usual, pulled it off with style and flair.

"Hi! You look beautiful, as always!"

"Oh you!" Belinda laughed, but she didn't blush. That was one of the things I liked about her; she *knew* she looked good in even the most outlandish outfits.

"Here's Hopper's paperwork."

"He's just down the hall if you want to give it to him."

"Actually I'm right here." Hopper came into Belinda's office. He accepted the file with a brief nod of acknowledgement. "So, I hear you broke Gibson's leg."

"*I* didn't break it. He did it to himself."

"Like Jack says, things 'happen' around you."

"I was just doing what I was told to do. It was Gibson's choice to chase after me with that stupid walker."

"Did it ever occur to you to stay out of sight in the trees? You probably could have gotten the pics and left without him ever being the wiser. Don't you know how to sneak?"

I'd heard this before, from Jack.

"Sneaky isn't really my thing."

"Too bad. You could be really good at this. No one would ever suspect you. With those skirts and no makeup you don't look anything like a P.I., more like a harmless hippie chick."

I'd heard that before, too.

"Well, I'm not a hippie, but I *am* mostly harmless."

"Not what I hear. Running people over, breaking knees, blowing things up…if that's you being harmless I'd hate to have you pissed off at me."

"Those things were all purely self-defense!"

"Okay, then." Hopper squeezed out another smile. Either that, or he had a gas bubble. "Anyway, you did a good job. I might pull you in on something else in the future."

"Okay, thanks."

Sounded good to me. The busier I stayed the less likely it was I would get pulled into any of Jack's craziness. There wasn't much I could do about getting sucked into my own.

I got home about six o'clock and walked through the front door to a heavenly smell. I couldn't quite put my finger on what all it was, but it definitely involved garlic and onions.

Jack poked his head around the kitchen door and gave me a wave.

"Hey, Rainie. Dinner will be ready in about fifteen minutes."

"Dinner?" Curious, I wandered into the kitchen.

Jack was back at the stove, stirring the pot that was producing the yummy smell. "Is that home-made spaghetti sauce?"

"Yeah. I had Rachel stop by the grocery store on the way home. No way I can survive two weeks on peanut butter and chicken breasts."

"Spaghetti has an awful lot of carbs in it."

"You need to quit obsessing about food. I sometimes worry you have an eating disorder."

"Me?" I laughed. "That's ridiculous."

"Really? Do you think it's normal for someone to go three days at a time eating nothing but an occasional bowl of cereal?"

"I haven't done that in a long time. I've been eating regular meals."

"Yeah? What did you eat last?"

I wish I could have just snapped back with an answer, but actually I had to think about it. I'd eaten an apple and a stick of string cheese on my way to Plymouth…

"I just ate chicken, right here with you!" I said defiantly.

"Okay, you ate one piece. That was Saturday, right?"

I nodded.

"Well, this is *Monday night*. What did you eat the last forty-eight hours?"

I grimaced. I couldn't remember, but I *must* have eaten something. Sure, Michael and I had lunch at the museum yesterday. I had a salad. I guess I'd skipped dinner. And breakfast and lunch today.

Jack figured out all he wanted to know from my silence.

"So tonight it's spaghetti, and as long as I'm here, you're going to eat."

"Look, it's not an eating disorder. I just get busy and forget."

"Right." Jack was clearly not convinced. "You want to butter the garlic toast? I made some garlic butter, it's in the fridge."

"Spaghetti *and* garlic toast? Are you trying to put me into a carb-induced coma?"

"I know, Eddie recommended the low-carb thing for you, but it doesn't hurt to eat this stuff once in a while."

"How do you know what Eddie recommended?"

"He told me."

"So now you and Eddie are discussing my eating habits?"

"Just in passing. He worries about you, too."

"I don't need to be worried about. I'm a big girl. I can take care of myself."

"Sure, no problem. Just butter the bread, will you?"

I sighed. Why was I even arguing? The truth was that sauce smelled so good I wanted to bury my face in it and slurp it up like a horse at a watering trough.

"We can at least have salad with it, right?"

Jack pointed at the fridge. "It's already made up."

I was sleeping soundly when my cell phone started playing "Long, Long, Way From Home" by Foreigner. Great. My brother Jason.

I peered bleary-eyed at my digital clock. One o'clock in the morning.

Seriously? What the hell!

With a sigh I answered it.

"What's up now, Jason?"

"Oh man, it's bad... really bad. You gotta come get us."

"Us?"

"Me and Terry. He's gonna go in and get her and he's gonna get shot so you gotta hurry up..."

"Whoa! Slow down, Jason!" I was sitting up now, already reaching for the jeans I'd discarded next to the bed. "Who's going after who? Who has a gun?"

"Oh man, hang on!" Jason must have dropped his phone, because I heard a small crash and a burst of what sounded like static, then the sounds of a scuffle and muffled voices. I could just make out a few words here and there: "...my girlfriend..." "...a gun..." "...wait a minute..."

I put the phone on my shoulder and held it with my chin while I maneuvered my pants up over my hips and buttoned them. I was wearing a T-shirt but no bra, but it didn't sound like I had time to worry about my underpinnings. I would be wearing a bulky coat anyway, no one would notice.

I had my socks on and was already stuffing my feet into my shoes when Jason came back on.

"Sorry, had to slow him down. We're in Niles, on that road that runs between the park and the old theatre."

"Okay..."

"Just turn onto the road, you should see us. Hurry!"

"But Jason..."

"Oh shit, there he goes again... hurry, Rainie!"

Jason disconnected.

I was just putting my coat on when Jack opened his bedroom door and peered at me through the gloom.

"You need some help?"

I thought of Jason saying "gun" and I almost told Jack yes. Then I thought of how everything got kind of crazy when Jack was around, and I reluctantly shook my head.

"No, it's just my brother. He needs me to pick him up."

"Drunk?"

"Yeah." But Jason hadn't really sounded all that drunk. "See you in the morning."

I hurried out to my car, shivering in the clear, cold night air. There were a billion stars above me, but I didn't have time for stargazing.

I drove to Niles as fast as I dared, knowing the Buchanan police wouldn't have much going on in the middle of a Monday night/Tuesday morning. I crossed the bridge over the St. Joseph River in Niles and drove two blocks to the road that ran behind the theatre. This little side street didn't get plowed, but there were ruts where cars had gone before me, and I was able to get down it okay.

I drove slowly, watching for Jason, not sure exactly where he would be. This road ran along the backs of a few businesses, all closed up for the night, and further along a couple of houses. I couldn't imagine what Jason and Terry would be doing down here.

Suddenly Jason was there, in my headlights, frantically waving me down. He was hanging on to Terry, who seemed to be favoring one leg, and there was a wild-eyed girl with them.

I hit the brakes and they rushed the car, Terry and the girl piling in back, Jason jumping into the front.

"Go! Go! Get us out of here!" Jason yelled.

"What the hell..."

"We'll explain later, just go!"

"But turn around first!" Terry urged. "Go back the way you came!"

So I went. I found a spot to turn around, and at their urging I drove back down the little road, a lot faster than I'd come in.

They didn't stop looking over their shoulders until we were back on a main road.

"Whoo-eee!" Terry yelled exuberantly. "That was some fun!"

"Maybe for you!" the girl exclaimed. "I was scared half to death!"

"I can't believe you did that, Terry." Jason was shaking his head in wonder. "Christ, you were like a secret agent or some shit."

"What?" I demanded. "You drag me out in the middle of the night, you at least need to tell me this great story!"

"Some guy kidnapped Terry's girlfriend, but he went and got her back."

"What? Kidnapped?"

"Yeah, he pulled me right out of the bar!" The girl sniffed. I glanced at her in the rearview mirror. In the flashes of light from passing streetlights I could see that her makeup had run under her eyes, giving her a raccoon-like appearance. No wonder she'd seemed so wild-eyed in the glare of my headlights.

"Had her in that building, but Terry went in..." Jason trailed off. "You tell it, Terry."

"Okay, so see, Kimmy called me...this here is Kimmy by the way. Kimmy, this is Rainie, Jason's little sister."

"Nice to meetcha." She sniffed.

"Same here." I think.

"So anyway, Kimmy was down at the bar singing karaoke and havin' a few beers, when Bobby – that's her ex-husband, Bobby – comes strollin' in, all up in her face and like 'you still belong to me' and shit like that, see?"

I nodded. I knew the type.

"So anyways, Kimmy tells him to get lost, but he just keeps it up and keeps it up, so she goes in the bathroom and calls me, so Jason and I get a ride to the bar."

"Where's your car?" I interrupted to ask Jason.

"At home. I had a few beers, didn't think I should drive."

"Well, good for you!"

"Thanks." Jason grinned.

"Anyways, if I can get back to my story…"

"Go ahead."

"All right. So we head on out there, but in the meantime Bobby goes all Rambo and just grabs Kimmy and drags her right out of the bar!"

"Didn't anyone try to stop him?"

"Naw, it's penny pitcher night. I don't think anyone even noticed." Kimmy answered me.

"So Jason and I get to the bar and find out she's gone, and I'm goin' all crazy tryin' to figure where she is, and she calls me. Only she ain't talking, you know? So I finally figure out she pocket dialed me, maybe on accident…"

"It was, but I'm glad I did!"

"Sure, good thing. So I hear Bobby talkin', and I know he's got her. So he lives right there, just a little ways past the old theater. That dirt road comes up on the back of his house. So then I hear her say 'why are we going into the garage?' and I don't know why, but at least I know where he's got her."

"Tell her about the gun, Terry!" Jason interrupted

"Yeah, yeah, I'm getting to that. So anyway, the phone disconnects, I don't know why, so Jason and I run quick down the road over to Bobby's place and I sneak up behind the garage to peek in the window. Sure enough, there's Bobby, hollerin' at Kimmy, and he's got a big gun laying on the freezer right next to him. He's tellin' her how he's gonna kill her and then himself if she don't come back to him."

"That's when I called you," Jason supplied.

"Right, when I came back to tell you what I saw. But I didn't want you to come too quick, not 'til I got Kimmy out of there."

"Let me get this straight," I stopped his recitation for a minute. "The guy kidnaps your girlfriend, he's holding her at gunpoint, and *you* have to get her out?"

"Well sure!"

"What about the cops? Did you ever think about calling them?"

"No. Why?" And the strange thing was, Terry seemed genuinely puzzled by the idea.

"Maybe because it their *job* to go after armed kidnappers?"

"But Kimmy's *my* girlfriend." Terry made it sound like that was the most obvious thing in the world.

"Okay, never mind." I was remembering the first time I'd met Terry, right after he'd beat the living daylights out of a man twice his size for sucker punching him, not once, but twice. Terry had been willing to let the first one go, which still baffled me. Apparently Terry went by some sort of code that I was never going to fathom.

"So I called Kimmy, and Bobby answered the phone, all shitty and whatever, telling me to get lost. And I tell him I will, but first I need to talk to Kimmy, make sure she's all right. So he hands her the phone, and all I say to Kimmy is: 'is his gun still on the freezer?' and she says 'yes' and I say 'okay, I'm coming,' and I hang up. Then I ran around the garage and go up to the door and BAM!"

I jumped when he yelled and slammed a fist into his palm.

"I kick the door and come flyin' in after it and I get Bobby down on the ground..."

"And he's yelling 'run, Kimmy! Run!' so I did."

"Yeah, so she was out of there so I jump off Bobby and grab his gun on the way out the door and I threw it hard as I could into the bushes and we just ran like hell!"

Now Terry and Kim were both laughing, and shortly Jason joined in.

"He was like some caped avenger!" Jason laughed. "Just ran in BAM! And took the guy down. It was great!"

"Great? The guy had a gun!"

"But he didn't get a chance to use it."

"He's probably still out there looking for it."

"So why the hurry to get away?" I asked.

"Just in case he already found it!" Terry laughed like that was the funniest thing in the world, and I couldn't help it, I laughed, too.

"Jason, did it ever occur to you that your friend is nuts?"

"Hell yeah, I know that," Jason agreed. "But he's a lot of fun!"

Well, fun is relative, I suppose. I mean, some people thought hitting a tiny ball around fifty acres of lawn trying to get it into a little hole was fun, too. Who was I to judge?

I finally got them all back to Jason's house and made my way home. I don't know if Jack heard me come in, but he didn't say anything. I dropped my jeans back on the floor and crawled into bed. It was three o'clock in the morning, and I was going to really hate it when the alarm went off at six a.m.

Oh well. As I'd reminded myself so many times before, Jason was my only brother, and at least I knew he was home safe.

I think I was asleep before my head hit the pillow.

I was stuck in a car wash and a warning buzzer was going off, a persistent rhythmic buzz that set my teeth on edge. I fumbled with the gear shift and the clutch, trying to break the car loose so I could escape.

Abruptly I heard a crash and suddenly the buzzing stopped.

I sat up, finally freed from the frantic dream, to find Jack standing next to my bed. My alarm clock was on the floor, smashed to pieces by his grinding heel.

"I hate those damned things. The FBI should blast that noise over their loudspeakers when they're practicing their psychological warfare. I guarantee those Branch Davidians at Waco would have given up in ten minutes." With that explanation he turned and strode from the room.

I blinked my eyes a few times, trying to clear the last of the sleep fog from my brain, and finally crawled out of bed. I stared at the carcass of my poor clock for a long moment before I finally bent down and scooped it up. It was quite dead. Its innards were hanging out, the little circuit boards like tiny organs, the broken wires like torn arteries and veins.

Okay, it was stupid to be so upset about a cheap clock, but it was one of the first things I'd bought for myself after Tommy and I divorced. I paid a dollar for it at the Salvation Army Thrift Store. I could probably get a brand new one for ten bucks. But it was mine, a symbol of my new independence.

I pulled the plug from the wall and dropped it into the wastebasket, almost feeling like I should say a few words of good bye. Okay, that was stupid, so instead I pulled on a pair of sweatpants and stumbled to the kitchen.

Jack was at the counter, his hands wrapped around a steaming mug. I wordlessly filled one of my own.

"Sorry about that," Jack mumbled. "That damned buzzing is like fingernails on a chalkboard."

"Yeah? Well I don't much like fingernails on a chalkboard either, but I was never tempted to throw a grenade at the board to make it stop."

"Maybe I did overreact a little."

"I guess it's just a good thing you aren't irritated by the gurgling of the coffee brewing."

"Hey, a man can put up with a lot if the results are a good cup of coffee." He tried a grin on me, but I answered with a scowl and went into the living room. I was in no mood to be charmed. I sat on the couch and stared at George, who stared back at me from the top branch in his cage, his eyes half closed, not saying a word. Reptiles make excellent early morning companions.

I heard Jack coughing, but I refused to be sympathetic. He should have gotten medical care for smoke inhalation. The cough sounded harsh and painful, and I couldn't really help a twinge of compassion, so I flicked on the TV to drown out the sound.

I turned on the morning news. Someone had been stabbed in a domestic dispute, expected to recover. There was an accident involving a drunk driver and a solid tree; only the tree was expected to recover. There was a warm front moving in, possibility of rain. Yuk.

I was almost finished with my first cup of coffee and considering going for a refill when Jack came out of the kitchen, carrying the pot.

"Warm up?"

I glanced at him, considering another scowl, but he was the bringer of fresh coffee, so instead I nodded and held out my cup. Jack was wearing a loose-fitting pair of pajama pants and nothing else. I had to admit he made a pretty cute waiter.

He poured and retreated to the kitchen but returned a moment later and sat next to me. We watched the news in silence.

There was a children's art fair going on in Niles. There had been a breakthrough in the treatment of migraines, but it wouldn't be available in the United States for several years. I wondered why they bothered reporting it? So migraine sufferers could moan and think 'if only?'

"I'm really sorry about your clock." Jack sounded sincere, and for some odd reason that made me tear up. "It was just buzzing and buzzing...made me crazy. I'll get you a new one."

"The clock is no big deal. The smashing, on the other hand, is."

"What do you mean?"

"You don't think that was a little over the top? It seems to me you have some anger issues."

"I don't think I was particularly angry."

"Impulse issues, then."

"You already knew that."

"Doesn't make it any better."

"I know. So what do I need to do to make it all right between us?"

That's what I like about Jack. Get to the point, take care of the situation and move on.

I stared at George for a few seconds, wondering just what it would take to make it right. I could replace the clock; it isn't as if it was an antique. And now that I was awake and not scared half out of my wits by some maniac smashing electronics in my bedroom, I realized I wasn't even really mad any more. Well, not very.

"Never mind. We're good."

"Yeah?" Jack gave me a little fist bump on the shoulder. "You're all right, for a girl."

I slapped his hand away.

"Thanks a lot."

"So you're with Thelma today, right?"

"Yeah. So what do you have going on today?"

"Rachel is picking me up at 7:30. We're working in Chicago for a couple days."

That was good news. I could use a break. I didn't tell him that.

"What's the job?"

"We're looking for a guy who skipped out on his bail."

"Glad it's you and not me."

"Hey, bounty hunting can be fun. You should come with me some time."

"That's okay. It seems to me that people who don't want to go to jail can get nasty about the whole thing. You know, guns and stuff. Not my thing."

Jack grinned. "Yeah, staying away from bounty hunting has really kept you out of danger."

I smiled back. "True enough. So when will you be back?"

"Wednesday or Thursday, I hope. Oh, and my new truck will be in on Friday."

"Great. Are you getting the same kind?"

"Yeah, Ford Ranger. I hope it comes in on time, because I've got a guy set to do some modifications on it next week."

"So how's the investigation on the house coming? Any news?"

"They've determined that it's definitely arson, but they haven't decided who did it yet."

"So you're still under suspicion?"

"Yeah, which holds up the insurance. Luckily I have some money put back. I'm going to have a trailer put up on the property, but it's going to take a couple of weeks. They have to run electric to it and hook it up to the septic system, and there's some question about whether they'll be able to dig with the ground frozen. I was thinking maybe I should go rent a hotel room until then."

"Why?"

"I didn't think you'd want me underfoot for that long. You've been great about all this, Rainie, and I really appreciate it, but I don't want to overstay my welcome."

"You haven't – yet. I think I can handle a couple of weeks." Really? My inner voice was bitching and moaning at me again, but it was far too late.

"I'll tell you what, we'll discuss it again Friday, when I get my truck. Just keep in mind, if at any time it gets to be too much, say the word and I'm out of here, no hard feelings."

"No problem." But, of course, it is. For one thing, I'm used to being alone. For another, this is *Jack*, and it seems I'm always on high alert mode when he's around. Why don't I just let him go?

I can't answer that. When it comes to Jack I seem to react from an unfamiliar place in myself, somewhere visceral that doesn't seem to have communication with my conscious brain.

Whatever, it was only a couple of weeks.

I was shivering on the porch, having my morning cigarette, when Rachel showed up to get Jack.

She was driving a sweet Chrysler LeBaron convertible painted a glossy black that had to be custom paint. It was an older model, on the smallish side, but it looked to be in mint condition, right off the showroom floor.

"Morning, Rainie!" She bounced up the sidewalk in a short, form fitting coat, full of perky energy. Her makeup was perfect as always, her hair curling just right around a stocking cap that would have made me look like a third grader.

"Good morning." I pointed at her car. "Nice ride."

"Thanks. It's a lot more fun in the summer, though."

"I'll bet. How does it handle in the snow?"

"Surprisingly well. I wasn't too sure. I bought it right after graduation when I was living in Arizona. If I had known I was relocating to Michigan I probably would have bought something more appropriate. Like a Hummer, maybe."

She grinned and I laughed, but I could actually picture her driving one of those huge beasts. She was small and perky, but she had a core of steel.

"Is Jack inside?"

"Yeah." I stubbed out my cigarette and led the way into the house.

Jack was just pulling on his coat, a black leather jacket he'd picked up somewhere, already broken in and comfortable looking. Maybe he'd beaten up a biker for it.

"Thanks for coming after me again," Jack told Rachel. She lived near the state line, so she had to go a distance out of her way to pick him up.

"I still think you should just stay with me."

"But you live in an efficiency apartment with nothing but one pull-out bed."

"Exactly." She gave him a look that would have turned an ordinary man's knees to jelly, but Jack only grinned.

"That's *exactly* why I'm staying right here."

Oh yeah? Why? Because he never had to worry about sharing my bed? Because I wasn't even a temptation? Maybe I needed to spend more time in front of a mirror, learning to do that come hither look. I tried to picture it on my face, but I feared it would just look like I was about to throw up. Besides, who would I use it on? Certainly not Jack. I wouldn't know what to do with him if he *did* come hither.

"I'll see you in a couple of days, Rainie."

"See you."

After they left I went around and shut off the last of the lights and took off for Thelma's.

Chapter Eleven

Thelma wanted me to take her to Niles to get a haircut.

"Niles? But you always go to the Curl Up & Dye in Buchanan."

"I know, but I'm pissed off at Suzie." Suzie was her hair stylist, and had been for twenty years.

"Why are you mad at Suzie?"

"Because she was rude to Morty. She told him he had no business driving anymore!"

"Um...well Thelma, that's kind of true."

"Maybe it is true, but that's no reason to hurt his feelings! Morty's a good guy, and he always gets me where we're going in one piece."

"Okay, so where are you getting your hair done?"

"The Cut & Curl on 933, in that little strip mall next to McDonalds. My appointment is at ten. What do you want to do until then?"

"I don't care," I shrugged. "I suppose if we left a few minutes early I could stop by the drugstore and get a new clock."

"A clock?"

"Yeah...mine broke."

"We can run by Beck's," Thelma suggested.

That sounded good to me. A clock might cost me a couple dollars more at Beck's Drugstore than it would at a chain store, but I liked to support small businesses. If we didn't, pretty soon we'd have

173

nowhere left to shop except one or two varieties of big box stores, cold, impersonal places with rude employees and questionable business practices.

We puttered around the house a bit, killing time before we left. Niles was only a twenty minute drive, maybe twenty five if there was any traffic on 933. We straightened the hall closet and Thelma set aside a couple of coats she thought might sell at "Next to You," and we took them along to drop off at the store.

There wasn't much traffic, so even after stopping to buy a new clock we were ahead of schedule when we pulled into the strip mall. It hardly qualified for the name. It was really just a low brick building built perpendicular to the highway that housed five small storefronts. There was a cell phone outlet, an insurance company, an empty spot, and strangely, two hair salons. One had tanning beds, the other a masseuse.

The parking lot was long and narrow. The whole operation had been slipped into the slimmest space possible, since frontage on 933 was costly. The lot was pretty full so I had to park near the back. I was happy to see they had done a good job clearing it of snow.

I put the car in gear and shut it off, a little concerned that I couldn't use the parking brake, since the parking slot was on a slight incline. On the other hand, the car no longer went into reverse most of the time, so I might need the incline to roll out of the space. I supposed I would have to get that brake fixed soon, or one of these days my little car was going to roll out into traffic. I didn't want to think about the transmission; that would probably cost more than the Blue Book value of the car.

I waited while Thelma patted her hair into place. It guess it wouldn't do to go into the hairdresser's with your hair a mess.

The lot was surrounded by low bushes, and beyond them was another parking lot that had seen better days. The asphalt was cracked and the snow had only been cleared in a narrow strip next to the building, apparently with a shovel. It had to be back breaking work with the heavy snow. The building was an old motel, one of those independently owned ones where you could rent the rooms by the week or the month. This one was shabby enough that it was probably used by alcoholics, drug addicts and poor retirees with no families.

I had never really noticed this one before. It sat back from the road, and its faded red brick façade didn't attract much attention.

From where I sat I could see six doors, the numbers faded or missing altogether. There was one old rusted car parked in front of what might have been room three. That didn't mean the other rooms weren't occupied. Most of the people who lived in such places had little or no money once the rent was paid, and a car, even an old and rusted one, was a luxury few could afford. I could see why the motel manager didn't spend money on plowing the whole lot.

"Okay, I'm ready." Thelma had fixed her hair and was climbing out of the car. I got out, taking one last glance back at the sad motel.

That's when I saw the sign. "The Golden Eagle Motel."

Whoa, wait a minute. Dave Swanson told his mom he was living with the eagles in Niles. Had he actually said he was living *at* the *Eagle* in Niles?

"What's the matter Rainie?" Thelma had stopped to look at me, and I realized I was gaping open-mouthed at the motel.

"Nothing," I lied, looking away from her. I couldn't keep dragging her along on my investigations. Unfortunately I was still a lousy liar. She narrowed her eyes at me.

"Rainie, what..." she turned her gaze toward the motel and frowned. "What about the motel? Are you thinking of telling Jack to stay here, or what?"

"No. Come on, you'll be late for your appointment." I got her moving and followed her across the parking lot.

I waited with an outward show of patience while Thelma got her hair cut, listening with some amusement while she debated whether she should dye her hair. She was thinking something in red, while the stylist was recommending a light brown with maybe a few auburn highlights. In the end Thelma decided to keep the gray, but went with a short spiky cut she saw in a magazine, intended for a French fashion model who would accessorize it with bold jewelry and bright make up. Funny thing was, Thelma actually pulled it off. It looked good with her jeans and her Rage Against the Machine T shirt.

She waited until we were back in the car to bring up my earlier lie.

"So tell me, what's with the motel? You thinking about bringing a date here, or what?"

I laughed. "Hardly. The truth is, I think that might be where Dave Swanson is staying. His mother said he was staying with the eagles in Niles."

"The eagles?" Thelma peered around and found the faded sign. "Oh, the Golden Eagle! Sure, this place was really nice back in the day. There used to be a little restaurant next door that featured fine wines from local vineyards. I had forgotten the place was even here."

"I'd never noticed it before. Anyway, I'm going to come back later…"

"Later? What's wrong with now?"

"Thelma…"

"Now don't be dragging out that old song about me not getting involved in your investigations. I've been in on this one since the start! Besides, I'll just wait in the car again if that's what you want me to do."

I thought about arguing with her, but really, what was the point? It wasn't like I was going to drag Dave out of the motel at gunpoint even if he was there. I was only going to talk to him, tell him about Davey and hopefully give him a ride to Pam's so he could see his son.

"All right, I'll do it now."

I started the car and drove next door, slipping and sliding into the snow clogged lot until I got to the shoveled strip and parked parallel to a glass door with dingy white lettering that read "of ice." Not being stupid, I guessed that if was supposed to say "office."

I reached into the back seat and grabbed the folder with David's info in it. After forgetting to take it to the nursing home I had thrown it in the car and left it there so I would have it.

"I'll be right back."

"Don't hurry on my account." Thelma flipped down the sun visor and was examining her new hairdo in the little mirror. "I'll be fine right here."

I went into the office, stomping the snow off my shoes on a small rubber mat just inside the door.

The office was really just a very tiny foyer with a plastic laminate counter that held a phone, an oversized bible, and an old fashion registry book.

There was a sign hanging off the fake wood front that said "Jesus Saves."

Behind the counter was a heavy set of drapes that closed off the room behind it. The tiny space was shabby but clean, the counter shiny where it wasn't scratched. I stood there for a moment before I noticed a small bell, the kind you used to see in diners to call a waitress when her order was up. I lightly tapped the little button on top to make the bell tinkle.

"Just a minute!" A voice called out immediately, but it was more like two or three minutes before the drapes parted and an old man slipped through them. I got a brief glimpse of a sofa and an old television set back there, and assumed he lived on the premises.

He was as shabby and clean as the foyer. He was freshly shaven and wore a white dress shirt with black suspenders, both a little frayed at the edges. His white hair was carefully combed but his pants were too big and I could see a carefully applied patch in one knee.

He smiled at me, revealing cheap dentures that were too perfectly sized and too white, and peered at me quizzically over a pair of rimless eyeglasses.

"Hello, how can I help you?"

"Hello, my name is Rainie Lovingston." I pulled my ID out and held it so he could see the B&E logo. "I'm a private investigators assistant, and I'm looking for a man who might be a resident here."

The man frowned. "I don't allow illegal activities on the premises. I run a clean place."

"I'm sure you do, Mr...?"

"Gentry. Bert Gentry. I'm the owner here."

"The man I'm looking for hasn't done anything illegal, at least so far as I know. I'm actually looking for him to tell him his son is sick. His wife lost contact with him some time ago."

"Lost contact?" The man was looking at me suspiciously. I suppose various authority figures came here on a regular basis looking for his tenants, and most of them weren't likely from the prize patrol, bringing good news.

"I'm not a bill collector or an agent for the police," I assured the man. "I really just want to talk to this man." I pulled out the two ten year old photographs and laid them on the scarred counter. "His name is Dave Swanson."

Mr. Gentry frowned at the pictures for a minute, then picked one up and peered at it carefully.

"I don't allow illegal activities on the premises, but I do try to provide a safe place for these men to stay, you understand?"

"Yes, I do. I suppose you wouldn't get much business if you were known as a stool pigeon," I nodded sympathetically. "I promise you, I am who I say I am. I'm not looking to hurt David in any way."

"Would you swear on the Bible?" He pointed at the big book.

Now, here's the thing. I don't actually believe in God, at least not like the Catholics or the Baptists do. My mother is a very spiritual person, and believes God is everywhere. I was raised to believe the Bible was just a collection of stories designed to get people to follow certain rules set by people who found those rules to be in everyone's best interest.

Still, I wouldn't want to lie with my hand on a Bible. Sort of a superstition thing, like not kicking black cats while standing under a ladder. Fortunately, I wasn't lying, so I shrugged and put my hand on the Bible.

"I swear I don't mean David any harm."

Mr. Gentry nodded reluctantly. Maybe he sensed my lack of connection to the Good Book.

"All right, I think I do know this guy, but his name is Dave Bell, not Swanson. And the guy I know is a lot thinner and has gray hair."

I was practically bouncing on my toes, I was so excited. I couldn't believe I'd actually found him! "These photos are about ten years out of date."

"Okay, then I'd say this is definitely him."

"What room is he in?" I prompted eagerly.

"Well, none of them right now. He only stays here on occasion."

"Oh." I felt the letdown as palpably as if I was a balloon with the air let out of me.

"You know," Mr. Gentry went on, "Dave is a nice guy, gentle and quiet most of the time, but he has some mental problems. I thought for a while he might have a problem with the drugs...I see a lot of that here. But I think maybe it was something else. He complained once that all these people kept talking to him, yelling until he couldn't hear himself think, but there wasn't anyone there. You know, he was hearing voices."

"I suspected as much," I nodded. "So do you know where he stays when he's not here?"

"No, and I haven't seen him for three months now. He used to come and stay for a week or so when he had a little money, but I'm not sure what's happened to him. I was actually thinking about him just the other day, worrying a little. You know, it's cold out there."

"Yeah." I sighed. "Well, thank you for the information."

"Wait a minute, I do have one idea for you. When Dave was having good days he used to help out down at the food bank at the Presbyterian Church. The pastor would pay him to sweep up and like that. You should ask there."

"Where is the Presbyterian Church? Is that the one across from the courthouse?"

"No, that's the Catholic church. You want the big one on Third Street, across from the grocery store."

"Oh sure, I know the place." I smiled and held out my hand. "Thank you very much for the information, Mr. Gentry."

He shook my hand and smiled back, tentatively. "You be careful when you find Dave, okay? I wouldn't want either one of you to get hurt."

"Hurt?" That statement worried me.

"I told you, Dave has some problems. It's possible he's a bit...delusional."

"Okay, I'll be careful." I nodded and turned for the door, and Mr. Gentry gave me a last little wave and went back behind his curtains, like a weathered and faded Wizard of Oz.

Just as I was stepping out the door a man was coming in, and I practically ran into him.

"Excuse me," I said, sidestepping, only he sidestepped in the same direction, in that awkward little dance so often played out by two strangers in a doorway. He flashed me a look of irritation, and something about his expression looked familiar.

I stepped past him and had just cleared the door when I suddenly remembered where I'd seen him before.

Last summer, on the sidewalk outside Thelma's new shop, right after he'd shot a bartender and just before he'd shot a Buchanan cop. I had gotten an up close look at his face, just before he pointed a gun at my face and pulled the trigger. If the weapon hadn't misfired my DNA would still be imbedded in the concrete on Front Street.

My insides threatened to liquefy and for a moment I thought my knees might buckle. They had never caught the guy, and I had always assumed he'd left the area, probably the state. Well, just because I recognized him didn't mean he recognized me.

I glanced back to find him already turning back to me, his eyes narrowed into slits, his mouth turned down in an angry grimace. Crap, he'd definitely recognized me!

I tried to hurry, but I had to cross in front of the car to get around to the driver's side, and it seemed in my panic that my little car had suddenly stretched out thirty feet. I slipped on the icy surface and had to catch myself on the hood of the car.

"Thelma!" I called out a warning to her, but she was already looking at the guy, her own eyes narrowed. She'd gotten a close up look at him too, when he'd knocked her down and broken her arm.

I cleared the front of the car, the guy right behind me. He had a gun in his hand, and he was raising it for a shot. I reached for the door handle, but I knew there was no time. Even if I got in the car he was going to shoot me before I ever got the car started, let alone had time to drive away. I didn't think I could rely on the gun misfiring again.

Thelma leaned over and I saw her reach toward the steering wheel, a strange little grin on her face. She turned the key in the ignition, and of course the car was in gear, so it lurched forward a few feet, just like when I'd hit the garage doors. Only this time there was no garage, there was just the guy with the gun.

The car hit him hard just below the knee and he slipped on the icy pavement and went down, his gun discharging into the air.

"Holy crap!" I ducked instinctively and pulled the door open at the same time. I dove into the car, Thelma yelling at me:

"Hit him again! Come on, back up and run him over!"

"No!" I fumbled with the clutch and the key and got the car started just as the guy was getting to his feet, the gun still in his hand. I tried to cram the Escort into reverse, but of course it wouldn't go there. I pushed it into first gear instead and rammed the wheel as far to the left as it would go, hoping to drive around him. I popped the clutch and the front tires spun a bit on the ice and then they bit and I almost got around him, but I clipped him with the right fender as I slid past, knocking him off his feet again. My intention was to speed out of the lot and down the few blocks to the Niles police station, but instead the Escort bogged down in the unplowed lot and I sat there spinning my wheels.

"He's getting up, Rainie! We need to get out of here!"

"I know, Thelma!" I let up on the gas and the car rolled back a few inches. I put it into second gear and lightly feathered the clutch out, and the car slowly moved forward.

"He's on his feet!" Thelma reported. She was twisted around in her seat, watching his progress, which was a lot faster than ours. "He's aiming!"

Jeez, who did she think she was, a play-by-play announcer?

The car bogged down again, and in desperation I tried reverse gear again. I was amazed to feel the satisfying little *clunk* when it went into gear. I let the clutch out and shot backwards, and once again I knocked the guy down. This time I heard a yowl of pain or rage or maybe both.

I was just getting back into first gear when I heard a siren blip and then start that familiar wail. Mr. Gentry must have called the cops at the first shot, and fortunately they must have been close by. Maybe at McDonald's, two doors down. Whatever, a few seconds later a police car pulled into the lot, plowing through the snow with a lot less effort than my little Escort required.

"He's gonna run!" Thelma declared, still watching the armed man. He had scrambled back to his feet and was trying to lope away, but he was limping severely.

I rolled my window down and shouted at the cops.

"He's got a gun! He's the one that shot the cop in Buchanan last summer!"

The cop stopped his car and rolled out behind his open car door, pulling his own weapon. "This is the police! Hold it right where you are!"

The guy took a few more steps but he was dragging his left leg and couldn't make much progress on the ice. He slipped and fell and his gun skittered away.

The cop came out from behind his door and hurried over. The guy was crawling toward his gun, and my heart was in my throat. I knew he wouldn't hesitate to shoot the cop if he got to it in time, but the cop was too fast for him. He stood over the guy and pointed the gun at his head.

"Give me a reason, asshole!"

The asshole in question looked up at the gun, and I remembered what that was like, looking down that black barrel, and I wondered if he felt like he was about to wet his pants or if that was just cowardly me who had reacted that way.

"God damn it!" The guy swore and dropped his head, admitting defeat.

"Woo hoo! That was some fun!" Thelma whooped.

I rolled my eyes. She was worse than Jack.

"Thelma, we just got *shot* at!"

"Shot *at*, but not *shot*!" Thelma laughed. "Close only count in horseshoes and hand grenades."

Okay, it's official. Thelma *is* as crazy as Jack.

It took some time to get everything sorted out.

The guy's name was Alex Truly, and he was also wanted for a bank robbery in Indiana. I figured the Hoosiers were going to have to wait a long time to prosecute him. No way Michigan was going to let a cop shooter get extradited.

Thelma and I had to give statements at the station, and Ned Gray, a Buchanan police officer, drove over to talk to us. He questioned us hard, wanting to be sure we would be airtight witnesses for the prosecution. There was some concern about the fact that I had run the guy down, not once but three times. They had been looking for this cop shooter for a long time and didn't want him getting off on some technicality. At the same time they seemed to think it was funny as hell, and they kept asking us to describe the incident over and over.

"So let me get this straight," Officer Cannon, one of the Niles cops, was questioning us about the original robbery. Officer Gray had already told him the story, but he wanted details. "You hear gun fire, and rather than ducking like most reasonable people would do, *you* run out on the sidewalk and try to tackle him?" He pointed at Thelma, and he seemed to be trying hard to keep his expression serious.

"I wasn't exactly trying to tackle him. I was just..." Thelma cocked her head and looked at me, as if *I* could explain her bizarre behavior. I just shook my head. She was on her own with this one.

"I can't really tell you what I thought for sure. I just saw a guy that needed to be stopped, and I stepped out to do it."

"And you thought you were big enough to do that?" Now he was smiling, looking at Thelma's birdlike frame.

"Thelma never thinks in terms of what she *can't* do." I knew *that* much about the way her mind worked.

"If you spend your life thinking about what you can't do you'll never get a chance to try anything." Thelma shot back.

"The guy could have shot you." The cop pointed out.

"Yeah, he almost did shoot Rainie, but his gun misfired."

Cannon clucked his tongue. "No wonder you ran him over three times."

"I didn't do that part on purpose..."

"Right, you were just trying to get away." Cannon nodded and looked at Officer Gray. "Well, the story works for me, what do you think?"

They finally let us go, with the assurance that we would be called upon to testify in the near future.

It was three o'clock by the time we left the station, and I was mentally exhausted from the past hours events, but I still wanted to talk to the Presbyterian pastor who sometimes gave Dave work.

I drove over to the church and parked out front.

"I'll be right back," I told Thelma.

She grinned. "See if you can get a guy with a machete to follow you this time. I can conk him on the head with a tire iron!"

I laughed. "I'll see what I can do."

I followed a carefully shoveled sidewalk around the church, directed by signs that read "Pastors Office." I went up a handicapped ramp and found a wooden door marked "Pastor John Rankin." I pulled on it, but it was locked. Sad sign of the times, that folks even have to keep their churches locked. There was a time when people could go in and pray pretty much any time of the day. I might not be a believer, but I respected other's right to believe, and I know they draw comfort from their churches. It seemed a shame that they had to schedule a time to seek that comfort.

Off to the side a smaller sign read, "Please ring bell." There was a little white doorbell push there, obviously recently installed. I pushed it and waited for a couple of minutes, and pushed it again when I got no response. No luck. I sighed and went back to the car. I would have to call and make an appointment.

Chapter Twelve

The next morning I got to Bob's to find him still in bed. He was pale and coughing and overall looked miserable.

"Just came on last night," he wheezed at me and went into another coughing jag.

"I'd better call the doctor."

"Now wait," he protested. "It's just a cold..."

"I don't think so." I shook my head and went to the bathroom for the thermometer. "That wheezing sounds more like bronchitis."

"If I go to the doctor he'll give me antibiotics and that'll give me the shits and I'll be sicker than I started!"

Unfortunately, that was common in the elderly. Antibiotics kill off good bacteria as well as bad, and while they can cause diarrhea in anyone, older adults were more prone to it. But I knew how to prevent it.

"No it won't, Bob. You still have those pro-biotics I brought you the last time, and those worked well keeping the diarrhea away."

"But..."

"Bob." I cocked my hands on my hips and gave him my sternest look. "Are we really going to have this argument?"

He looked at me for a minute, then cut his eyes away and sighed. "I guess not. You'll win anyway."

"Exactly. Now, put this under your tongue. They'll want to know your temp when I call the doctor."

I took his pulse and counted his respirations while he held the thermometer under his tongue. Everything was pretty good except his temp: 102.3.

"I'm surprised you have the energy to argue with me!" I admonished him.

"Just hand me that bottle of Tylenol. I'll be fine."

I handed him a glass of water and the pill bottle. "I'll call the doctor."

The doctor's office fit him in at eleven o'clock. I drove him over, listening to his complaints all the way. I sympathized, but I remained adamant.

Sure enough, he had bronchitis, but also the start of pneumonia.

"You need to go over to the hospital," Doctor Kresky said. "I'll admit you for a few days..."

But Bob was already shaking his head. "No. No hospital." Bob glared at me. "See what you did? Why couldn't you just leave well enough alone?"

"Bob, she did the right thing," Dr. Kreske argued. "This sort of thing can get on top of you pretty fast."

"I don't care. I'm not going to the hospital, and that's final!" Bob shouted, bringing on a heavy coughing spasm that left him breathless for a minute.

"Doctor, do you think he'd be all right if he went home with twenty-four hour care?"

"What?" Bob had recovered his voice. "No! I don't need a nursemaid!"

"Actually, you do." Doctor Kreske was firm. "I'd prefer you went to the hospital, but if you have someone with you I'll send you home. With the understanding, of course, that if you don't show *noticeable* improvement in twenty four hours you *will* go to the hospital."

Bob started to protest again but I cut him off. "It's a good deal, Bob. You should quit while you're ahead."

He grimaced but finally nodded. "All right."

I took him home and got him settled in bed and ran back to the drugstore to fill his prescriptions.

I called Daryl to let him know what was going on.

"That stubborn old man...well, thanks for taking care of it Rainie. I don't know where you find the patience."

"I guess I just understand where he's coming from. I prefer my own bed, too, especially when I'm not feeling well."

"If he needs twenty four hour care I can call that service I used before. I hope they send someone better than that last lady though. Dad didn't like her much."

"Actually I know a lady who's looking for some extra hours right now. She could probably stay for a couple of days."

"Hey, that would be great!" I could hear the relief in Daryl's voice. It was a crapshoot when you called a home care service as to whether or not they'd send someone both competent and likable. Or either one, for that matter.

"I'll give her a call. If she's not available I'll let you know, otherwise you can just assume she's here."

"That's great. I'll stop by after work to check on things."

I hung up and found Bob glaring at me.

"You don't need to call anyone. I'll be just fine alone."

"No."

I didn't even listen to his objections. Whether he wanted to admit it or not he was weak, and his cough was liable to get worse before the antibiotics kicked in and made it better. Left to himself he'd probably lie in bed and dehydrate until I got back on Friday.

I was already dialing Gretchen, a lady I knew who had been providing homecare for years. She was sturdy, dependable and compassionate, and she wouldn't put up with any crap. She was exactly what Bob needed.

I explained what I needed to Gretchen, and she agreed to come right away.

"Give me a few minutes to pack a go bag and I'll be there in about an hour."

"No hurry. I can stay as long as necessary."

Gretchen was there in just under an hour, carrying a bag with a change of clothes and an afghan she was crocheting. She came into the bedroom and introduced herself to Bob.

"I don't need you here, you know!" He told her.

"I'm sure you don't, you look pretty capable to me. But do you really feel like getting up to fix a meal or fetch a glass of water?"

"I don't have much appetite anyway."

"That's because you haven't tasted my homemade chicken and noodles yet." She held up a canvas grocery sack. "I raided my cupboards and brought everything I need for some good old-fashioned comfort food."

Bob snorted. "Home made. That just means you open a bag of noodles and throw them in some chicken broth."

"No, that means I start with a whole chicken and fresh vegetables and make chicken broth, and I roll out my own noodles."

"Real homemade noodles?" Bob's expression brightened a little. "I haven't had those since Rainie made me some last fall. Do you use the whole egg in the noodles?"

"Of course. You're past ninety, I'm not going to nag you about cholesterol. Now, if you don't need anything at the moment I'll leave you to rest and I'll get started in the kitchen."

He nodded and Gretchen left the room.

"So, do you think you'll be okay with Gretchen?"

"I suppose." Bob settled into his pillows. "I'll just reserve judgment until I try her chicken and noodles."

"Fair enough. I'll see you Friday. Remember to drink lots of water."

"Yes, mother." Bob grinned and closed his eyes. I left for B&E, two hours late, but confident Bob was in good hands.

I stopped to say hello to Belinda on my way through the office. Today she was dressed in a short black A-line dress and black leggings with a pair of the highest heels I'd ever seen outside a magazine. Her hair was back to blonde and fell to her shoulders in shining waves, her make up was well done and understated except for some incredibly long false eyelashes. It was like a mix of sixties and eighties, but as usual Belinda pulled it off well. She was gorgeous.

"Damn, I wish I could get away with that stuff."

"You like?" She held out one foot. "I found these on line and couldn't resist. I put the rest of the outfit together to showcase the shoes."

"Maybe that's my problem. I hate shoes, so I'd never think to accessorize around them."

"Could be. Hey, how's it going with the new roommate?"

"Fine. He's out of town right now."

"I know, but I meant when he's there. Anything I need to know for the rumor mill?" She waggled her perfectly sculpted eyebrows suggestively and I laughed.

"Not a thing. He's staying in my guest room and I hardly ever see him."

"Huh. And he's okay with that?"

"Why wouldn't he be?"

"Oh, I don't know..." Belinda shrugged. "Just thought he might have had other ideas about the sleeping arrangements."

I blushed. "Don't be ridiculous. We're just friends. Besides, I have a new boyfriend, remember?"

"Oh yeah. How is the accountant?"

"Michael is fine. Things are going pretty well with us."

"Really? Give me details!"

I laughed. "There aren't any details yet. But we're going out again Friday, so who knows?"

"I'll be expecting a full report on Monday."

"We'll see. I'd better get to work."

I looked up the number for the First Presbyterian Church in Niles, wondering if somewhere there was a Second and a Third Presbyterian Church, and called Pastor Rankin. He was in his office and agreed to see me that afternoon if I could be there by four.

No problem. I spent an hour running some data checks for other cases, emailed the results to the P.I.s in charge and hit the road for Niles at 3:15.

Pastor Rankin was a tall, thin man with a distinctive bearing. He was soft spoken and shook my hand gently, as if afraid he might injure me if he squeezed too hard.

"Please, have a seat." He indicated one of two captain's chairs that sat in front of his desk, a wide expanse of dark wood that was well-polished but scarred by a lot of years of use. It was cluttered with files and paperwork, making me wonder just what a pastor's job was. Apparently they did more than just preach on Sundays and visit the homebound.

"So, Miss Lovingston, you're here to ask about David Bell?"

"Yes, but I know him as Dave Swanson." I handed him the outdated photos. "These pictures are from ten years ago, but I want to be sure we're talking about the same man."

Rankin looked at the pictures for a moment and nodded. "Oh yes, that's definitely David. He has a very distinctive nose, don't you think?"

"Sure. So, when is the last time you saw him?"

"Well." Pastor Rankin sat back in his chair and steepled his fingers under his chin. "First of all, could you tell me why you want to find him?"

I launched into Pam's story, letting him have every sad detail. I watched his expression change as I went on. He was good at showing concern and compassion, I'll give him that. When I finished he leaned forward.

"This is tragic! How terrible for this little family! Do they belong to a church that might help them out?"

"I don't know, but a friend of mine is helping them out a little. She hired a caregiver to give Pam and her mom a rest a few mornings a week."

"My, that's very generous!" Rankin's eyes widened in appreciation. I was afraid he was about to ask me what church Thelma belonged to, hoping to recruit her, so I got us back on the subject.

"Anyway, if you can help me find Dave…"

"Of course, of course." Rankin sat back again. "You understand that David has some…issues. Mental health issues."

"So I've heard. Do you know what his diagnosis is?"

"I'm afraid not," Rankin shook his head. "I've tried to get him to go to a doctor, but he refuses, and I worry that if I push him he won't come around at all anymore. Dave is a very suspicious person."

"Suspicious or paranoid?"

"Well, he often rants about government conspiracies and listening devices in the hymnals, so I suppose paranoid is closer to the truth. Nonetheless, he's usually a very gentle man."

"Usually?"

"We had one incident a couple of months ago." Rankin sighed. "We had a meeting of several church leaders here, and one of the Catholic priests called David 'my son.' David...well, frankly, he freaked out. He started ranting and screaming, and when the priest touched his shoulder in an effort to calm him David punched him right in the nose and went running out of the church. I'm afraid I haven't seen him since."

"A couple of months? Aren't you worried?"

"Of course I am, but understand, David was never here on a regular basis. He would come every day for a week, work around the building or out in the yard...he's a very hard worker, and it seems he knows how to do just about any minor repair you can name. I let him sleep in a room in the basement, but I paid him cash at the end of every day, because I never knew when he would just stop showing up for a few weeks. I've actually been expecting to see him again soon."

"Do you know where he stays when he's not here?"

"Have you tried the Golden Eagle Motel?"

"Yes. He hasn't seen him for a while either."

"I'm not sure then, but I have a couple of ideas. We don't have a big homeless population around here, thank the good Lord, but the ones we have tell me that the old paint factory out by the tracks has some nice rooms for squatting."

"Okay." I nodded, thinking about the big old place. I'd hung out there all the time when I was a teenager. It was a collection of huge old abandoned buildings, all the windows and doors long gone, and we used to party down there. Never mind the possibility of toxic waste or the dangers of broken glass and exposed, rusted metal. The place was just too cool to stay away from. At least, it had been when I was sixteen. It should be no big deal to go search it for a crazy homeless guy.

"You said you had a couple of ideas."

"Well, the other one might be nothing, but a couple of times I saw David duck into the woods off 933, just down from the credit union. You know where I mean?"

"Sure, there's a decent sized stretch there that blocks the subdivisions from the highway."

"That's the place. Now, I can't imagine David is sleeping outside in this weather, but who knows? I'm pretty sure I saw him a few weeks ago walking on the side of the road, but by the time I got up to where he was he was gone. I can't imagine where else he disappeared to if not the woods."

"All right, thank you." I stood, ending the interview. "I appreciate your time."

"I hope you find him. Poor little Davey...you tell Pam if there's anything I can do, she should just call."

I was impressed by his sincerity, and shook his hand.

"I will. Thank you again."

I considered driving straight to the paint factory for a quick search, but it was already late in the day and the sun would be down soon. All I had was the miniature mag light I kept in my glove compartment, hardly enough illumination for a real search.

Besides, I didn't think I should go there alone. Even as a kid I found the place spooky, which in truth was part of the charm of hanging out there, but being spooked wasn't much fun when you were alone.

I drove home, on the way giving Eddie a call.

"Hi Rainie, what's up?"

"I have a favor to ask. I got a tip that a guy I'm looking for might be squatting at the paint factory, and I wondered if you'd go with me to check it out."

"The paint factory? Damn, that brings back some memories!" Eddie laughed, and I wondered which memory he was recalling. We'd been there lots of times, but once in particular Eddie and I had been off in a dark corner by ourselves, and there'd been some groping going on. I blushed at the memory, but we were just kids, just coming in to our sexuality. I know Eddie was as glad as I was that we'd never taken it any further. We were good as friends. "I wish I could go," Eddie spoke again, "But I've got to be on a plane tonight, and I'll be gone at least a week."

"Oh, where are you going?"

There was a slight hesitation before he answered. "B&E business. I can tell you about it when I get back."

"Gotcha." I was getting used to him going off without being able to disclose details, but it made me wonder sometimes if B&E weren't a front for something far more complicated than private investigations and personal security. Silly, I know, because Eddie almost always told me about his assignments after the fact, usually leaving out the names of the principal players. A suspicious person might think he used the time away to make up a cover story, but I preferred to accept what he told me at face value. I worried enough about him without hearing he'd been sent to break up a terrorist cell or invade the compound of some drug cartel.

"Why don't you ask Jack?" He suggested.

"He's in Chicago with Rachel until tomorrow night."

"Can you wait?"

"Probably," I hedged, not wanting him to worry.

"Rainie, that place has been empty for a long time. The structure probably isn't sound anymore, and who knows who or what is living in there? You'd better wait until you have someone to go with you."

"I will."

"Rainie..."

"Really, Eddie, I promise. To tell you the truth I don't think I have the nerve to go alone. That place is pretty spooky."

"That's what made it so fun!" Eddie chuckled, sounding a lot like the teenaged Eddie that used to delight in telling outrageous scary stories about the place, getting our whole group half terrified even before we snuck into the place after dark.

I laughed. "I'm not going for fun this time. But don't worry, I won't go alone."

"All right. I'll call you when I get back into town."

"Be careful, Eddie, whatever it is you're up to."

"I always am."

He disconnected and I drove on home, considering who I should ask to go with me.

I went in and let George out and got him some fresh food.

"I don't suppose you want to go with me?" I asked him. George just kept shoveling bits of apple and Romaine lettuce into his prehistoric maw, not even blinking at me. "I should have trained you to walk on a leash. Then I could have strapped a flashlight on your back and taken you along." I grinned at the image, but George didn't look particularly amused. I guess the P.I. life wasn't for him.

Instead I called Tommy, who would be much better with a flashlight.

"The old paint factory? I haven't thought about that place in years."

"Did you ever hang out there?"

"Sure, I went to a couple of parties there. Almost got busted by the cops once, but I made it out the fire escape with Shirley Chase just in time."

"Shirley Chase? You mean two-bit Shirley?" I was shocked. Shirley had a reputation in junior high for being willing to do almost anything for a quarter, although I'd been told her price was really closer to five or ten dollars. Still...

"Hey, a guy has needs you know? And remember, back then I had no idea what those needs were." Tommy laughed. "Besides, I never got a chance. The cops got there before we could finish negotiations."

"They did you a favor."

"Yeah, probably. Anyway, yeah, I'd love to go with you. You want to go tonight?"

I thought about it. The place would be a lot less scary in the day time, but if David was squatting there he was more likely to be "home" at night.

"I guess so. I need to find him sooner rather than later."

"Okay, I'll grab a flashlight and come on over. I'll see you in about a half hour?"

"Sounds good. Oh, wear something dark."

"Oh, I get it, stealth clothes! This should be good."

I hung up and went to change into my black jeans and sweatshirt, and dug my heavy flashlight out of the kitchen drawer. I was just putting fresh batteries in it when Tommy knocked on the door.

He was also dressed in black jeans and a black jacket, with a black watch cap covering his blonde hair. He was carrying a huge flashlight, big enough to be used as a club if necessary. I nodded approval and we headed for Niles.

Chapter Thirteen

The paint factory was near the tracks, and the best approach had always been the back side, where a narrow dirt road ran near the railroad bed. There wasn't much back there, just a storage facility and a small tool and die shop, but it was enough that the road was plowed more or less regularly.

I maneuvered my little Escort down the dark road. It was plowed only one lane wide, and I followed the packed tire tracks of cars that had passed before me heading for the storage facility. I parked in the U-Store lot and Tommy and I got out in the cold, our breath puffing out in little white clouds. The sky was clear and filled with stars but the moon had not yet gotten high enough to cast much light.

"Where do you want to start?"

"We'll try the loading dock on the east end," I answered. "That was always open."

Tommy nodded. "Can't imagine they've boarded it up. No one really cares about the place anymore."

We crunched through the snow to the factory, making our own way across until we came to a path that had been beaten down before us. Clearly there were still plenty of people using the place for one reason or another.

The loading bay loomed before us, the double wide entrance a darker shape against the dark building. To get in you had to skirt the ramp, which angled down to bring the bed of a truck even with the floor. A trampled snow path led us right to the top. We stepped over into the blackness of the building and flicked on our flashlights.

The snow continued for a few feet into the building, and I shone my light over it, noticing the wide variety of shoe prints. They came in all sizes and treads, so it wasn't just a couple of people coming in. This place seemed to be getting more traffic now than it did when it was up and running.

Tommy moved his flashlight beam over the room in front of us. It was an empty, cavernous room, much as I remembered it from my younger years. There was nothing there except the rusting hulk of a forklift that had been too far gone to take with them or to sell at auction when the factory closed. It was just a skeleton now, all the removable parts taken for scrap when the price of metal soared.

We moved across the room to an open doorway on the far side and paused to shine our lights down the hallway. Again there wasn't much to see, just a little trash and a lot of dirt gathered in the corners. There were several small rooms off this hall, old offices that had probably once housed the shipping and receiving employees.

Tommy led the way, stopping at each open or missing door so we could shine our lights in. A couple of the offices still had broken remnants of office furniture and piles of old papers. I suppose no one cared about invoices from a bankrupt business, so when the place closed the office workers packed up whatever personal effect were on their desks along with any useful items such as staplers and paper clips and walked away.

We moved on. Somewhere a door suddenly banged shut, and I jumped about a foot. Tommy chuckled softly. "Might have just been the wind." He whispered, and I nodded.

"Let's keep going." I whispered, too. Not only did I not want to scare David away if he was in here, but it just seemed the better part of caution to not announce our presence. I kept telling myself there probably wasn't anything more dangerous than a few drunken teenagers in here, but in the dark and silence it was possible to imagine just about anything. The leaping shadows produced by our flashlights didn't help much.

This whole experience was bringing back a lot of memories. It had always been scary, which had been a big part of the attraction back then. Where the hell had my sense of adventure gone? Why wasn't this fun anymore?

Of course, before I'd only been a teenager, and like most people of that age I thought I was immortal, too young to be touched by death no matter how stupid I got. I had also always come here with a group, as few as five or as many as a dozen, and there had seemed to be safety in numbers.

Now I had passed my thirtieth birthday and I was all too aware of how easily death can come raging out of the dark, and there was only me and Tommy. I resisted the urge to walk behind him, clinging to his shirt, which is how I had usually entered this building. It might have been a different guy every time, but I'd always preferred the reassurance of a broad back to hide behind. Now, of course, I was a grown, independent woman, and I didn't need that sort of protection.

Really, I didn't.

So I walked beside Tommy, shining my light left when he went right and vice versa, and reminded myself that this had all been *my* idea in the first place.

We got to the end of the hallway and passed through yet another missing door to step out onto the factory floor.

This room was huge, the ceilings soaring up a full two stories. The darkness was nearly absolute, no light penetrating from the line of narrow windows forty feet above us. We ran our lights over the room, but the beams wouldn't reach the far end. There had once been a metal stairway leading to a catwalk that encircled the room, but the lower half of the stairs was missing, maybe dismantled and taken for scrap.

Most of the equipment had been taken out, but there were a few hulking metallic beasts that were bolted to the concrete floor, the skeletal remains of machines I wouldn't have recognized the purpose for even if they were still complete and in motion.

Now they just cast mysterious shadows across the floor and walls when our lights passed over them and provided hundreds of nooks and crannies where someone –maybe a deranged killer – could hide. Tommy and I moved across the floor slowly, shining the light at the floor now and then in search of hazardous obstacles, and the whole distance I expected an ax to come down on my neck from the darkness. Silly, I know, but the place was definitely creepy.

We reached the far side of the room and Tommy pointed at the concrete staircase that led upwards into the impenetrable blackness. "There's more offices on the second floor," he whispered. "That's the most likely place to find someone."

I nodded and started up the stairs, Tommy close beside me. The second floor was really the third, since the factory ceiling was so high. The stairs switched back on themselves, each turn causing my heart to leap into my throat, sure that now was the time someone – or thing – would come leaping out of the dark to tear my throat out.

Several times we heard what might have been footsteps or whispered voices, and we would both freeze, listening intently. The old building creaked and moaned with every gust of wind, and sound echoed strangely in the empty rooms. There was no way to be sure where a noise was coming from, or to identify its source.

"You okay?" Tommy whispered, and I realized I had unwittingly snatched a corner of his t shirt and I was clinging to it like Linus clung to his blanket. Thank goodness I hadn't also stuck my thumb in my mouth.

Embarrassed, I let go of his shirt. "I'm fine," I whispered back, and to prove it I moved a little faster, taking the lead.

I came to the top of the stairwell and poked my head out into the hall. The moon must have risen, because there was a slight gray cast to the gloom, enough to make out large shapes but certainly no detail. I used my flashlight to illuminate piles of trash and a long, wide corridor. The floors here were varnished wood, at one time likely highly polished but now scuffed and coated with dirt.

There were a lot of individual rooms up here, many of them with their doors still intact. Oh goody.

"Let's go left first." I whispered to Tommy, trying to take charge of myself and the situation.

He nodded and we moved to the first door, which was hanging open on one hinge. The floor creaked ominously under our feet, the old wood protesting our weight. Inside the room there were more piles of trash, a lot of it broken beer bottles. There weren't any aluminum cans. I suppose they had all been collected for the deposit or the scrap value.

The next two rooms both had closed doors, but there was nothing behind them but more trash, although one also held the bottom of a metal barrel that had clearly been used as a fireplace. I shuddered, thinking of the wooden floors, aged and dried to tinder. One of these days the old place would probably be burned out, just like all those joints I'd smoked under its spooky roof.

We searched several more rooms, finding nothing but more trash, mouse droppings, and more used condoms than I ever wanted to look at in my whole life. In some rooms the roof had leaked, leaving ugly stains running down the walls that could easily be mistaken for dried blood if one's mind was given to such gruesome images – which of course, mine was. In one room the ceiling had caved in, leaving a view of the starry sky shining down on piles of wet, moldy plaster.

At the end of the corridor a closed door gave way to a larger room, what might have been a conference room back when there was something to confer about here. I stood in the door and played my light over the room. On the far side there was an old mattress and a crumpled blanket. This was probably Dave's place!

"Hey," I whispered to Tommy and pointed with the beam of light, and he nodded. I started across the floor eagerly, hoping for some sign that this really was Dave's home, or even better, maybe a note saying where he'd gone. You know, something like: "ran to the store. Back in twenty minutes."

Tommy was a couple of steps behind me, shining his light into the corners.

I heard the loud crack a half second behind the sensation of breaking wood and I fell through the floor!

I think I cried out. I know I dropped my flashlight and tried to throw myself forward, but my lower half had already passed through the newly torn hole. I scrabbled for something to hold onto, but there was nothing but smooth floorboards, and beneath me nothing but a forty foot drop to the concrete factory floor. I slipped past my waist, still frantically feeling for something to hold onto, when suddenly I felt Tommy's strong hand grasp my wrist.

"I've got you!" He shouted, no longer worrying about stealth.

He had thrown himself flat on the floor, like a rescuer on an icy pond, distributing his weight so he wouldn't fall through the fragile floor. I grabbed his arm with my other hand and for a few seconds just hung there, my heart pounding, my mind trying to catch up to the fact that I wasn't an ugly splash of blood, tissue and bone on the factory floor.

"Are you all right?"

I tried to process the question and come up with a coherent answer. Was I all right? Well, I wasn't squashed on the floor below like a bug on a windshield, and that was good. I guess the phrase "all right" was relative.

"Y-yeah, I'm okay. C-can you pull me up?" I finally stammered. I seemed to be having trouble controlling my tongue. It kept wanting to stick to the roof of my mouth.

"Yeah." Tommy pulled, and I cried out as the sharp ends of splintered wood stabbed through my jacket.

"Ow! Wait! Stop!"

Tommy quit pulling. "What's the matter?"

"Sh-sharp..." I was still stuttering. I took a deep breath and tried to get a grip on my fear, tried to get that excited rush adrenalin had sometimes brought me, but I couldn't get past the fact that one wrong move and I was going to die horribly. I think it's a little different when I have some control over the situation, when I can choose to run or fight. Right now I had a choice between a fatal fall or being impaled on a floor board, and neither option was making me very excited. I was hyper aware of my legs dangling over empty space, and I had to resist the urge to flail them around in search of something solid to put my feet on.

"The boards," I finally managed. "They're splintered and I'm getting hung up on them." I was pretty proud of that sentence. I thought I sounded remarkably calm. "I think I'd better get myself up. If you hang on, I think maybe I can swing my leg up."

"Okay, whatever you need. I've got you."

I tried to swing my lower body around and get a leg up through the hole, but it became immediately apparent that wasn't going to work. For one thing, the hole wasn't big enough; it was only a few inches wider than my hips, which so far had been the widest part of me to fall through. Secondly, my twisting had made my wrist slip in Tommy's grip, and for one heart-stopping second I thought I was falling again.

"Okay, wait!" I commanded, taking another deep breath. "There has to be another way."

"I'm going to have to stand up and pull you straight through."

"No!" I protested. "You'll probably just fall with me!"

"I don't think so. Look," Tommy gestured with his head at the floor. "I think I see a joist, right there. It should be solid enough to hold me."

I looked, and thought he was probably right. I could see the wooden beam under the splintered boards. My chest was practically on top of it, which was likely all that had saved me from falling straight through.

"I'm going to move, but I promise I won't let go, okay?"

"Okay." But it wasn't nearly. I didn't want him to move. I knew that eventually one or both of us would get tired and our grips would fail, but I wanted to live until eventually came to pass. I saw no need to hurry it along. Then again, if Tommy could pull me out of this predicament so I didn't have to die at all that would be even better. So I kept my mouth shut and hung on tight to his wrist as he shifted himself to a sitting position.

The movement pulled me hard against the splintered wood, and I felt something pierce my skin just below my breasts, but I bit my lip and didn't say anything. I could handle a little pain. Okay, a lot of pain. A small cry escaped my gritted teeth.

Tommy made it to a sitting position and scooted over the creaking boards until his butt was firmly on the joist.

"Tommy," I stared at the joist, my mouth dry. "The beam is bending."

"I know, I can feel it," his expression was grim. "The whole damned room must be ready to go. I'm going to stand and pull you up as fast as I can, then we need to run for that door like our asses are on fire. You ready?'

"Do it!"

I clung to Tommy's arm with every ounce of strength I had while he swung his legs around and in one smooth motion got to his knees and then his feet, all the while bending at the waist, his hand firmly gripping my wrist. We were both sweating profusely, and I felt his grip slipping, but I had my nails dug into the sleeve of his coat and I wasn't letting go come hell or high water.

He didn't hesitate to ask if I was all right this time. He just bent his knees and grabbed my other wrist and jerked me up like a weightlifter clearing barbells off the floor. I popped out of the hole like a cork from a bottle and fell against him. There was an ominous crack and I felt the floor giving way.

I got my feet under me and leaped toward the door, trying to clear as much floor as I could. Tommy was right behind me, barely getting his weight off the beam as it broke and a five foot diameter hole appeared in the floor. I didn't see the hole until I was relatively safe on the other side of the door, looking back in, leaning on my knees and gasping for breath.

Tommy was next to me, his own breath chugging in and out like a freight train.

"God damn! God damn!" he shouted.

I looked at the hole, then at him, then back at the hole, barely visible in the dark, a cloud of dust like a dirty mist obscuring most of the room.

"Huh! That was something else!" I grinned at him and he looked at me like I'd just waved good bye to my last shred of sanity.

"Jesus, we almost died in there! What are you grinning about?"

Now that it was over I was finally enjoying the rush, and I wished Jack was there to share it with me. "Almost isn't a bad thing!" I laughed. "Almost dead just means you're alive!" I hugged Tommy. "I sure am glad you joined that gym!"

"Rainie, are you hurt? Did you hit your head?"

"No, silly! I'm fine!" Although actually there was a pretty intense pain just below my left breast and my shoulders felt like they'd been nearly dislocated. Tommy hadn't been gentle when he jerked me up, but I wasn't about to complain. "I'm thinking we should get out of here, though. I don't think David was still staying in that room or we'd have found him plastered to the floor downstairs, and if he was anywhere else I'm sure he cleared out after hearing all that."

"All right, let's go." Tommy turned toward the stairs, and I was glad of the moonlight. We'd both lost our flashlights.

There weren't any windows on the stairs, so we felt our way down slowly in almost total blackness, hanging tight to the rail.

"I hate this. I can't even tell if we're near the landing."

"Here, wait." I pulled my cigarette lighter out of my pocket and lit it for a few seconds. There, yet another argument for not quitting! Always having a lighter in your pocket could come in handy. The landing was only three steps away, but I couldn't keep the lighter going for long; it got too hot.

I let it go out and we made our way down, stopping to check our progress with the lighter now and then. It was a relief to finally reach the ground floor, but then we had the cavernous room to cross, and the moonlight didn't penetrate the gloom.

We shuffled slowly across, our hands moving in front of us like kids playing pin the tail on the donkey. It seemed to take hours to make it to the far wall, and then another long search before we found the door and the hallway that led to receiving.

At last we stepped out into the cold night, and the moonlight seemed as bright as a lamp after the blackness of the abandoned building. We didn't say anything until we got back to the car and I started driving home. I was wishing I'd asked Tommy to drive. The pain in my ribs was bad, and it was taking a good portion of my concentration not to sob out loud.

"Geez, Rainie. Is this what your job is always like?"

"What? No, of course not. I hardly ever have to explore abandoned buildings. Well, there was the abandoned house where the meth lab was, but I didn't go in there. And I guess technically the fourth floor apartment they moved the meth lab to was abandoned, but there were people living in the building."

"Rainie, I think you know what I mean."

I blew out a sigh. "Yeah, Tommy, I do. I just didn't want to hear the lecture."

He shook his head. "No lecture. I just..." he looked away for a minute, then turned back and I could see his grin out of the corner of my eye. "Hell, you were amazing in there! I was all freaking out, and you were just cool as a cucumber!"

"Ha! Are you kidding? I was about to wet my pants!"

"You didn't show it." Tommy shook his head. "You were like Jane Bond, double-O C cup in there!"

I started laughing and I couldn't stop. I finally had to pull over to the side of the road and let it out, tears streaming down my face, as much from the laughing as from the pain. This was the Tommy that I had married, the irreverent, silly guy that could always make me laugh.

"Man, I really love you, Tommy!"

I said goodbye to Tommy outside. I didn't want him to see me in the light, because I knew my coat was torn, and I wasn't sure what sort of wound was underneath it. I did love Tommy, but I didn't want him fussing over me.

I went straight into the bathroom and peeled off my jacket. It had a long tear down the front, good for nothing but the trash.

Underneath the coat there was blood. Lots of it. Worse, there was a blood-soaked piece of wood sticking out under my breast.

For just a few seconds I saw little flashes of color behind my eyeballs and I thought I might throw up or pass out or both, but instead I took a deep breath and sat on the edge of the tub. I looked at the chunk of wood. It was no bigger around than a pencil, and sticking out about an inch. The question was, how far was it sticking *in* me?

Only one way to find out.

I clenched my teeth, grabbed the end of it, and pulled.

My fingers slipped off the bloody surface and I didn't pull nearly hard enough. All I got for my effort was a searing jolt of pain. I broke out in a sweat and leaned over the toilet and threw up.

I hung there for a long moment, sobbing, thinking it was time to call 911. I needed an ambulance! I needed a surgeon! I needed...

"Get a grip on yourself!" I admonished myself through gritted teeth. I couldn't afford to go to the hospital if this was just superficial, and I sure didn't want to explain the night's escapades to the police.

I sat up, breathing deeply, and reassessed the situation.

I was sure I hadn't punctured any major organs, or I wouldn't still be walking around. It was high enough that it might have gotten my lung, but I was fairly certain I wouldn't be able to breathe properly if it had punched through to one of them. I wasn't obese anymore, but I still had a healthy layer of fat, and I suspected the splinter – I chose to call it that, for my own mental health – was simply lodged in that.

I didn't need a doctor, I needed a tool. A pair of pliers ought to do it.

I got up slowly, and once I was sure I wasn't going to pass out and knock myself unconscious on the edge of the sink I made my way out to the kitchen and opened my tool drawer. I kept several sizes and types of screwdrivers, a hammer, wire cutters, box knives and pliers there. Okay, I also kept a good amount of other things that weren't technically tools, like a stapler, a few loose keys, a length of phone cord, several boxes of matches, a worn pot holder, and, inexplicably, a book about outdoor survival.

I pushed everything around until I located the pliers and I pulled a stool over to the sink. I sat there for a minute, breathing deep, getting my nerve up.

"Just do it!" I told myself, and I sounded pretty firm about it. I grasped the wood with the pliers and took another deep breath. I let it out in a cry of defiance and pain and jerked as hard as I could. The bloody wood came free with a strange little pop that I felt as well as heard, and once again I thought I might throw up.

I sat there, breathing hard, for a full minute, until I noticed blood was dripping on my kitchen floor.

"Oh crap!" I got off the stool and grabbed a kitchen towel and wadded it up against the wound. I hadn't yet taken my shirt off, and I wasn't sure I wanted to. Of course, cowardice wasn't really an option in this case. I got the bottle of Vicoden out of the cupboard over the sink, left over from my gunshot wound. A painkiller would be welcome, but unfortunately I was a lightweight when it came to drugs, and I was afraid if I took one I'd fall asleep before I finished what I had to do. At least I could take one when I was done.

I went back to the bathroom, still holding the dishtowel in place, and dug out my first aid kit. I had a good supply of sterile gauze pads, and I opened several of them with my teeth and one hand and set them in a neat pile on the edge of the sink.

I dropped the dishtowel in the basin, appalled to see how soaked it was with my blood. I pulled my shirt over my head, leaving a wide streak of blood on one side of my face and into my hair, and dropped it on the floor.

I couldn't see the wound looking down; my boob was in the way. I looked in the mirror instead, and grimaced. There was a definite hole there, just under my bra line, and it was still oozing blood at a goodly pace. I clapped the gauze pads over it and held them, pressing hard.

I sat on the edge of the tub again and waited for the bleeding to stop. I forced myself to wait ten long minutes, not peeking, waiting for my platelets to do their job and clot the wound. The body is an amazing machine, and given even basic maintenance and repairs it will pretty much take care of itself. In fact, it's a testament to American decadence that we manage, time and again, to trash our bodies beyond redemption. It takes a lot of abuse to break one of these babies, but a lot of us sure manage it.

I carefully pulled the gauze away, pleased to see that most of the bleeding had stopped. Now came the awful part: I had to clean the wound.

I got a plastic basin from under the sink and filled it with soapy water. It was half-full when I heard a light tapping on the bathroom door.

"Rainie, are you in there?" It was Jack.

"What are you doing home?"

"We got our guy already. Told you we were good. Are you okay?"

"Of course, why wouldn't I be?"

"There's a pair of bloody pliers and a blood-soaked wooden stake in the kitchen sink. I thought that might mean bad news."

"Oh. I'm just getting cleaned up."

"Can I come in?"

"I'm not dressed."

"So, can I come in?"

"No!"

"Look, throw a towel around yourself or whatever. I want to see how bad you're hurt."

"I can handle it."

"I'm coming in three..." Jack started counting off and I snatched a towel off the rack and threw it around my shoulders just as the bathroom door opened. I'm not sure what I was so worried about. I was wearing a plain white bra made of thick cotton material that covered more than most women's tank tops. I guess it was more the idea that it was a bra that bothered me.

Jack frowned when he saw me, and stuck a hand in my bloody hair, running his fingers over my scalp.

"My head is fine. That's just blood transfer from taking my shirt off."

"Okay, let's see the wound."

I tugged the towel aside and Jack leaned in close. He turned me toward the light to get a better look.

"Damn, Rainie, you need to see a doctor. That needs stitches."

"No. The only thing stitches are good for is minimizing scarring and keeping out infection. I don't care about the scarring and I have good bandages, but I don't have insurance. I can take care of it myself."

"Were you on B&E business?"

"Yeah, but I had Tommy with me, and technically we were trespassing. I don't think Harry wants the B&E name associated with this."

"He'll still take care of it..."

"No, Jack. I'm not going to sit for hours in an emergency room and then more hours being questioned by the police. I already have all the cops in Buchanan and half the cops in Niles watching me like I'm some dangerous lunatic. I'll be fine, really."

Jack sighed. "All right." He picked up the plastic box I used for a first aid kit. It was a good sized box, a little bigger than a shoe box, and always well stocked. I highly recommend such a kit for anyone who is uninsured.

Jack found a pair of tweezers and a small magnifying glass I used for finding splinters, usually in my fingers. An image of him digging in the puncture wound with them filled my head and once again I felt a little woozy. I sat down on the tub.

"Are you okay?"

"Yes!" I snapped. "Just go on...I can do this myself."

"You know, Rainie, I happen to have more than a little experience in field medicine. In my line of work there's rarely a medic around when you need one. Now, either let me help or I'm going to carry you to the ER."

I blew out a hard breath. The truth was, I wasn't sure I could see the wound well enough to clean it properly, and I was thinking of all the dirt and the varnish on the wood floor I'd been pierced with.

"Okay, but first I'm going to get in the shower and wash the blood out of my hair. I won't be able to once the bandage is in place."

"Okay." Jack leaned on the sink. "Go ahead."

"Well, you need to leave."

"What if you pass out in the shower?"

"Don't be ridiculous. Get out."

"All right, but I'll be right outside the door, and I want you to talk to me the whole time."

"Fine. Just go."

"Hey, did you take one of these?" He held up the bottle of Vicoden I had set on the sink.

"Not yet. I was afraid it would knock me out too fast."

"You'd better take one now."

I swallowed it willingly enough, now that Jack was taking over the actual wound care.

Jack stepped out and pulled the bathroom door partly closed, leaving it ajar.

"Close it."

"Damn it Rainie, I'm not going to peek! Just get in the shower already!"

I started the water and stepped into the tub fully clothed. I pulled the curtain shut and undressed, dropping my jeans and bra and underwear in the tub. They were all soaked with blood and probably destined for the trash.

"You doing okay?"

"Yes. I'll let you know if I feel like I'm going to pass out."

I washed my hair and the rest of me, hanging on to the towel bar for support. I was a lot weaker in the knees than I wanted to admit. I dried off behind the curtain and finally stepped out with the towel wrapped around me. The running water got the wound bleeding again, so I held a fresh gauze pad on it while I dressed.

I had a pair or pajama shorts and a tank top hanging on the back of the door and I put them on.

"Okay, you can come in."

Jack swung the door open, picked up the first aid kit, and pulled a fresh towel from the linen closet.

"Come out and lie on the bed."

I grimaced but did what he asked. He tucked the towel under me and I lifted my shirt, which was already stained with blood. The good news was the Vicoden was kicking in, and I was feeling pretty good.

Jack had brought the small plastic tub I'd filled with warm soapy water and he started with that, gently washing the wound. It hurt, but I could take it. I was taking deliberate, deep breaths and doing my best to relax.

Jack pulled the bedside lamp closer and bent over me, tweezers and magnifying glass in hand. I started counting in my head, imagining neon numbers glowing behind my eyelids, anything to keep the image of him digging in that puncture wound out of my head.

"How deep is it?" I asked, not sure I really wanted to know.

"Deep enough," he answered grimly. "Looks like it got stopped by a rib, luckily enough."

Yeah. I felt lucky.

He started probing and I gritted my teeth and sucked air in, hard, determined not to cry out. Vicoden was not a substitute for a local anesthetic.

"Sorry," Jack murmured, but he kept going, diligently searching out every last sliver of wood. He pulled out several, wiping them off the tweezers onto a gauze pad before going back in search of more. It seemed like he was excavating clear to my spine, and I couldn't help a whimper or two. I had my eyes closed, but I could feel tears squeezing out from under my eyelids.

Finally he stopped digging and washed the wound again, and held a fresh pad on it for a few minutes until the fresh bleeding stopped.

"I think I got it all."

I nodded, not trusting myself to speak. Jack wiped away the tears running down my face. "You want another Vicoden?"

"No." I shook my head. Actually, now that he had stopped carving on me the pain was diminishing rapidly.

I felt him working with gauze and tape, but it was all distant now. I was starting to drift away on that pleasant Vicoden ocean, the one where there are no big waves or sharks, just pleasant blue water to float on under a perfect sky...

I think I fell asleep before Jack finished bandaging me.

Chapter Fourteen

My first thought when I woke up was: pain. That's rarely a good start to a day, so I didn't rush to get up. I stayed where I was, nestled under my feather quilt, and peeked at the glowing numbers on my clock.

My brain was still fogged from the painkiller, so it took a minute for the time to register: seven-fifteen. I had forgotten to set the alarm on my new clock. Oh well, at least I didn't have Jack in here smashing the stupid thing.

With a groan I threw aside my warm covers and sat up. I stayed on the edge of the bed for a minute, assessing myself. I was groggy and I felt like someone had kicked me in the ribs, but overall it wasn't too bad. I'd felt worse.

There was a light tap on my bedroom door.

"Rainie?" Jack called my name softly, maybe trying to make up for the rude way he'd woken me the last time. "Shouldn't you be up?"

"Yeah, I'm getting there."

"I have coffee."

"Come in!"

He came in carrying my favorite cup, and I took it eagerly, the fragrance rising with the steam almost making me whimper with pleasure. He didn't say anything, just smiled a little and left again. He was learning.

By the time the cup was half gone I felt ready to face myself, and I went into the bathroom and turned on the light. I immediately regretted that decision.

I'd gone to bed without drying my hair, and it had dried like a fright wig, sticking out in all directions. My tank top still had a patch of dried blood on it, and my eyes were underlined with dark circles.

"Lovely." I murmured to my reflection.

I used the toilet and brushed my teeth and tried to make some sense of my hair, but it was pretty hopeless. Some people have bad hair days. I have a bad hair life.

I pulled up my shirt. A little blood had soaked through the bandage overnight, but not enough to worry about. A dark bruise was spreading from under the edges, and I suspected that was where most of the pain was coming from. I decided to go have another cup of coffee before I changed it and got dressed.

Jack was sitting at the kitchen counter, already dressed and ready for his day. When I came in he was bent over, coughing hard.

"You okay?"

"Yeah." He cleared his throat and took a drink of his coffee. "I only do that in the morning. No big deal." His glance took me in head to toe, but to his credit he didn't smirk when he saw my hair. "How are you feeling?"

"Not too bad," I answered honestly. "I slept well."

"You need help changing that bandage?"

"No thanks, I'm good."

"You going to work today?"

"Sure, why not?"

He grinned. "Yeah, why not?"

There was a knock at the door and Jack went to let Rachel in. She perked into the kitchen, every hair on her head where it belonged and her makeup flawless.

There ought to be a law against women looking that good before eight in the morning. It made it too hard on the rest of us.

"Good morning, Rainie!" She greeted me brightly.

"Morning, Rachel."

"Hey, are you okay?" Her expression looked genuinely concerned, so I decided to forgive her for being so damned cute.

"Yeah, just a rough night."

She put her hands on her hips and put on a mock expression of sternness. "Jack, were you two out playing again after dark?"

Jack laughed. "Not me, this time! I just helped clean up the aftermath."

"I was sneaking around an abandoned building with my ex-husband."

"Mm, I've seen him around. He's pretty yummy," Rachel looked at me, and I couldn't quite read her intentions. "You should have hung on to that one."

"We're better as friends."

"Huh. Too bad." She glanced at Jack.

"You ready to go?"

He was sliding into his leather jacket, suppressing a cough.

"I always am!"

She laughed and waved goodbye and followed Jack out into the cold morning.

Reluctantly I dragged myself in to get dressed. I would just be able to get to Thelma's on time if I hurried.

I called Gretchen while I drove, and asked about Bob.

"His temp is down and his wheezing is letting up," she reported. "I'm fixing him breakfast right now. He wants eggs and toast."

"Well, that's a good sign."

"If the snow is too bad tomorrow I can stay an extra day."

"Snow?" I hadn't watched the weather, but right now the sun was rising in blue skies.

"The weather guy said twelve to twenty four inches tonight. Lake effect, so you know how that goes."

"Yeah, we could get anything from a few inches to six feet." Gretchen and I both laughed.

"Anyway, I'll be happy to stay if you want me to. Bob and I are getting along just fine, so give me a call in the morning."

"I will. Thanks again, Gretchen, and tell Bob I said hello."

Thelma took one look at my hair and burst out laughing.

"Whoo, girl! Did you have a cat fight with a blender?"

"Very funny, Thelma. I went to bed with wet hair."

"Really? Who was in the shower with you?"

"No one!"

"Hey, I just assumed. I mean, the only time I was ever in that big a hurry to get to bed after a shower was when I had someone in there with me, soaping up my back!"

"Thelma, please!"

"Okay, okay, you showered alone. So why did you go to bed with wet hair?"

"It's a long story. How about a cup of coffee while I tell it?"

"Fair enough."

We settled in her comfortable old kitchen and I told her the whole story, which of course required showing her the bandage on my ribs.

"Hm, Jack did that for you? That's hot!"

"It wasn't hot, Thelma. I was in pain and half asleep from the painkiller. And believe me, there's nothing sexy about a guy digging around an open wound with a pair of tweezers."

"Maybe not. So, have you updated Pam recently?"

"No. I wanted to wait until I had confirmation that David is still around. I hate to get her hopes up for nothing."

"She might appreciate a ray of hope or two."

"I suppose." I sighed. "I guess I should call her."

"Why don't we go over and talk to her? I wouldn't mind getting out of the house for a while."

"I don't know if she'll be home today. Heidi should be there."

"It's early enough, maybe she hasn't left the house yet."

"Okay, let me call and see if it's a good time to stop by."

Pam's mother answered the phone, sounding rather cheerful. "Of course, come by. Pam has been hoping for some news."

"I don't want to interrupt if she has plans to go out."

"That's okay, dear, she's not going anywhere this morning. You just come on over."

Thelma and I trundled into the car and drove on over. The sun was shining and the roads were clear, the temperature hovering in the mid-thirties. All in all, not a bad day for the end of January.

Pam answered our knock with a smile, and I was once again surprised by her appearance. She hadn't magically regained her lost weight, but she had dyed her hair a fresh auburn color, and her face seemed a couple of shades less pale.

"Come on in!" She stepped back to let us in, and we stomped the snow off our shoes and entered the living room.

"Your hair looks great!"

"Thanks! Heidi suggested it, and I went and bought a home kit. I have to admit, it does make me feel better."

The curtains were open, and the living room had a freshly scrubbed feel, not a speck of dust to be seen. Little Davey was on the couch, propped on pillows and reading a book. Gus was sitting in a recliner, playing checkers with Heidi.

"Hi!" Heidi called out cheerfully.

"Ha!" Gus grunted. He reached out a slow, shaky hand and moved one of his checker pieces.

"You sure you want to do that?" Heidi asked, and Gus glared at the board, concentrating hard. After a few seconds he reached out and moved the piece back.

"That's what I thought." Heidi smiled and patted his hand. "Take your time, Gus, it's a game, not a race."

"Pop-pop is getting better." Davey announced.

"That's good to hear," I answered sincerely. Unfortunately, it was apparent Davey was not. He was wearing a knitted cap to hide his bald head, and his skin was so pale it looked almost translucent. He was so thin I could see the shape of his bones, the knobby joints looking like they might burst through the fragile skin. My chest constricted and I felt tears burn the backs of my eyes.

"Let's go into the kitchen," Pam suggested, leading the way. "Would you like some coffee?"

"Always!" I agreed enthusiastically.

Thelma and I both accepted a cup and the three of us sat at the scarred kitchen table.

"I won't be able to thank you enough for Heidi if I live six lifetimes." Pam smiled. "She's transformed this house. And it's not just the deep cleaning she gave it, although that certainly made a difference. Heidi seems to see Daddy and Davey differently than Mom and I do. Her very first day she insisted on getting both of them out of bed, and Daddy hadn't done that for weeks! She makes him do his exercises and she refuses to just lift him into his chair. She makes him do it, and guess what? He can!" Pam laughed. "He's back to using his bedside commode instead of asking for the bedpan. I can't tell you how much easier that is on us, and he's a lot happier about it, too."

"That's great, Pam. I knew Heidi would be good for you."

"She's taking care of all of us." She patted her hair self-consciously. "I had forgotten what it was like to really care about what I look like." Her expression turned serious. "So, any news on David?"

"Maybe. I don't want you to get your hopes up too much, but I have reason to believe he might still be in the area."

"What?" Pam looked startled.

I went on to fill her in on what I'd learned, and she listened, incredulous.

"You mean he's been right here in Niles all these years and I never knew it?"

"He's been keeping a pretty low profile. The consensus seems to be that he's mentally ill, paranoid with possible delusions. If that's true, he might have a very good reason for staying away...at least, in his own mind."

"That's awful!" Pam looked close to tears. "You mean he's been wandering around out of his head for all this time...I should have been there to help him!"

"It isn't that simple." I shook my head. "David might benefit from the right prescription, but he'll have to agree to take it, and that can be a tough sell to someone who's paranoid and out of touch with reality. Besides, you had no way of knowing. You can't blame yourself."

"But I thought he was doing drugs. I blamed him."

"You were a young, scared mother, not a psychiatrist. Come on, Pam, you have enough on your shoulders. Don't go looking for something else to load on just because your burden has been eased a little."

"You sound like Heidi." Pam smiled. "It must be a caregiver thing."

"Or just a common sense thing. Anyway, I'm hoping I'll locate him soon."

"If he hasn't left the area. You said no one has seen him for a couple of months."

"But Pastor Rankin seems sure he'll be around soon. Give it a few more days, okay?"

"I don't have much choice." Pam's eyes drifted toward the living room, and I knew what she was thinking. Little Davey didn't have much choice, either, or much time.

I parked in Thelma's driveway and we stepped out into newly falling snow. Thelma put her hand out and caught a few flakes on her palm, smiling. "Definitely lake effect. Big, fat, wet flakes. Good snowball fight weather."

Abruptly the snow started falling faster, and we turned for the house. By the time we reached the porch we were both covered in white. When the snow really cranked up like this it could bring two inches or more in an hour. I glanced back at my car and could barely see it through the thick curtain of snow.

Thelma and I hung around the house the rest of the day. We worked for a while on a jigsaw puzzle, chatting and listening to music. We ate lunch, me a tossed salad and Thelma a tuna salad sandwich, heavy on the onions.

Now and then we would stop at a window and look out at the falling snow. It hadn't let up, and by two o'clock there was a good six inches on the ground.

"I think you'd better leave early," Thelma declared after watching a plow rumble down the road, throwing huge gouts of snow onto the curbs.

"It's no big deal. I only have to drive a few blocks."

"Yeah, but that little car of yours is going to be dragging its bumper in this mess."

"Won't be the first time." This was, after all, Michigan. Our weather wasn't for wimps.

"Still, I'd prefer to know you were home safe. It's not just your driving you have to worry about, you know. There's plenty of folks out there without a clue how to drive in the snow."

"Are you sure you aren't just trying to get rid of me? You've never worried about me driving in the snow before."

"It just seems silly t hang out for another two hours when we aren't really doing much of anything. Go while the gettin' is good."

"All right, Thelma, I'll go."

"Call me if you hear anymore about David."

"I will."

Driving home was slow going. Visibility didn't extend more than a foot or two past my hood. Some of the roads had been plowed but the snow was falling too fast to keep them clear, and I was guessing they would pull the plows off all but the main emergency routes until it slowed down. It was a good afternoon to hunker down.

My house was extra quiet with the muffling blanket of snow. I let George out of his cage and turned the stereo on low before going in to change into flannel pajamas and thick fuzzy socks. I checked my bandage, saw only a tiny spot of blood had seeped through, and decided it was fine. See, I hadn't needed stitches at all!

I made myself a cup of hot chocolate and curled up on the couch to read. I hadn't had much time for that lately, and this unexpected free afternoon was a nice luxury. I was five chapters into my brother's book, and so far it was pretty amazing. It was a thriller involving a bartender pulled into a kidnapping plot against his will and better judgment. The characters were well defined and believable, the plot was building at a good pace and so far following a twisted but somehow logical line. I could hardly believe this had been written by my own brother.

The quiet only lasted a few minutes. The front door opened and Jack swept in on a blast of cold air. He stopped on the little square of tile by the door and brushed snow off his head and shoulders.

"Ha! It's really coming down out there!"

"So I noticed." He unlaced his boots and left them on the mat.

"Rachel didn't want to drive in this stuff anymore. She says her car isn't designed for it."

"It isn't."

"Is that why you're home so early?"

I smiled. "Thelma was afraid the snow would get higher than my bumpers if I didn't get home, so what the heck. I thought I'd enjoy a little quiet time."

"Oops, sorry!" Jack grinned. "Didn't mean to stomp all over your 'me time.'"

"That's okay. I'm just reading."

He came over and looked at the thick sheaf of pages on my lap.

"What are you reading?"

"It's called 'One More for the Road,' and my brother wrote it."

"Really? Is it any good?"

"It's excellent!"

"Want to share? Let me read what you've finished."

"I don't think I should without asking Jason. Why don't you grab a book off the shelf?"

"Huh. I haven't sat down and read a novel in...well, let's just say I think I had a teacher standing over me with a yardstick threatening bodily harm if I didn't do it."

"I saw all kinds of books at your house!"

"Yep, all non-fiction. Politics, war, a little science, now and then an autobiography, although most of *those* probably count as fiction."

I laughed. "Probably. But once in a while you need to read a good novel. It's like junk food for the brain. It's as soothing as chocolate."

"Yeah? What kind of books do you have? Lots of sappy romance?"

I gave him a look. "*Really*, Jack?"

He smiled. "Hey, I didn't think you'd be into that, but everyone has their little secret vices, right?"

"I guess so." I briefly considered what Jack's might be, but I cut that line of questioning off. I really don't think I want to know.

"Why don't you try Lee Child? His are always a good read."

I pointed at the bookshelf on the far wall. "Top shelf. Start with "The Killing Floor."

"Start with?" Jack laughed and looked at the row of Lee Child books. "You must really think I'll like it if you believe I'll get through all of them."

"Trust me."

"I always have."

Jack pulled the book off the shelf and settled into a side chair, his feet on the coffee table.

An hour went by, the comfortable silence broken only by the whisper of pages turned.

Suddenly Jack laughed, and I looked over at the sudden noise. He was looking at the clock on the wall.

"Okay, you win, Rainie. This book is really good! What a great character!"

"I thought you'd like him."

"And Child must really do his research. Either that or he's exceptionally talented at making up bullshit facts and making them sound right."

"What do you think of the fight scenes?"

"Accurate, detailed and interesting. Just graphic enough to be exciting, and more or less plausible, if you believe Reacher is what he is."

"An oversized ex-soldier with an intimate knowledge of human anatomy?"

"Well, an intimate knowledge of how to *break* human anatomy, anyway."

"Close enough!"

Jack stretched and set the book aside. "I think I'll go fix dinner. You like pork chops?"

"Not really."

"You'll like them the way I make them." Jack got up and went into the kitchen, as confident about his cooking skills as he was about everything else he tackled. But pork chops? I hadn't had one in years. Well, I guess one won't kill me.

I set Jason's book aside and decided to get my laundry caught up.

Chapter Fifteen

I got up the next day to find the outside world obliterated by white.

At seven a.m. the sun wasn't quite up, so I flicked on the porch light for a better view. The snow was still coming down, but worse, the wind had picked up. I couldn't see anything but blowing snow past the edge of the porch. I couldn't really see the edge of the porch; the snow had drifted up over the steps until it appeared the porch was at ground level.

Jack appeared beside me, silent in his bare feet. "Harry already closed operations for the day, except critical functions. You'll find a text alert on your phone; he sends mass texts on the rare occasions he closes the office."

I thought about David, and the urgency of locating him. "What's considered a critical function?"

"Ongoing security and bodyguard duties. All P.I. stuff is shut down."

"Huh." I peered out, looking for my car, but it was just another hump of white somewhere out in the whiteness. I guess it would be a little difficult to get into Niles.

"Guess I'll check the weather."

I turned on the TV and found a local news station. Weather reports tended to annoy me. They were sensationalized and exaggerated, a play for ratings more than public information, but it was all we had to work with. The key to getting anything useful out of them was to listen for the facts, such as temperature, wind speed and recorded snowfall, and ignore such phrases like "dangerous conditions" and "severe weather."

They showed a graphic with reported snowfall around the area, and as usual the lake effect had dumped on some places and not on others. Buchanan was reporting twenty-six inches, but Niles had only gotten fourteen. The west side of South Bend had been hit hard, but to the east it wasn't as bad. Snow emergencies had been declared in most of the nearby counties, which meant you weren't supposed to be on the road unless it was absolutely necessary.

Of course, "absolutely necessary" was open to interpretation.

I sighed. Authorities in the Michiana area had the know-how and plows to get the roads cleared, but the logistics of getting twenty-six inches of wind-blown snow off all the roads meant it was going to be a while before my little Escort could make it any real distance. I was sure I could make it to Bob's, but Gretchen had said she was willing to stay over, and it was quite possible she would prefer not to drive home until the roads were cleared.

I called her, and she answered cheerfully.

"Good morning, Rainie! Pretty out, isn't it?"

"Pretty messy. I was wondering if you still wanted to stay over."

"Bob and I were just talking about that. He doesn't think either one of us should drive until the plows get a chance to get at the roads. He says you should stay home. I think he wants to beat me at Scrabble again."

"He must be feeling better if he's playing games."

"Not just playing, winning!" Gretchen laughed. "Tell me, is 'xi' a real word?"

"Yep, it's in the Scrabble dictionary."

"That's what Bob says, but he conveniently can't find his."

"Well, he won't really cheat you, but if you want to browse through it in self-defense I happen to know it's on the bookshelf in the den, bottom shelf, right between "War and Peace" and an autobiography of Bob Hope."

"Ah ha! All right, I'll go dig it out. So how late do you think I should stay?"

"I'll call Daryl in a while and ask him. If Bob is doing that well you can probably go as soon as the roads are clear."

"Okay, let me know. I'll talk to you later."

People from outside the Midwest could never appreciate the quiet joy of an unplanned snow day. For the kids, it was an unexpected break from the school routine, and often meant building snow forts and snow men until cold fingers and toes drove them inside for hot chocolate and an afternoon of video games. If the parents were stranded at home as well, there might even be board games brought out, and rousing games of Monopoly might break out all over the state.

Then there were us single folks. We could catch up on housework and reading, or take a nap. Once the roads were open a lot of people would probably hit the slopes for skiing or sledding, but I wasn't much for either one.

Jack called about his truck, which was supposed to be delivered by noon. He hung up, pissed off.

"My truck is sitting on a flatbed, stranded at a truck stop. They're hoping it'll arrive tomorrow, but if not I'll have to wait until Monday."

"If the snow lets up I'm sure it'll get through tonight."

"I should have rented a car. I hate being stuck all weekend."

"I don't think you'd be going anywhere today, anyway."

"I guess." Jack went off to his room.

The wind and snow both stopped around mid-morning, and Jack and I went out and shoveled the walk and the driveway and cleaned the huge mound of snow off my little car. The road had been plowed to one lane, but there wasn't any place I particularly needed to be, so I went back in to warm up.

Jack was doing his best to be a good house guest, staying out of my way. He spent some time on line and a little more time reading, but by lunchtime he was prowling the house like a caged tiger, peering out the windows every few minutes to check the weather. Finally he pulled on his coat and hat.

"I'm going out for a while."

"Okay." I watched him go, wondering where the hell he was planning to go. Oh well, not my business.

I put away the last of my laundry and cleaned George's cage. I stood in the living room, hands on hips, deciding what to do next. I wasn't in the mood to write any poetry, and I could only sit and read for so long. I wanted to do something.

It occurred to me Jack had been gone for over an hour. I wondered where he went. I looked out the front window, half-expecting to see him coming up the front walk. Nope, no Jack.

The kids next door seemed to be involved in building a snow fort. In fact, it looked like every kid in the neighborhood was over there, swarming over the snow covered yard. Wait a minute, that tall kid in the black coat...it was Jack! What the heck was he doing with a bunch of kids?

Curious, I threw on my coat, hat, scarf and gloves and ventured out.

"Hey Rainie!" Jack saw me standing in the driveway. "We're about to get started with our snowball fight. Want to join?"

"I don't think..."

"Oh, come on, Miss Lovingston!" Cheryl, the twelve year old who lived next door, called over to me. "We hardly have any girls!"

"That's because girls can't throw snowballs for crap!" That teasing comment came from Phil Christopher, an adolescent from down the block.

"Is that right?" I took up the challenge. "We'll see who can throw and who can't!" I slogged through the snow to join up on Cheryl's side.

The snow fort was surprisingly elaborate, with three sides tapering down in the back and spaces left here and there to look through. "Those are for engaging the enemy without exposing yourself to fire," Cheryl explained, and I nodded. I could see Jack's influence all over this.

"All right guys, gather around here!" Jack called his crew over behind the wall.

"I think he's discussing strategy," Mike Anton observed. He was fourteen, a solemn kid with plastic framed glasses. "You know any good strategies, Miss Lovingston?"

"First of all, please call me Rainie. Secondly, as a matter of fact I *do* know a few tricks. My brother was all about winning snow ball wars. Gather round here, and I'll tell you what we're going to do..."

Fifteen minutes into the fight Cheryl's parents came out on the porch to watch. Five minutes after that, Cheryl's dad had joined our side and her mom had scooted over to Jack's.

Before I knew it half the parents in the neighborhood, all home for the snow day, had joined in the fun. I'd never seen anything like it. New forts sprang up in neighboring yards and even across the street, and snowballs were flying from and to all directions. Someone's dog, a big black lab, got into the fray, snatching snowballs out of the air. It was obvious he thought they were tennis balls, and I laughed at the repeated look of confusion on his face when they crumbled and dissolved in his mouth.

Even Mrs. Haggerty, who at eighty-nine had no kids to join the fun, decided to get involved. She declared her porch the "Red Cross/med-evac tent" and dispensed hot chocolate from a thermos to those who needed to warm up or even just take a breather. Snow ball fights were hard work!

Sadly, even the most entertaining days must come to an end, and as dinnertime approached we all started drifting back to our respective homes, exhausted but reluctant to see it end. It had been a spontaneous day of fun and camaraderie, and it wasn't likely to ever happen again. We would all retreat back into our heated homes for the remainder of the winter, and wave to each other on our way to work or school, but probably not come together like this again. It didn't seem possible to plan this kind of event. They seemed to get started by some cosmic force unseen and unheard, and then to grow and expand under their own momentum.

"That was a lot of fun." Jack said as he stripped off his wet gear.

"That...magical!"

"Magical?" Jack started to laugh, but he must have seen something in my face. "I don't know about magical, but it was a rare day. Not something you could plan on ahead of time."

"Just like I said. Magical."

Michael called at five o'clock. "Hey, I've been trying to reach you all day. Is everything all right?"

"Sure. I was outside all afternoon. We had a snowball fight."

"We?"

"The whole neighborhood!"

"Sounds like fun." His tone was doubtful, and it was clear he didn't get it. There was no point trying to explain just how terrific it had been. You had to have been there.

"It was. So what's up?"

"Well, we had a date tonight, remember?"

"Oh! Yeah, of course! Are the roads clear enough to go?"

"The plows have been out all afternoon. I called the bar, and the band is still planning to show up."

"All right, I'd love to go."

"Great! I'll pick you up at seven thirty then?"

"I'll be ready."

I dressed carefully for my date. I wore a black gauze skirt and a black shirt that showed a little more cleavage than I usually exposed, and I took the time to blow dry my hair so it would have some lift and shine. As usual I didn't wear any make up. I had never gotten the knack of putting the stuff on without looking like a six year old who'd gotten into mommy's make up bag.

Jack was in his room when Michael got there, so once again I didn't mention our temporary living arrangements. As much as I believed that honesty was generally the best policy, I didn't want to blow our date. I'd been looking forward to it all week.

I ate a cheeseburger and a salad, foregoing the fries. I felt guilty about the cheeseburger, but I'd learned my lesson well about drinking on an empty stomach. The plates were cleared away and we ordered beers and chatted while we waited for the band to set up.

By the time they started playing I was two beers into it, and they didn't sound too bad. By their second set I was four beers into it and I decided they were pretty damned good. Michael and I even got up and danced, something I hadn't done since my party days. Most guys I had dated didn't dance, and I have to admit Michael was pretty brave to try it. He didn't so much *dance* as shuffle his feet and throw his arms around a lot while making funny little faces like he was really getting into it.

We sat down at the end of the second set, a little overheated. Michael looked at our empty beers.

"Ready for another?"

"I don't know..." I did a head check on myself. Four beers was quite a lot for me. I had a pleasant buzz, but thanks to the food I wasn't drunk yet. I thought it best to keep it that way.

"I don't think so. Maybe a Coke or something."

"We could go back to my place. I have Coke in the fridge."

He said it casually, but I felt my breath catch just the same. Back to his place. For a Coke...and maybe a tour of his bedroom?

I didn't say anything for a minute, considering the question. Finally I smiled.

"Sure, I'd love to have a Coke with you."

Michael dropped me off at home at nine o' clock the next morning with a promise to call me later. Our kiss goodbye was brief. Unlike Jack, Michael didn't keep a supply of new toothbrushes on hand for unexpected overnight guests, and I'd cleaned my teeth with a smear of toothpaste on my finger. My mouth still tasted like stale beer and old shoes. Or at least, what I imagined old shoes must taste like. I'm happy to report I've never actually tasted any.

I practically floated into the house, feeling light and ridiculously happy.

"Hey, George!" I went to let him out of his cage, but he was already basking under his light on the shelf. Oh yeah, I'd forgotten about Jack. He must have let him out.

And speaking of Jack, there he was, standing in the kitchen doorway, looking as pissed as I've ever seen him.

"Where the hell have you been all night?"

"With Michael..." I answered automatically before it occurred to me he had no right to ask.

"And you couldn't find the time to call me?"

"Why the hell would I call you?"

"Didn't it occur to you that I'd be worried?"

"No, it didn't! Why would it?"

"Because I was expecting you home, and with your lifestyle, who knows what trouble you might have gotten into?"

"My *lifestyle*? You mean the P.I. crap that *you* got me started in? Besides, you knew I was on a date with Michael. I'm sure you're bright enough to figure out where I was, and that I was perfectly safe. I only gave you a room to sleep in, I didn't adopt you as my surrogate mother!"

"You're right, I'm sorry." Jack lifted a hand to stop the tirade. "It just freaked me out a little when I woke up at three and you still weren't home."

"You went in to check on me?" I was outraged. How often did he sneak into my bedroom at night when I was sleeping?

"I never heard you come in. I *am* sorry, really."

"Fine." I waved him off. I wanted to get back to the good mood I'd been enjoying when I got home.

Jack offered me a little grin. "So, how was the accountant in bed? Calculating?"

"What the hell! That's *really* none of your business!"

"Hey, sorry, just kidding around!"

"Well that's not funny!" I went to my room and slammed the door.

I brushed my teeth and took a long hot shower, and by the time I'd dried off and dressed my temper had cooled. Maybe Jack even had a point. I didn't have the greatest track record lately when it came to staying out of trouble.

I came into the living room to find Michael standing there, talking to Jack. Actually, it looked more like Jack was talking to him.

"Michael, what are you doing here?" Okay, that was probably rude, but he *had* stopped by without calling first, one of my pet peeves. On the other hand, I'd never told him not to, because the issue had never come up. Truth was, I was just freaking out a little bit that he'd found out about Jack being here, and it wouldn't be a problem at all if I had just told him about it. How was I supposed to explain not telling him for a whole week?

"I just stopped by to bring you this." He held out my cell phone. "I found it under the couch."

"Oh, thanks." I blushed, remembering our frantic fumbling on the couch.

"Yeah, no problem." He took a step toward the door.

"Sorry to hear about your house." He glanced at Jack. "I hope it works out okay."

"I'm sure it will. I have good insurance."

"Well, I'll see you, Rainie."

What, not even a quick kiss?

Nope. He glanced almost furtively at Jack, and went out the door.

Huh. That was weird.

I looked at Jack. "What did you say to him?"

"Me? Nothing. Just told him about the fire and how you let me stay here. I was kind of surprised to hear you hadn't told him yet."

"I just haven't gotten around to it."

"Yeah, well he was pretty surprised." Jack grinned.

"I'll bet." I sighed. Had I really thought I could keep these living arrangements secret? And really, why had I wanted to in the first place?

"I'd better go talk to him." I shoved my feet into my shoes and grabbed my coat on the way out the door. Michael was just getting into his car.

"Michael, wait!"

He hesitated, and for a minute I thought he was going to just drive away. He reluctantly got out but didn't close the car door, as if he was keeping his line of quick retreat open.

"Michael, I'm sorry. I should have told you he was here."

"You think?"

"I almost told you a few times, but then...I don't know. I just didn't."

"Well, now I know."

"It isn't anything, really. He's just staying in the spare room."

"It isn't anything?" Michael's look could have peeled paint off a wall. "You spend the night with me while you have another man waiting at home and it isn't anything?"

"He's just a friend."

"Really? Then why didn't you tell me about this?"

"Because..." I stopped. I really didn't have an explanation. Not a good one, anyway. Well, that was easy enough to deal with. I just wouldn't. "Oh, to hell with it! You can think what you want!"

I spun on my heel, ready to make a dramatic exit, but I slipped on the icy driveway. I would have fallen on my butt if Michael hadn't reached out and grabbed me just in time.

"Whoa, are you okay?"

"I'm fine." I straightened out my coat and my dignity and started to turn away again.

"Wait, Rainie...I don't want to leave it this way."

"Whatever." I started to walk away.

"No, really...you know, that Jack is a really scary dude."

That stopped me. I blinked, processing that statement, and slowly turned back to face him.

"What do you mean?"

"He just had a 'talk' with me. I know you really like him, but he's really not a nice guy."

"He is when you get to know him."

"Okay, but still...I mean, there are hotels, you know."

"He's a friend and his home just burned to the ground! I couldn't just dump him off somewhere."

"I get that, but...are you sure he's just a friend?"

"Michael, I've explained our relationship to you already. Are you accusing me of lying?"

"No, it's just…why didn't you tell me he was here?"

"I don't know," I answered honestly. "Maybe because our relationship was kind of new and I thought it might be hard to explain. I guess I was right, because here we are."

"This isn't really about him staying here. I'm kind of wondering…well, does Jack know he's just a friend?"

"Just what did he say to you?"

"He said you have a lot of friends, and they wouldn't be happy if I did anything to hurt you."

"Well, that's not so bad, even if it is none of his business."

"It wasn't just *what* he said. You had to see his *eyes* when he said it." Michael grimaced. "Like I said: a scary dude."

"Jack always looks scary." I was still trying to play this off as nothing, but actually it was kind of freaking me out. Since when did Jack have the authority to go around threatening my boyfriends? And why would he want to?

"That isn't all," Michael went on. "He knows things about me."

"Knows things? Like what?"

"Like where I went to high school, and what kind of grades I got. Did you know he ran a background check on me?"

Now I was clenching my teeth, my blood boiling.

"No, I didn't know that, and I can't imagine why he did."

"I don't know either, but it's pretty weird. I don't have anything to hide. I've actually lived a ridiculously normal life, but that isn't the point, is it?"

"No, it's not." I stared at the driveway for a minute, watching the steam from my breath rise in long streams as I pulled in cold air to cool my temper. "I'm sorry, Michael, I don't know why he did that." I looked at him, and my temper hadn't cooled much at all. "But the fact is he only warned you not to hurt me. If you didn't plan to do that you didn't have anything to worry about, so why run away?"

"I'm not running away…"

"Of course you are! You couldn't get away fast enough. Were you even planning to talk to me about it or just ditch me over the phone?"

"I just needed to think about things first."

"You mean think about Jack, and whether I was worth the trouble."

"Well…" And then Michael said something that endeared him to me: he told the truth. "Yeah, I guess that's exactly right."

I frowned, not sure what to say. I had expected him to deny it.

"I'm not a fighter, Rainie. I mean, I don't consider myself a coward. I'd step forward to defend myself or someone else if necessary. I guess the question in my mind is this: is this a fight worth waging? Is Jack really just a friend to you or am I risking an ass-kicking for nothing?"

"I've told you…"

"I know what you've told me. You like working with him and he's a good friend, but you can't imagine it ever going anywhere other than that. The thing is, you don't seem to think he would ever take it further, that you aren't his 'type.' I think you're wrong. I think you're exactly what he wants."

I had been told this before, and I still didn't believe it. Besides, the fat girl in me was cringing at the image of getting intimate with Jack. Even if he did think I looked all right with my clothes on, he would be turned off fast enough if he saw me naked. I couldn't bear the image of his look of disgust, of him turning away from me. And the humiliation would go on long afterward, every time I saw him around the office…nope, never going to happen.

I didn't say any of that to Michael, of course. I just shook my head.

"I have no interest in having that kind of relationship with Jack, even if by some wild chance you're right. I'll even admit he's flirted with me now and then, but I don't have any interest in becoming another one-night notch on his bedpost."

"You mean he's tried to…sleep with you?"

"Not really. I think he just finds me amusing. His flirting isn't serious."

"Okay, I believe you." Michael took a deep breath. "So, do you want to continue or did I screw it up too bad?"

I considered that.

"You really should have just talked to me in the first place. It was pretty cowardly to just walk away."

"Like it was cowardly not to tell me Jack was staying with you?"

"Okay, you're right. We both screwed this up."

"So what else can I say? I'm sorry."

"So am I." I held out my hand. "So, we forgive each other?"

"Really? A handshake?" It was his turn to shake his head. He ignored my hand and kissed me instead. "Do you want to come over for dinner tonight? I'll cook."

"I have some work to do in Niles, but then I'm free for the evening. So, seven o'clock?"

"I'll see you then."

He got in his car and drove away. It was only then that I remembered how pissed off I was at Jack. I stomped into the house.

"Jack! I need to talk to you!"

"What's up?" he came out of the kitchen, looking so cool butter wouldn't melt in his mouth.

"Who the hell do you think you are, threatening my boyfriend?"

"You mean Michael? I didn't threaten him."

"He says you did. And what's this crap about a background check?"

"Oh that. Hey, I just wanted to make sure he checked out all right..."

"Checked out all right? What business is that of yours?"

"I was worried you were moving too fast with the guy. You haven't known him all that long, and you were already talking long term."

"No, *you* were talking long term! *You* were the one asking if I was in love with him."

"Well, now you've slept with him, so I guess you made up your mind."

"If you think so then why threaten him now?"

"Because I don't want him to hurt you."

"And you thought breaking us up wouldn't hurt me?"

"I wasn't trying to break you up..."

"Bullshit, Jack! This isn't the first time you've gotten between me and a guy I liked. I'm sick of you interfering in my life! It was a mistake to let you stay here. You need to get out."

"My truck will be in on Monday..."

"No! Not Monday. Today. Now. Call Rachel or someone and have them take you to a hotel. I'm done with you, Jack! Get the hell out of my life!"

I snatched up my car keys and stomped out the door.

Chapter Sixteen

I drove to Niles, taking it easy on the snow packed roads in Buchanan. As I neared Niles the level of snow dropped off considerably, and the roads were almost clear, thanks to the quirks of the snow bands coming off the lake.

I was still so mad I was shaking, so I went through the Burger King drive thru in Niles and ordered some breakfast food. I needed the carbs to calm me down and clear my head.

I parked in the lot to eat it, shoving it into my mouth and barely bothering to chew. Binge eating was one of my worst habits, one I only resorted to when I was really upset, and this morning qualified.

I wasn't pissed off at Jack only because of what he'd done, but for the results. I really did like hanging around with him, and now he'd ruined it. What the hell had possessed him to interfere in the first place? Why did he care who I was dating?

I didn't have an answer, and I needed to put it all aside. I was hoping to find David today, and I wanted to concentrate on that.

My stomach full, my mood chilled by the overload of fat and carbs, I got my mind on business. I pulled out onto US 933 and drove south, past the crowded business district, to the section of woods where Pastor Rankin had last seen David.

I slowed as I passed the credit union and peered at the stretch of woods.

It was only a couple of hundred yards long, but it went back quite a ways. Behind it there was a relatively new subdivision, and the woods served as a sound buffer from the road. Even so, I figured it was only a matter of time before this area was taken over by redevelopment, and the trees would be gone. They would probably put in some kind of complex and give it an ironic name like "Woodland Acres."

The woods looked pristine and untouched by man, covered in a mantle of fresh white snow. The tree line started about twenty feet back from the road, and the snow was smooth and bright in the sunshine. There was too much traffic for me to go slower than forty-five miles an hour. If I had any hope of seeing signs of David I was going to have to do it on foot.

There was no parking on 933, so I parked my car on a side road. I checked to be sure I had my cell phone and walked the short distance back to the highway.

There was no sidewalk, and the snow was piled in a dirty line just off the curb, a formidable obstacle should I find myself needing to leap out of the way of a speeding truck. I had to keep an eye out for oncoming traffic while at the same time scanning the edge of the woods for signs that someone had passed this way.

Then again, how much of a path would one man make, even if he came and went at least once a day? I wasn't sure. I wasn't even sure he came out once a day.

But then I saw it: a clear trail of footprints in the smooth snow, leading into the woods.

I stood and stared at the path for a minute. Did I really want to go in there alone in search of a possibly delusional man?

Eddie was in Chicago, so I couldn't call him, and Jack...well, I simply *wouldn't* call him. The last time I asked Tommy to help I almost got him killed. I guess that left me. Well, what was the big deal? I was just going to talk to the guy, right?

I climbed awkwardly over the snow pile, sinking to my knees here and there where the snow wasn't packed as tightly. I was glad for my leather gloves. The snow under the fresh layer was ice encrusted and sharp.

I made it over and followed the trail into the woods. It was rough going. Yesterday's snow fall had left a fresh layer calf deep over the hard, frozen stuff below. About every third step my foot would break through the crusted snow and I'd sink to my knee. On another step the snow might be packed down to ice, and I would slip and slide until I got back to the crusty stuff again. It seemed like I trudged for an hour that way, but it probably only took about ten minutes to make it into a small clearing.

The first thing I noticed was the vague shape of a car buried under a winter's worth of snow. I had no idea how the car had gotten here; certainly not down the narrow path I'd walked in. I wasn't sure if it was an Oldsmobile, but I would have been willing to bet on it if someone had been around to take my action. It looked like it had been parked here for years.

The second thing I noticed was a man getting out of the car, sliding through the passenger side window, which had been covered by an old white tarp. He slid through with the speed and agility of long practice and stood about five feet away from me. He was tall and his face was gaunt. I couldn't tell about the rest of him. He was wearing a dirty, shin-length trench coat over what looked like several more layers of clothing. Clumps of filthy blonde hair stuck out under a black wool watch cap, and his long beard was matted and graying.

"Who are you?" He asked.

"My name is Rainie Lovingston..."

"Livingston? What, are you some explorer? If you are, these woods aren't much."

"No," I replied. As often as I'd gotten that nonsense, in this case I didn't think the guy was kidding. He seemed very sincere. "It's Lovingston, with an 'O.' Are you Dave Swanson?"

His eyes narrowed. "That information is need to know. Do you?"

"Do I what?"

"Need to know." He spoke patiently, as if he was used to dealing with ignorance, maybe even expected it.

"Yes, I do need to know. I'm here about your son..."

Apparently that was exactly the wrong thing to say. As if I'd ignited some inner raging engine he rushed at me, his eyes burning with hatred, his arms raised, and belatedly I saw the fist size rock in his hand.

I screeched and ducked, but not fast enough.

A dazzling burst of light and pain exploded in my skull and then...

I came to in darkness, my teeth chattering from the cold. I tried to sit up and moaned from the pain in my head. In my early twenties I had suffered from migraines, pounding, nauseating headaches that made even the dimmest of light and the smallest of sounds rip through my skull like wolves tearing into the soft underbelly of a deer.

That's what I felt like now. I was disoriented and confused, and for a few moments I thought I was home in bed, the curtains drawn, waiting for a migraine to pass.

I closed my eyes and held absolutely still until the worst of the nausea and throbbing subsided. I wondered why I didn't have an ice pack on my eyes. I always had an icepack when the migraines got this bad. I cautiously cracked my eyes open again.

I could see the dim outline of the back of a car seat, and slowly everything came back. This wasn't a migraine; it was more likely a concussion delivered from a large rock. I guessed I was in the snow-covered Oldsmobile.

I didn't guess anything else. I went back under, into the absolute dark of unconsciousness.

I came around again and opened my eyes to more darkness.

I think I had been awake a couple of times, but I'm not sure. There were vague impressions of gray light, always accompanied by the crushing pain and rolling waves of nausea, followed by longer periods of nothing.

I took a moment, trying to get my bearings. Once again I saw the back of the car seat, and slowly the memory of where I was and how I got here came back to me. I didn't want to go under again; I had to get out of here!

I tried to sit up, and only then realized I couldn't feel my hands or arms. In a panic I started to thrash around, but that only brought on a fresh wave of pain, nausea and dizziness, and I dropped my head back to the leather-covered seat and moaned.

After a few minutes I tried moving my hands. They were trapped underneath me, so I slowly rolled to the side and wriggled them a little. Shortly I was rewarded with that tingling sting that meant my hands were tied and asleep, not permanently paralyzed. I moved my legs, relieved that at least my feet weren't tied.

"Hello?" I called out softly. Immediately someone popped up from the front seat and peered back at me.

"Where's my son?" Dave's hoarse voice demanded.

"W-with Pam!" I stammered.

In a flash he'd reached across the seats and his hand was clutching my throat. He squeezed and I felt a flash of fear more intense than the pain in my head and I tried to jerk my head away.

"Don't lie to me, devil! Tell me where you're keeping him!"

I gasped for air but couldn't speak with his hand constricting my airway. I tried to kick him but I couldn't get any leverage and he hardly seemed to notice the ineffectual blows. He realized I couldn't speak and lightened his grip.

"Tell me!"

"I- I'm not keeping him! He's with Pam…she sent me to find you…"

"You think I'm stupid? Of course you do. You all thought that. Fucking government, thinks we're all sheep…think none of us know what you're doing…you just take and take and use us all like pawns on a chessboard…" He was rambling, clearly talking more to himself than to me, his words coming out in a rapid staccato. "You take my son, you chase after me, and all for nothing… I was never going to do it…I wouldn't have taken over the world no matter how much they urged me… I just wanted little Davey safe…"

Suddenly he let go of my throat and dropped his head on the back of the seat, sobbing as if his heart was breaking.

"I just wanted him safe, and you took him...my little Davey...just a baby, but you don't care...you don't care..."

I wasn't sure what I was dealing with here, but he was clearly delusional. I've dealt with such things before. It's more common than you'd think among the elderly, who can be pushed over the edge into more than confusion by well-meant prescription drugs or in response to illness.

"He's not a baby anymore," I said as gently as I could. "He's ten years old..."

"You do have him!" He launched himself across the back seat and straddled me, grabbing my shoulders and pressing me into the seat, his face inches from mine, his breath smelling like carrion and rotten eggs. "What have you done with him!"

"Please!" I gasped and squirmed. "I'm trying to help..."

"I know about your kind of help! Just tell me where he is!"

"I can take you to him!"

That made him stop. He glared at me, calculating.

"It's a trick. You just want to get me, too. It's always been about that, hasn't it? You never wanted him, you just wanted to trick me into coming in."

"No, not a trick!" I wheezed. It was hard to take a real breath with him kneeling on my diaphragm. "I'll take you to him, I swear..."

"If I go with you, turn myself in, will you let him go?"

"Yes!" I decided to play along with his delusion, anything to get him to take his weight off of me. "We never needed him...come with me, we'll let him go..."

Dave abruptly scooted back into the front seat, babbling a hundred miles per hour. "Tricky...won't do it...probably dead, but if I don't, gotta think, think,

255

damn it!" He slapped himself in the head four or five times. "Gotta get him out of there...but if they have me...little Davey...poor little Davey..."

In a flash he slipped out of the tarp-covered window and I heard his babbling voice fade into the distance.

I rolled back onto my side and started wriggling my hands again in hopes of determining how tightly they were bound. The headache hadn't subsided much, but it had become a lower priority now that it was clear I was probably about to die at the hands of a madman.

I struggled to a sitting position. I twisted my wrists and instantly regretted it. They were tied with some sort of coarse rope and I could feel it cut into my skin. Even so I pulled and twisted for a minute, hoping to break free.

No such luck.

Okay, I would have to do it the hard way.

I leaned forward and pushed myself over the back of the seat. It would have been an awkward movement using my hands. Without them, it was a humping, gasping maneuver, and I went over face first, my head banging into the arm rest on the passenger side door.

I swallowed a cry of pain. I couldn't hear Dave at the moment, and I hoped he'd wandered far away, but just in case I didn't want to attract his attention.

I squirmed around until I was on my knees, facing the tarp over the window, and had to stop for a long minute, holding back sobs. My head was throbbing like the bass drum in a rock concert and I was in imminent danger of throwing up. I forced myself to take a few deep, cleansing breaths and pushed the pain back with a reminder that if I stayed here I was going to die.

Freshly determined, I stuck my head through the window opening and pushed off with my legs. I stopped halfway through, my top half dangling out the window, my bottom half still in the car. There was no way to make this easy. I took a deep breath and pushed off again, twisting at the same time so at least I wouldn't land face-first.

I dropped two feet onto the crusted snow, landing on my back. The impact jarred my head and dragged an involuntary moan out of me, but I cut it off in a hurry and rolled over onto my knees.

It was full dark, but there was a three quarter moon overhead that made it possible to see basic shapes and outlines. I held still for a minute, listening. At first there was total silence, but then I heard the bare *swish* of a car going by on the distant road. Well, not so distant if it was a clear spring day and I was in top form. But in the dark and snow and with my head throbbing and my hands tied, it seemed that it might as well have been thirty miles away.

Well, as Confucius said, "a journey of a thousand miles begins with a single step."

Yeah, but did Confucius ever try it in two feet of snow with his hands tied behind his back? I doubt it, or he would never have taken that first step. He would have crawled back onto his pallet on the floor and gone back to sleep! I nonetheless pushed myself to my feet and took a step.

And immediately fell again. The snow was well packed from Dave's frequent coming and going, and it was like climbing an ice sculpture, and without my hands free I had no sense of balance.

Fine. I got to my knees and moved slowly away from the car at an angle to Dave's path until I was in the fresh snow. My heart was pounding, and the little voice inside me was urging me to hurry, but I knew I had to take my time now. I would probably only get one chance at this.

I stood and took a tentative step, then another. I was sinking just past my ankles with each step, but if I moved slowly I was able to stay on my feet.

I moved toward the tree line and the barely discernable path I followed in, slow step by excruciatingly slow step. I swear I could feel eyes on my back. I was sure I would feel Dave's hand clutch my shoulder any second, dragging me back to the car and certain death.

I picked up my pace, too scared to keep up the deliberate speed that I knew was required. A panic was building up in me, a frantic need to run. I tried to force it down, knowing it was probably just an overload of adrenalin. I trudged on, concentrating on where I was putting my feet, trying not to think about what – or who – might be coming up behind me.

The path seemed to stretch for miles. Time and again my feet punched through the frozen crust and I bogged down, and without my hands it required a combination of twisting, pulling, and a lot of cursing under my breath to get my foot free again for the next step.

I made progress, though. Eventually I could see cars passing on the road ahead, their headlights as welcome as the lighthouse beacons of old must have been to ships looking for shore. I was going to make it!

For some reason the sight of safety so close at hand made me want to hurry even more. Maybe it's from all those years of watching horror movies where the girl is almost safe, maybe even has her hand on the doorknob where her family waits inside...but oh no! The door is locked...she fumbles for the spare key...too late! The killer slashes her to death right on the front steps, inches from safety.

Okay, not the best thoughts for me to be having right now. It was making my imagination run wild. I could almost feel Dave's breath in my ear, right behind me...

"You! Stop!"

Oh crap. It was Dave, not so close I could really feel his breath, but close enough that he was probably going to catch me before I reached the road.

Caution was no longer an option. I lifted my knees as high as they would go and really started chugging through the snow. I screamed for help once, but realized how stupid that was. The people driving by probably had their windows closed tight and their radios at top volume, and screaming was only going to use precious air that I needed to keep my lungs functioning.

"Government bitch!" Dave growled behind me. "You'll give me my son or..."

I don't know "or" what. I had finally reached the road, but the pile of plowed snow at the edge seemed an almost impassable barrier. I tried to run up it and fell, and I felt Dave clutch the shoulder of my jacket.

"No! Let go of me!" I jerked away and rolled toward the road. I fell off the other side and landed with a grunt on the pavement, only to find headlights bearing down on me. I tried to roll back out of the way, but I knew I was going to be too late...

I heard the squeal of bad brake pads and the headlights started slewing back and forth, the car skidding out of control as the driver tried to slam on his brakes on the slippery road. I pulled myself into a fetal position, ready to die in the same shape I'd been born in.

There were more headlights and horns honking and the sound of metal on metal and Dave was swearing and trying to drag me to my feet and people were shouting and I think I might have been screaming for help...

"Hey, you! Let go of her!" It was a woman's voice, confident and commanding, a voice that was accustomed to being listened to.

Dave was trying to drag me back over the hump of snow, but now he let go of me and instead leapt over the embankment and started running for the woods.

"Someone stop that man!" The woman demanded, and then she was next to me, helping me to sit up. "You!" The woman pointed at an onlooker, a scared looking teenager with a pierced lip. "Call 911, police and ambulance, stat!"

I was bathed in the bright glow of headlights. The skidding car had come to a stop three feet from me, its rear end in the other lane. The woman kneeling over me was maybe sixty, with steel gray hair and a stern face. She was wearing flat heeled shoes and a long coat, which she pulled off and put over me.

"Miss? Can you tell me your name?" She was holding my chin and looking me in the eye.

"R-R-Rainie..." I replied through chattering teeth.

"Can you tell me what happened?"

"Hit me...tied...up..." I was having difficulty getting words from my brain to my mouth. It seemed like some of the wires were crossed up.

"Does anyone have a pocket knife?" The woman asked the gathering crowd. In the distance I could hear sirens. Someone must have produced a knife, because the woman cut the ropes on my wrists and examined them in the headlights.

"Nurse?" I asked, making another one of those brilliant deductions that would someday make me such a great detective.

She smiled for the first time. "I'm a surgical RN at St. Joseph Hospital. I think you might have a concussion, and your wrists are badly abraded, but I think you'll be okay."

"Been...worse..." I tried to smile back. The ambulance arrived, and before I knew it I was wrapped in blessedly warm blankets on my way to the hospital. Relieved, I fell asleep.

Chapter Seventeen

They didn't let me sleep for long, since they were pretty certain I had a concussion. I was pretty sure, even without the tests they insisted on running, that they were right. I was nauseous and disoriented and I was really wishing my head belonged to someone else right now.

"You'll need to stay the night," the doctor informed me. "If all goes well you can go home first thing in the morning. Is there anyone we can call for you?"

"I can…" I looked around, suddenly remembering my cell phone. "My phone…" As soon as I said it I realized it was ridiculous. Dave had certainly taken it. I was surprised when the nurse spoke up.

"It's right here." She held up a plastic bag that held my phone and my car keys. Huh, I wondered why Dave hadn't taken it away from me. Hadn't he even searched me for weapons? And what the hell, you mean I could have called for help any time? Assuming, of course, that I could have reached the phone in my pocket with my hands tied…

"Miss Lovingston?" The doctor prompted me, and I realized I was drifting down that meandering mental path that so often took me away in times of stress.

"Sorry. Yeah, I'll call my mom." I took the phone out of the bag and made the call.

"Rainie! Where have you been! Everyone has been frantic all weekend…"

"All weekend?" I blinked, trying to process that. "What day is it?"

"It's Sunday. When Michael called looking for you..."

"Michael called? Mom, wait, I'm having a little trouble here. Why did Michael call?"

"You were supposed to go to his house for dinner, and you didn't show up and you weren't at home and he called everyone, but no one knew where you were, and the *cops* didn't even want to go looking right away, although I'm sure if they thought you had a little *weed* they could bust you for they'd have looked quick enough..."

"Mom...please, I'm having a little trouble following you."

"I'm sorry, honey, we've all been so worried..."

"I know mom, I'm sorry. I'm all right, but they want me to stay overnight for observation."

"I'll be right there!"

"No Mom, don't do that. I feel like crap, I just want to sleep if they'll let me. But could you come in the morning and give me a ride home?"

"Of course, sweetie. Are you sure you don't want us to come now..."

"No, Mom, really. I just want to rest, okay?"

"All right, honey. I love you."

"Love you, Mom. I'll see you tomorrow."

The nurses woke me up every hour to check my vital signs and to shine a light in my eyes to check for proper pupil dilation. Apparently I did all right, because first thing in the morning they told me I could check out.

I called Mom to be sure she was on her way and got dressed.

While I was waiting for my mom a police officer came to ask me a few more questions. He informed me that a search of the woods revealed the abandoned car and signs that someone had been living there for some time, but there was no sign of Dave Swanson. He was gone again, maybe for another ten years.

I felt tears prick at my eyes. Poor little Davey. It was too bad his mother couldn't afford a *real* detective, one that wouldn't have screwed up what might have been his only hope for survival.

Mom and Jedediah came to take me home. I had no sooner settled on my couch when Eddie showed up, not looking so much concerned as pissed.

"What the hell were you thinking, going off on your own that way?"

"Hey, don't yell at me! I'm a big girl, I can go where I want, when I want!"

"Not doing this kind of work, you can't! One of the first rules of this game is *never* go into an unknown situation without backup, or at the very least without letting someone know where you're going."

"I didn't have anyone to tell."

"Bullshit! You could have called me or Jack..."

"You were out of town, and I didn't *want* to talk to Jack."

"I don't want to hear about whatever petty shit is going on between you and Jack..."

"*Petty*? He threatened my boyfriend..."

"Whatever, I don't care! This isn't junior high, this is serious business, *literally* a matter of life and death! If you want to do this work you need to take it seriously and not let your emotions get the better of you."

"I *do* take it seriously!" I protested, but maybe not as hotly as I had a minute ago. The truth was it hadn't really occurred to me that I would be in that much danger. I mean, I was just going to talk to a guy. Okay, a possibly crazy guy who was hiding out in the woods...

Geez, maybe I *hadn't* taken this seriously enough.

Eddie was still talking, and I realized I had tuned him out to go along my little mental jaunt. I focused on him again.

"...could have called Tommy, or even Thelma, for God's sake! At least then we would have known where to look..."

"Okay, okay!" I held up a hand in surrender. "You're right, I get it. I should have left my itinerary with someone. I'll do that next time. Now, could you *please* stop yelling at me? I have a blasting headache!"

"I'm sorry," Eddie immediately lowered his voice. "I was just so damned scared for you..."

"Thank you, Eddie." I squeezed his hand. "It's nice to be cared about."

"There are plenty of us who care about you. Jack is almost frantic..."

"I don't really feel like talking anymore." I interrupted, putting a hand to my head and closing my eyes. I was being a bit overly dramatic, but I really didn't want to hear about Jack, and besides, my head really did hurt. It felt something like I imagined it would feel to have a couple of guys in steel-toes boots kicking me in the skull, and none too gently.

"Okay, I'll go." Eddie squeezed my hand this time. "Love ya."

"You too." I closed my eyes and he slipped out the door.

He no sooner left than my mom came out of the kitchen with an herbal icepack for my head. I accepted it gratefully, but I was over being babied.

"Mom, I love you, and I really appreciate all your help, but really, I'd rather be alone for a while."

"The doctor said..."

"Mom, since when do you put any stock it what a doctor says?" I grinned. "Really, I'm fine, I just need to rest."

"Oh honey, I love your independence, but sometimes you take it too far."

"I'm just going to sleep. I promise I can do that without damaging myself."

Finally convinced, mom kissed me on the forehead, extracted my solemn word that I would call her if I needed *anything*, and left.

I did lie on the couch for a few minutes, but in spite of the slamming in my head I was restless. I had unfinished business to tend to. For one thing, I had to call Pam, to let her know I had at least found her ex-husband. Of course, then I'd lost him again...

I called Pam and told her what had happened.

"Oh my god, I just can't believe it. He really tried to kill you? David was never violent, *never*!"

"I believe you, Pam. He's clearly delusional, and if I was hearing him right he thought I was a government agent who was keeping his son in custody. He has no idea that Davey is still with you."

"Do you think you can find him again? Davey needs him..."

"I think the police will find him. He assaulted me...they'll look for him now."

Pam sobbed. "That's just great! Now that he's *hurt* someone they'll finally take time to look for him, but when they find him they'll just put him in jail!"

"Maybe not. I'm hoping they'll put him in a psychiatric facility. He needs help."

"I'm sorry he hurt you."

"Don't be, it's not your fault. It's not anyone's fault, really, not even his. Anyway, I don't think he'll get far on foot. The police will probably have him in a couple of days."

"I hope so. Keep me up to date, will you?"

"Of course. I'll call if I hear anything, but the cops will probably call you first if they arrest him. You're still his wife."

"Okay." Pam's voice sounded small and defeated. I hung up and decided to lie down again, feeling a bit defeated myself.

I was dreaming about being back in the Oldsmobile. I knew it was a dream, because I was warm and I could smell bacon frying…

Bacon?

That brought me awake, and I sat up, too abruptly, and had to fight off a wave of nausea and dizziness that threatened to topple me off the couch. When it passed I sat still, sniffing the air and listening.

I could hear someone moving around in the kitchen.

"Who's here?" I called out, a little pissed off.

"It's me." Jack appeared in the dining room archway, a spatula in his hand. "How are you feeling?"

"What the hell are you doing here?"

"Hey, you're pretty cranky. Must still have a headache, huh?"

"You didn't answer my question."

"Just a minute." Jack went back into the kitchen and came back a minute later without the spatula. By that time I'd gotten off the couch and was heading in after him. He met me halfway

"Hey," he said softly, and touched the bruises on my throat, his fingers so feather light they sent shivers down my spine. "Why didn't you call me?"

I swallowed, wishing he'd get his fingers off of me, but wanting him to keep on touching me at the same time.

"I'm mad at you, remember?" I finally managed.

"Oh yeah." He gave me his "shucks, sorry about that, ma'am" grin, and I felt something deep in my belly melt a little. "Still, you shouldn't have gone out there alone." He took my hands and lifted them up, his thumbs lightly brushing the bandages on my wrists. "We've talked about the need for back up before, haven't we?"

"Eddie was in Chicago, and you…well, I didn't want to call you."

"I'm sorry." He sounded sincere.

"Don't be." I pulled my hands away from him, but I wasn't having much success maintaining my mad. "So why are you here? I told you to stay out of my life."

"Yeah, but I didn't think you meant *forever*!"

"It's been two days!"

"I know, I wanted to give you a little extra time to get over it."

"Are you kidding?"

He smiled. "Anyway, I thought I'd stick around for a day or so. You shouldn't be alone with that concussion."

"That's ridiculous. It isn't that bad."

"Even so, here I am."

"And if I tell you I don't want you here?"

"I'll pitch a tent in the backyard and come in every hour to check on you anyway."

"You can be a real pain in the ass, Jack."

"So I've been told." He shrugged. "So, you up for a BLT?"

I stared at him for five seconds, ten...he had no right to be here after I clearly threw him out. I needed to tell him to get lost.

Instead I said: "I'm starving!"

"Okay, give me five minutes." He turned to go back to the kitchen and I went back to collapse on the couch. Okay, so I'm a wimp when it comes to being mad at Jack. I don't know why I keep forgiving him so easily. Maybe it's because that bacon he was cooking smelled so heavenly.

Not long after dinner Jack went off to the spare room and I went off to my bed, exhausted even after a day of not doing much of anything. I barely had time to think "I'm falling asleep" before I was.

I woke up to a sticky hand being slapped over my mouth!

I jerked away and tried to scream, but the sticky hand was actually a piece of duct tape, and all that came out was a high pitched "MMMMM!"

Hands were dragging me off the bed and I twisted and kicked, trying to dislodge them. A smell assaulted my nose at the same time, the smell of something rotten and unwashed body, and I realized it was Dave Swanson. What the hell?

He'd managed to get my arms behind me and pulled me off the bed. He was dragging me toward the window, mumbling about his boy and government agent bitches and who knows what else. I kicked at the bedside table, hoping to break the lamp and make enough noise to wake Jack up, but the lamp fell to the carpeted floor with a muffled thump and remained intact.

"MMMM!" I was still trying frantically to scream, but I couldn't get any volume through the heavy tape. Dave threw me onto my stomach and shoved a knee into my back. He let go of my hands and I heard duct tape being ripped off a roll. No way was I going to let him tape my hands behind my back! I bucked and twisted and got turned over, but I hadn't dislodged him.

My bedroom door flew open and a dark shape moving sleek as a hunting cat came streaking across the room. Seconds later Dave was off me and Jack swung at him and I heard the loud *thwack* of the impact and Dave went down. Jack jumped on him, arm raised for another hit, and I tore the tape off my mouth.

"Don't hurt him!" I screamed. "Don't Jack! He's sick, he can't help it!"

Jack froze, one arm still raised, and glanced back at me.

"Don't hurt him? Are you kidding me?"

I fumbled for the lamp and righted it and turned it on. Dave was struggling now, and Jack needed both hands to keep him pinned to the floor.

"He needs meds, not a beating," I implored Jack. "He thinks I have his son! In his mind his behavior is totally justified."

"Christ, Rainie..." Jack was gritting his teeth with the effort of holding Dave still. I scrambled around and found the duct tape.

"Here, use this. I'll call the cops."

Jack shook his head, disgusted, but he did what I asked. I found the phone and called 911.

"911, what's your emergency?"

"This is Rainie Lovingston. A man broke into my house..."

"Is he still in the house, ma'am?"

"Yes, but he's...secured." Well secured. Jack had made short work of taping his hands and feet. "I need you to send an ambulance."

"An ambulance? What is the nature of your injury?'

"Not me, him...the guy who broke in. But he's not really injured, he's sick."

"What is the nature of his illness?" the dispatcher was rolling with it, his voice cool and professional.

"He's mentally ill...you should send someone..."

"The police are already on the way, ma'am. Please stay on the line until..."

"No, no, I'm not going to do that. I'll watch for the cops."

I disconnected. Jack stood up and moved away from Dave, who was flailing around to the best of his ability with his hands and feet tightly taped. He was screaming obscenities and nonsense, alternately pissed off and crying, a total mess.

"Only you would worry about the well-being of your kidnapper." Jack gave me a crooked grin. "Christ, Rainie, this guy tried to kill you – twice!"

"But only because he's trying to protect his son. He's clearly delusional, Jack. He's not responsible for his actions."

Jack sighed and lifted my hands again. The bandages had been torn away and my wrists were bleeding again.

"Damn it..."

"Never mind, Jack, it's okay." I heard sirens out front. One advantage to living in a small town, there might not be very many cops, but they were usually close by when you needed them. I went to let them in.

I knew the police officer first on the scene. In fact, I was getting to know all the Buchanan cops, probably better than they liked. This was Brubeck, and he'd been the one who came in response to the disturbance at Bob's last year. He remembered me, too.

"You're the caregiver detective, right? You got shot last year, and you helped some old guy who was getting robbed, right?"

"More or less."

I had to argue with him about arresting Dave, telling him that I thought it would be better if they transported him to a mental health facility for evaluation. The evidence of Dave's violent tendencies was all over me, though.

"He choked you?" the cop noted the bruises on my throat.

"No...not tonight, anyway. That was last night."

"He was here last night, too?"

"No, this happened in the woods. In Niles."

"So he's stalking you?"

"Sort of...he thinks I'm a government agent and that I have his son. The truth is, I was trying to find him to take him to his son."

I briefly explained the situation, and the cop listened, nodding now and then. The ambulance arrived and the paramedics had a moment of confusion over the duct tape.

"He's delusional and violent. Be careful," Jack warned.

More cops arrived and we stepped out of the bedroom to give the paramedics room to work. One of the officers grinned at me, and I recognized him. It was Officer Gray, the one who'd come to Niles when they'd apprehended Alex Truly at the Golden Eagle Motel.

"Hey, I know who you are," he said. "You found that cop shooter!"

"Well, he kind of found me."

"She's the one that ran him over!" Gray told Brubeck, and they both laughed.

"That was a good job," Brubeck shook my hand. "We're not allowed to beat suspects up anymore."

"Glad I could help. Now, about David..."

By the time they had him sedated and on a stretcher I thought everyone understood the situation, and they agreed to transport him to the hospital for evaluation.

"You should probably get checked in the ER, too." Brubeck told me. He seemed much more kindly disposed toward me now. It would be nice to think I had at least a few Buchanan cops on my side for a change.

"I'm okay, I don't need to go to the hospital."

"You're bleeding."

I looked at my wrists. The bandages had torn loose and the rope burns were oozing blood again.

"I'll wash up. It's just superficial."

"Okay. We'll probably need to see you again later for a follow up report."

"Can someone call David's wife?" I knew I should probably do it, but I was just too damned tired.

"I'll go talk to her," he promised.

"Thanks, Officer Brubeck. I appreciate you taking it easy on David."

"Call me Ken." He grinned. "I have a feeling we're going to keep running into each other."

I sighed. "Yeah, you might be right."

After they were all gone Jack took me into the kitchen and had me sit on a stool next to the sink. He got my first aid kit and went to work re-bandaging my wrists.

I sat silently, wincing a bit now and then. He cleaned the blood away and wrapped fresh gauze around the wounds.

"Thank you."

"You're welcome." He started putting stuff back into the first aid box. "So, do you still hate me?"

"I never hated you," I answered honestly. "I just don't want you butting in where you don't belong."

"I get that. I'm sorry about the whole thing with Michael. You want me to apologize to him, too?"

"God no! I don't want you anywhere near him."

"Hey, come on! What do you think I'm going to do to him?"

"Geez, I don't know." I didn't want to admit the truth, but what the hell. If nothing else, I did consider him a friend, and he deserved the truth from me. "You're pretty damned scary."

"Me?" He looked more than surprised. He looked shocked, and more than a little offended. "Do you really think I would ever do anything to hurt you?"

"No! Not me." And that was also the truth, although I hadn't actually realized it until he verbalized it. Somewhere along the line I had come to accept that for whatever reason Jack was genuinely fond of me, and he would likely go to great lengths to keep me from being hurt. But...

"The thing is, I don't think you hesitate much when it comes to hurting other people, and that's sort of...well, it goes against the grain with me."

"You think I go around breaking people's arms just because it's Tuesday or because Starbucks served me cold coffee?"

"No, but face it Jack, you live a whole secret life that I know nothing about. You disappear for weeks at a time, working on stuff you can't tell me about..."

"So does Eddie. You aren't afraid of him."

"That's different. I've known Eddie since we were kids. I don't know anything about you since before the first time you came to play poker. I don't know about your family, your other friends...it's like those scars on your back. I won't pry, because you obviously aren't comfortable talking about them, but that's the kind of thing I mean. I don't *know* you."

"I'll tell you about the scars if you want to know." He said it softly, and I could hear the reluctance. The scars in question were very faint lines across his back, and I probably would never have noticed them if he hadn't once pulled up his shirt to show me the scars from an old shrapnel wound. I *did* want to know about them, if only because he was so reluctant to tell me, but I also wanted to respect his privacy, so I shook my head.

"That's your business. You don't need to tell me."

"I wasn't ready to tell you the first time you asked, but things are a little different now." He shrugged. "I guess I have some trust issues of my own. Anyway, it was a long time ago."

"Not so long ago that it doesn't bother you any more."

"You got any beer? It tends to be a thirsty story."

Beer? That was a first. I'd never seen him drink before.

"I don't want you to tell me if…"

"Rainie, really, I'll tell you." He stepped over to the fridge and pulled two beers from a six pack. He offered one to me and I accepted it. It probably wasn't a good idea with a concussion, but I had I feeling I was going to want it. He opened his and leaned against the counter.

"It happened when I was eight. My father…" he grimaced. "Hell, he was a mean bastard. Looking back, I realize he was probably a sociopath, but what did I know then? I was just a kid." He took a pull on his beer. "Anyway, he knocked me and my mom around from as far back as I can remember. I'd get it for not putting my toys away, mom would get it for leaving a dirty dish in the sink or...hell, I don't know. For breathing, I guess.

"Anyway, my mom died when I was five. She fell down the basement steps carrying a basket of laundry down to wash and broke her neck. It was ruled an accident, but I always wondered...still, I was only five, right?"

I nodded but didn't say anything. I was picturing him, a vulnerable little boy, his mommy gone, left to live alone with the fearsome man who might have killed her. I took a hard swallow of my beer to keep the tears at bay.

"So when I was seven my father married Ursula. She was a quiet little thing, gentle and soft spoken. She told me she knew she couldn't replace my real mom, but she hoped she could fill in some of the empty spaces.

"And she did. She was not only kind to me, she was fun. When my father wasn't around we laughed together a lot. She taught me how to ride a bike and play a little on a flute, and we cooked together.

"But when he was home, it was always ugly. Ursula couldn't do anything right in his eyes, and he was always finding an excuse to smack her. Then she got pregnant with Casey, my little sister. He was more careful, then, just pushed her around some. I think he liked the idea of another kid to smack around.

"So I was eight years old and Ursula was six months along and it was a Saturday. Ursula had gone shopping. I came running in for a drink of water, and I left my bike on the front walk. I knew the rules: put it in the back, lock it up. Every time, no exceptions."

He took another long swallow of his beer before he went on.

"So my father saw the bike and he grabbed me, right there in the entry hall, and tore my shirt off. He had a willow switch, strong but flexible for maximum bite, and he started beating me with it. He was hanging onto my arm so I couldn't run, and I remember screaming, and I remember little sprays of blood on the white walls…you know, the cast off."

I shuddered and closed my eyes. I didn't want to hear any more. I wanted to live in ignorance, and not be reminded that such horrors happened to children. Especially not to ones I knew, even if they were all grown up and bad-assed now.

"So Ursula came home from the store, walked in and saw my father beating me, saw the blood. She didn't even hesitate.

"She was carrying two plastic grocery sacks. She dropped the one that had the eggs and the bread, took a two handed grip on the other one. It had canned goods in it. Canned peaches, actually, my favorite. I was a picky eater, and she was good about keeping things around that I would eat.

"Anyway, she swung that sack back as far as she could and brought it around and hit my father in the face with it. He dropped like a stone. Beating over."

Jack finished his beer. "So? Now you know about the scars."

"I'm sorry." I could barely raise my voice above a whisper. "I shouldn't have asked."

"It's okay, it has a sort of happy ending." He smiled, but not like he meant it. "My father suffered a traumatic brain injury. He was in a coma for two months, and when he woke up he had to re- learn everything from scratch: how to walk, how to talk…how to wipe his ass.

"He never fully recovered. Last I heard he was living in a group home, but his stay there was iffy. Seems even that hard blow to the head couldn't knock the asshole out of him, and he still has anger issues.

"Ursula wasn't prosecuted. It was a clear case of defending me. Even better, she got custody of me, and she did a damned fine job of raising me and Casey."

He pulled his wallet out and slipped a photo out. "This is them, taken a couple of years ago."

They were both pretty. Casey was on the tall side, with dark hair and mischievous eyes. Ursula only came up to her daughter's shoulder, a tiny woman with black hair and sad, gentle eyes.

"She's so little!"

"I know. Five foot one, only weighed maybe a hundred and twenty the day she knocked out my father, and a lot of that was baby." Jack grinned, and this time his amusement was real. "My father preferred picking on people smaller than him. I guess he just never calculated that crucial law of physics: something heavy propelled by a mother protecting her young is equal to the force of a baseball bat in Babe Ruth's hands."

I laughed in spite of myself. "I never studied that law in science class."

"It's not a law that scientists can really quantify. Ursula is usually so gentle she'll carry spiders outside rather than squash them, but when it came down to it she did what she had to do." He smiled again. "Like you."

"I don't know about that."

"No? Think about it." He rinsed his beer bottle out and carried it to the return bin on the back porch. He came and stood close to me. Very close, well within my personal space. "So, am I a little less scary now?"

"I don't know about that." I wanted to back away, but I was up against the counter with nowhere to go.

"I'll have to work on that." He kissed me on the forehead, a friendly gesture. "Well, I guess you don't need anyone watching over you anymore. Unless you've pissed off some other psycho I don't know about?"

"Nope, I made a resolution to stick to one psycho at a time."

"I'll get my things and get out of here then. Call if you need anything."

And he was gone.

Chapter Eighteen

Six weeks later I knocked at Pam's door, and she opened in a hurry, welcoming me with a hug. I was almost getting used to that. In fact, I think deep down I was beginning to like the whole hugging thing. It was just one more thing my mom was right about.

"Come in!" Pam ushered me in from the cold. It was late February, and the sky was cloaked in that gray perma-cloud we were so often subjected to in the month before spring began to reassert itself. It had been snowing on and off all morning, but it wasn't enough to hide the dirty gray snow that was piling up on every corner. Spring couldn't get here soon enough for me.

"Hi Davey!" I greeted the boy, who was sitting on the couch, playing a video game. "You're looking good." And he did. David had proven to be a good match, and Davey had spent a few weeks in the children's hospital in Indianapolis, getting his bone marrow transplant. He had just come home the day before.

"Hi Rainie! Hey, have you seen my dad?"

"I did, just yesterday. He's doing better."

"Mom says he might get to come live with us again!"

"Well, not for a while, honey," Pam admonished him. "I'm going to go into the kitchen to talk for a few minutes, okay?"

"I'm not a baby anymore. You can talk about dad in front of me."

"You're too smart for your own good, Davey." She kissed him on top of his head. "Be a kid for a while longer, okay?"

"But I want to know about dad!"

"I'm not going to keep any secrets from you, but let me choose when to tell you stuff, okay?"

Davey frowned but grudgingly said, "Okay."

We went into the kitchen and Pam closed the door.

"Did you talk to the prosecutor?" she asked.

"I just came from there, and there's good news and bad. He said it really doesn't matter whether I want to press charges or not. They have plenty of evidence even without my testimony. He did say he would take David's mental state into consideration, and he won't pursue the kidnapping or criminal confinement. There's still the assault and home invasion charges, though."

"I suppose he'll do some jail time." Pam had tears in her eyes.

"I don't know, his doctor is doing what he can, too."

I had gone to see David, and it was hard to believe he was the same man. He had been taking the proper meds for weeks, and although he was still struggling with the voices, he was gentle and sweet and couldn't stop apologizing for hurting me. I didn't think he needed to be in jail, either.

"The prosecutor was talking about time in the state mental hospital. It isn't the greatest place, but at least it's better than prison. At least he'll get treatment."

"Prison would tear him apart. I told you, he's really a gentle man."

"I can see that, Pam. I think the court will see it, too. We'll just have to wait a while longer."

Pam smiled. "I've waited nine years. I guess I can handle it."

"Are you really thinking about having him come home?"

"I know it might seem strange, but now that he's taking the meds I can see the sweet guy I fell in love with. And if I don't take him in, where will he go? I can't let my son's dad be homeless."

"His illness won't be easy to deal with."

Pam smiled. "No easier than leukemia or stroke, I imagine."

"You're a good person, Pam."

"Well, as good as I have to be, anyway!" Pam laughed, and I saw a shadow of the party girl she used to be.

And that was a good thing.

I drove home, feeling a little blue but not sure why. It was probably just the weather. The lack of sunshine can get to you after a while.

I turned the radio on just in time to catch the forecast: There was a warm front moving in, and we would have overnight rain mixed with snow.

I sighed and wondered what the weather was like in Florida. Or Tibet. Or anywhere outside the Midwest.

Just as I was walking in to the house my cell started chiming with Michael's ring, and I answered it. He often just called to chat now, and it seemed we were slipping into a pretty comfortable relationship rhythm.

We had only been talking a few minutes when I heard the alert that I had another call coming in. I pulled the phone away from my ear for a second to glance at the read out. It was Jack. Huh, I'd seen him around the office, but he hadn't called me since that night David broke in and assaulted me. I wonder what he wanted?

It probably wasn't a good idea to hang up on Michael to talk to Jack. Michael was still pretty touchy about the whole subject, and was just as glad I wasn't hanging around with Jack. But then again...

"Hey Michael?" I interrupted him mid-sentence, and to tell the truth I had no idea what he'd been talking about. That probably wasn't good, either. "I have another call coming in. I think it's my brother. Can I call you back later?"

"Uh...sure, I guess."

"'Kay, talk to you later!" I hit the button to accept Jack's call. "Hey Jack!"

There was a moment of silence, then Michael's voice, sounding *really* unhappy. "This is still Michael. You didn't switch over."

"Oh..." The phone wasn't beeping anymore. Jack must have given up.

I heard Michael sigh.

"Yeah...'Oh.' I'll talk to you later." Michael's tone made it sound like later might be *much* later. Like never.

He hung up.

I looked at the phone, thinking I really should call Michael right back to apologize. I wasn't sure how to do that; I mean, I had obviously lied, hadn't I?

My phone started ringing again and I smiled and answered it, pleased that he had called me back.

"Hey Jack! What's up?"

Made in the USA
Charleston, SC
14 December 2011